Sworn Shift

by

AJ Skelly

The Wolves of Rock Falls

Sworn Shift

Cover Art by *Jennifer Greeff*

The Wild Rose Press, Inc.
PO Box 708
Adams Basin, NY 14410-0708
Visit us at www.thewildrosepress.com

Publishing History
First Edition, 2022
Trade Paperback ISBN 978-1-5092-4112-5
Digital ISBN 978-1-5092-4113-2

The Wolves of Rock Falls
Published in the United States of America

As the wolf opened his mouth right over Cade's throat, saliva, pink with Cade's blood, dripped down wickedly long teeth that flashed under the pale beams of moonlight filtering into the clearing.

A shriek not quite wolf and not quite human ripped from my mouth as I crashed through the remaining underbrush into the clearing.

The big wolf startled and looked me right in the eye.

And then I knew.

Heat exploded down my limbs, curling in my belly, fanning into hot flames that licked all over my body as every cell I possessed focused on the dark wolf with the soulless brown eyes. I skidded to a complete stop as the big wolf stared at me hungrily.

Terror and desire clouded my mind making it hard to think… This hulking brute was my mate.

Praise for AJ Skelly

"You'll fall head over tail in love with this story of family, revenge, and the power of forgiveness. You won't be able to resist reading 'just one more page' until the dramatic conclusion leaves you howling for more."

~ *Sarah Harmon*

"Sworn Shift once again immerses us in the world of Rock Falls and the two packs that live there. The book brings back all the old favorites while also exploring some newer faces. It kept me engaged from start to finish and showed how even the most unlikely of relationships can bloom into something spectacular!"

~ *Lacey R. Scott*

Dedication

Because the story wasn't done yet.

And for every girl who has felt she was "less" because she was not exactly the same as her peers. You are seen, valued, and special just the way you are. And for every guy who has ever struggled with the labels put on him. Labels don't make a man. Integrity does.

Acknowledgments

Mihi Pater, gratias ago tibi quoniam donum verba.

Husband, thank you for being my enabler. I couldn't write without the time you give me.

Mom, Dad, Landon, Grandma, your encouragement is invaluable.

My sweet kids, I'm so honored that you want to write books, too. Yours will be far greater than mine ever could be.

My cheerleaders and launchers—I could not do this without you. Your willingness, encouragement, and stickwithitness has superseded anything I could have imagined. I'll be forever grateful. Particularly, all three Sarahs, Lacey, Brandy, Alyssa, Portia, Aunt Bonnie, Erin, Meghan, both Jessicas, Teri, Krisy, Brittany, and Kristie.

Karen, you get your own line. No one has been more influential on my writing than you. The things I've learned from you could fill their own book. You have my eternal gratitude.

My "home folk." Once again, I find myself utterly humbled and grateful for your support. There is something mighty to be said for small-town community.

The Wild Rose Press, thank you for book three. I wasn't sure I'd get here. Thank you for believing in my dream, too.

Finally, you, dear reader. Thank you for picking up my book. Thank you for reading it, for caring about my characters, for falling in love with Rock Falls. A book isn't much good without readers to enjoy it. Your comments on social media, your reviews, your emails, and messages just make this author heart go pitter-pat. Thank you. From the bottom of my heart, thank you.

Chapter 1
Raven
Friday night

Blood. Thrashing. Night. Breaking. Howls.

The tang of blood and the shrieks of war crashed in on me as I ran to my spot on the battlefield. I winced at the echoes of teeth ripping into flesh, yips of warning, and howls of pain.

I was in the second wave of the pack, intended to further maim the wounded while our stronger wolves attacked in the first wave, wiping out the fiercest enemies.

Bodies writhed on the ground, healing, shifting, breaking, dying. A dark wolf glared up at me from the ground, hate radiating off every hair on his hide. With a slash of teeth and a snarl of rage, he flew at me, his right leg covered in blood.

Wolf took over, and I let the animal instinct encase me completely. Twisting to the side, the wolf just missed ripping into my face and instead found himself with my teeth sinking into his haunch. He yelped and went down hard as I hung on. Coppery, pungent blood filled my mouth, and the rational bit of human left wanted to gag and spit it out. Forcing myself back down and letting the wolf have her head, she growled, and I shook the flesh in my mouth, reminding the injured animal that he was no longer his own.

He tried to turn and bite my side, but I was quicker. Without letting go of his leg, I sidestepped. More howls filled the air. I needed to help the others. There were too many from Victor's pack. We needed everyone from our pack that could fight. My father never would have allowed me out otherwise.

Keeping hold with my mouth, I shoved down the remorse I knew was coming, and with my front legs, found purchase on the wolf's legs. I heaved all my weight against them, using my muscular hind legs as leverage. A resounding *crack* and yelps of pain echoed around me as his legs broke and the wolf went down to stay.

Turning, I had less than a second to dodge the next set of teeth coming at me. Then another. I couldn't take two on my own. Not when they were both bigger, more experienced, and heavier-muscled males intent on my life.

I used the only weapon in my arsenal of any use to me at the moment. Seeing the perfect opening, I leaped up high and landed on the other side of the big gray. I was slim and built for speed. With a burst, I was off. I glanced around, trying to find where I could help the most. For a wolf, I was small and somewhat delicate. I was great at guerrilla warfare—run, strike, retreat. But I wouldn't last long in an all-out fight.

There–a lone brown wolf ready to pounce on Jake from my pack. I could head off the brown wolf so Jake could focus on the battle he was currently winning. Changing directions, the wind blew toward me. With so much blood choking the air, it's amazing I caught the scent.

Cade's blood.

My brother.

The rest of the world faded as I honed every sense in on finding Cade. I couldn't see him, but I could smell his blood. And if he was bleeding...I stopped the thought.

Stepping back into the trees to scan without being seen and further engaged in the fight, I searched, heart pounding in my chest. The smell of his blood was stronger here. Sniffing, I found a faint trail. There were other wolf scents crisscrossed over the path, but Cade's scent was more familiar to me than any other. I could single it out in the middle of the ocean.

Nose to the ground, I followed, picking up the pace as I began to hear the isolated sounds of another fight not part of the melee I'd left behind.

Cade yelped, and I sprinted for all I was worth. Two wolves came into focus in a clearing up ahead; both were black and matted in blood. Cade was big, but the other wolf was bigger. He was a huge mass of muscle covered in mud, fur, and blood. They danced around each other, fangs out, swiping with paws, slashing with teeth. Cade reached out to bite into the other wolf, but just as he did, he tripped over a root. The bigger wolf was on him in a second, and I heard the snap of a rib just before Cade howled. The big wolf pinned Cade to the ground as Cade thrashed, in pain, trying to either get purchase from the ground or reach the other wolf with his teeth.

My heart thundered as I pounded over the ground. I wasn't going to make it in time! Desperation flooded my system with adrenaline. I shuddered, frantically trying to hold it together.

As the wolf opened his mouth right over Cade's

throat, saliva, pink with Cade's blood, dripped down wickedly long teeth that flashed under the pale beams of moonlight filtering into the clearing.

A shriek, not quite wolf and not quite human, ripped from my mouth as I crashed through the remaining underbrush into the clearing.

The big wolf startled and looked me right in the eye.

And then I knew.

Heat exploded down my limbs, curling in my belly, fanning into hot flames that licked over my body as every cell I possessed focused on the dark wolf with the soulless brown eyes. I skidded to a complete stop as the big wolf stared at me hungrily.

Terror and desire clouded my mind making it hard to think.

This could not be. The big wolf had forgotten Cade the moment I stepped into the clearing. His attention was completely fixed on me. He stepped off Cade's chest, and Cade wheezed, too weak in the moment to fight.

Muscles rippled beneath dark fur in slow motion as the beast prepared to launch himself after me.

Terror overrode any irrational desire in my brain. I wheeled around and ran faster than I ever had in my life. I didn't know where I was going—just away from the hideous, desirous creature hot on my trail.

Trees came and went in a blur as I dashed wildly through the underbrush, the smells of pine and rotting earth mixing with the fear and blood that coated the back of my mouth.

His paws thundered over the turf behind me, and I risked one fatal glance back. He was on me in an instant. The moment I looked back, he leaped into the air, crashed into me, and knocked me over. He pinned me to the earth. His expression changed from one of bloodlust to one of awe. Part of me thrashed, trying to get away; the other part longed to be closer to this maniac. Horrified longing welled up in my chest as I watched, almost like a spectator outside of my own body, as his nose came down and ran up the length of my neck, scenting me. I squirmed under the weight of his bulk, and he altered his position, growling softly deep in his chest. He stared me straight in the eye, his dark and violent, but tempered by what I knew would be my death sentence. Possession.

With a grace that belied his massive proportions, he leaned down and gently closed his mouth over my muzzle, biting down just enough for me to feel the pressure and know that I had been Claimed.

This hulking brute was my mate.

I had been so distracted, I'd lost awareness of all else around us, and I yelped when the dark wolf was battered from the side and toppled off me. I glanced around wildly and saw Cade, covered in more blood than fur, wheezing. He'd used his head to hit the dark wolf and ram him off of me.

Instantly, the black wolf was on his feet, and I knew, thanks to our new unwanted connection, that he would protect me at all costs. He would kill Cade in an attempt to keep me from harm, even though I knew perfectly well that Cade was no threat to me.

Snarling with teeth glinting, the big wolf advanced on Cade. I scrambled to my feet and put myself between Cade and the mountain stalking nearer.

Cade hissed at me through his clenched teeth.

I growled at him, unwilling to take my thoughts from the brute for even a second.

Mania emanated from the black wolf as our gazes locked. My knees trembled, but I held my ground. All at once, the big wolf shook his head, pawing at it as if trying rid himself of something painful. When his head came back up, his eyes were tortured, looking back and forth from Cade to me, lingering on me. He whined as his eyes cleared. With one more agonized whine toward me, he bolted, leaping clear over both Cade and me and dashing into the trees, back toward the battle.

Chapter 2
Bowen

Victor was dead. I knew it before I reached the fight ring where my half brother had challenged him for Alpha not an hour before. Wolf stopped us in our tracks in the outskirts of the forest. Emotion overwhelmed me, and I fought for breath. The black tether that tied me to Victor—my father—disintegrated, and for one glorious moment, I was free.

My eyes slid shut, and I tried to process the emotions slamming through me. Mate. Victor dead. Free. Nearly committing murder.

I heaved and wretched in the grass until there was nothing left in me. In a way, it was cleansing in more ways than one—like purging a physical representation of my father's hold over me. He had it no more. He would *never* control me again. Everything of his that I could purge was gone.

Even as I thought it, I felt the constricting tethers realigning themselves. Strengthening the cords that bound me to my pack, I recognized the rush of power spinning over my shoulders. My nose tipped to the moon, and I let the power take hold. I was Beta of the pack once more. Kyp, my brother, was now my Alpha. Relief, hot and sweet, boiled through me. I would follow Kyp. I would be his Beta willingly, unlike when Victor forced me into the position.

Creeping to the tree line, I saw Kyp standing tall and straight in his human form.

My wolf ears had no trouble picking out his words, projected widely over his new pack. "I am not your enemy. But I am your Alpha. I will not hold anyone here who wishes to leave. But those of you who stay *will* obey me." I scanned for Drew, Victor's second-in-command outside the blood hierarchy. My lips curled back as I found him, poised and ready to lunge at Kyp.

I was in motion before the snarl ripped from his throat. With no small degree of satisfaction, I dove at him, tackling his dirty brown fur to the dirt and letting my teeth clench tightly against his neck.

A low growl of warning declared my full willingness to rip his throat out if he so much as moved. I detested this wolf.

I'm with you, I sent through our mental link to Kyp. He nodded, our eyes connected, and a silent affirmation of brotherhood passed between us.

Kyp turned to speak again to the gathering of wolves. I shook Drew's scruff in my teeth and released him from my mouth but put a heavy paw on his chest to keep him down. He stared balefully at me from the ground. Hateful, but for the moment, powerless.

A few minutes later, Kyp resumed his wolf form and turned to Drew, still cowering in the dirt under my paw. Kyp's wolf towered over Drew, lips curled back in a menacing snarl. A tremor went through Drew's chest and vibrated up my leg.

Get out. Kyp's words, spoken through the link, echoed inside my chest, and the tether that kept Drew tied to the pack was effectively severed and thrust back at him. He'd been cast out. He was Rogue.

Drew yelped as I let him up. He scrambled for the trees, tail between his legs.

Relief swept over me again. I did the next instinctual thing that came to me. Showing Kyp my fealty, I quickly tipped my chin up, exposing the silvery-white patch on my chest, matted now with blood and dirt, then scented him. Solidifying Kyp's woodsy scent to memory—Alpha, liberator, brother.

****

The next morning, I woke to the phone. I'd opted to crash in the mobile home I'd been living in rather than go back to Kyp's house. Kyp was my brother, but we'd only known of each other's existence for a few weeks.

"Hello?" My voice crunched like gravel.

"This is Alfred Dewson, Victor Atwood's lawyer. Is this his Beta?"

My senses jerked to high alert. "How did you get this number?"

"Mr. Atwood left it in his will. A source has informed me that Mr. Atwood is, in fact, quite dead."

"He is," I confirmed tightly.

"And you are his Beta?"

"I was."

"Oh. Oh dear. I'm going to need to get in touch with Mr. Atwood's Beta immediately. There are things to take care of regarding the will."

I needed to call Kyp.

****

Three hours later, the pack had been reassured with their Alpha's presence and were left to rest and lick their wounds while Kyp, Kyp's mate Rachel, and I drove one town over to a brick building where Mr.

Dewson waited for us.

Plush maroon carpet and soft velvety chairs one shade lighter were positioned around a mahogany desk. All the red in the room reminded me of blood, making my stomach dip uncomfortably.

A receptionist wearing too much perfume and hairspray led us in and closed the door behind her.

"Welcome." An older bespectacled man with thinning gray hair stood behind the desk. He bowed slightly and motioned to the chairs.

Sitting stiffly, my eyes flitted around the room. Aside from an obnoxious amount of maroon, it simply appeared to be the office of a well-to-do gentleman.

"I'm sorry for your loss," Mr. Dewson intoned. I resisted the urge to roll my eyes. "I've been Mr. Atwood's attorney for many years. You are, were, Mr. Atwood's Beta then?"

"I was," Kyp said.

"In that case, it is my duty to inform you that you have inherited all of Mr. Atwood's five properties, his car, and the 1.27 million dollars in his accounts."

Silence reigned the room.

"What did you say?" Rachel found her tongue first.

A smile ghosted over the old man's lips.

The roar in my ears was just as deafening the second time the lawyer repeated himself. I'd lived with Victor for four years, and I had no idea he'd had those kinds of resources at his disposal. I didn't envy Kyp. I wanted nothing of our father's.

"May we have a few moments to speak alone?" Kyp asked. Mr. Dewson's eyebrows rose, but he nodded graciously and exited the door.

"I think I may hyperventilate," Kyp confessed as

the door snicked shut.

Rachel smiled encouragingly and leaned over to kiss his cheek. Wolf nudged me, wanting to see our mate again. Today. We needed to find her today.

"Bowen, I—" Kyp's eyes held a helpless look. "—I was his Beta for a week and a half. This all belongs to you."

I shook my head. "No. You're the oldest. You were the Beta when he died. It's yours."

We looked at each other, both of us at a loss for words and unsure how to feel about this revelation of our father's wealth.

"I won't keep all of this. It's rightly yours."

"I'm no more or less son of that man than you are. Keep it."

"Why don't you split it?"

Our gazes swung to Rachel. She shrugged.

"What? It's the logical thing to do, right?" Her red curls bounced.

Kyp looked at me. "If you won't take it all, you're at least talking half."

My middle twinged uncomfortably. "I really don't want it."

"My conscience won't let me keep all of it anyway," Kyp answered with a grin.

"What about Shelby?" I asked. Shelby was our younger half sister. Victor had let her have a risky operation to have her werewolf scent glands removed, so she could infiltrate the Wolfe pack. She was able to get close with no one being the wiser, but the removal of her glands had resulted in her madness. She'd taken things into her own hands, and in the end, Victor had written her off, cut her, bled her like a stuck pig, and left her as a warning for the Wolfe pack. I shuddered. She remained in a coma at the hospital.

"We'll take care of her any way we can," Kyp said softly. Rachel took his hand. Kyp had been the one to discover her shredded body. "We'll use whatever money she needs to make sure she has whatever she requires. Mom may be able to make some good care facility suggestions, too."

I nodded. Jennifer Kypson, though fully human, was a force to be reckoned with, I'd recently discovered.

Kyp continued. "Shall we each pick a house? Dewson said there were five?"

"I only knew about two of them," I confessed with a shrug.

"It's settled. I won't command you to take half but consider it a very serious request that you do. And that you pick a house. I spoke with Dominic last night. Maybe early morning. I don't know," Kyp said with a wry grin and rubbed the heel of his hand over his right eye. "I'd like to stay in the area for a while and learn from him. I don't know how to be an Alpha. I know what kind of Alpha I don't want to be, but I think, especially as broken as our pack is, we need help. If we're staying in the area, assuming the properties are around here, I vote we each pick one and settle in for a while."

My mate was here. It was unlikely after the way she ran from me that she wanted to leave the area immediately. I sighed. "All right."

****

We walked out of the lawyer's office, each of us with one hundred fifty thousand dollars of Victor's cash from the lawyer's safe. We went straight to the bank.

"Kyp, I need to ask you something."

"Shoot," Kyp responded as we parked in the bank parking lot.

My mouth dried, and suddenly I had no words.

"I need to know who this is," I rasped. I sent him a mental image of my mate. Wolf form, since I didn't know what she looked like in human form yet.

"That's Raven Rivers." Two sets of eyes suddenly pinned me to my seat.

"Why do you need to know who Raven is?" Rachel eyed me suspiciously.

Chapter 3
Raven

Saturday afternoon, Dominic put out an all call that everyone available should come meet our newest allies that night. Since Kyp took over Victor's pack last night, the pack that wanted to annihilate us were now our allies. The thought didn't sit well with me, and I knew I wasn't alone in thinking it. Probably why Dominic wanted us to intermingle sooner rather than later. It wouldn't do either pack any good for the animosity between us to steep.

Tonight's all call also meant that the hulking brute—my mate—would be there, too. In human form. The thought both terrified and exhilarated me. Dread clawed at my middle while Wolf skipped around like a pup inside me, excited to see our mate in his human form—to find out who he was.

****

We met outside Sam's cabin back by the fire pit. Sam, Dominic's son and Beta of our pack, heaved another log onto an already blazing fire while his mate, my friend Megan, stood off to the side next to a table set with cookies and a percolator of coffee. Dozens of wolves already roamed the area—all in skin. Most were from my own pack, but some were from the Thornehill pack, our allies from New York. I turned to go over and talk to Megan, but I picked up Rachel's scent and turned to scan for her.

"Raven!" Rachel called me over. "How are you?" Her eyes looked me over carefully.

"I survived last night. How are *you*?" Rachel had been kidnapped as part of Victor's attempt to control Kyp.

"Still reeling a little bit, if I'm totally honest." She gave me a rueful smile as the firelight danced over her red curls.

"How does it feel to be the Alpha's woman?" I attempted a grin of my own, but I'm not sure it came through the layers of dread and anxiety building up inside me.

Rachel's smile lit up a three-foot circle around us. "I would have loved him just as much if he'd stayed a Rogue or been an Omega, but I think having an Alpha for a mate is going to be a lot of fun." She gave me a conspiratorial wink.

"Hey, ladies." Cade sidled up, still favoring his healing rib. "Anyone seen Sam out yet?"

"He was just over by the fire pit," I said.

We glanced over, but he seemed to have vanished. Rachel said, "He's probably grabbing something for Megan in the cabin. I'm sure she's been baking most of the day. Actually, I was on my way over to help her but saw you and wanted to see how you were." She turned her last words to me.

I offered a smile.

"I appreciate it. I'm glad you're not hurt."

Kindness radiated from her as she squeezed my arm. "Oh, and Joanie's coming home over the weekend!"

Joy flooded me. Rachel's sister Joanie had been in

a drug rehab that heavily involved both their parents, so Rachel had been staying with Kyp and Jennifer. I hugged Rachel.

"I'm *so* glad, Rach!"

She squeezed me back then headed across the clearing to Megan and the table of refreshments.

I swallowed thickly. The hairs on the back of my neck stood on end. *He* was here. Somewhere.

"Rave? You okay?" Cade asked as I felt the blood drain from my face.

Ignoring him, my eyes scanned the groups of people milling about. There. Coming up the path behind Kyp.

My stomach dropped to my toes as Wolf tried to propel us forward.

Intense brown eyes locked with mine. Prominent brows and a thick fringe of dark brown hair shadowed them, but I saw the glint of those endless depths as the firelight flickered in them. My blood turned to ice as fear crept up my spine. Wolf panted, wanting to be near him, wanting to Claim him back, but shock held me to my spot.

He was horrifyingly *gorgeous*. Wide shoulders tapered to a trim waist. Square jaw and full lips. Nose with just a slight bend in the middle. And those eyes. Pinned on me.

My heart hammered. My palms sweated.

Cade stiffened beside me, and a low growl crept into his throat. He subtly angled himself in front of me.

My mate nodded to both of us, his face devoid of emotion, but he did not come any closer. The breath I'd been holding left in a rush as the dark eyes lingered on mine, but then he turned and followed Kyp toward

Dominic.

****

I stuck close to Cade. Without explanation, Cade understood that I needed my big brother, and he didn't object.

Not long after, Dominic stood up on a stump and surveyed the group of werewolves gathered in the clearing. There had to be close to one hundred of us between the three packs.

"Thank you all for coming tonight," Dominic opened. A hush fell over the crowd. "We felt it was important that everyone understand that we are *all* allies. Yesterday's events happened, but they will not determine the future relations between the three packs gathered here tonight."

A log broke, and crackling sparks soared upward.

"I'd like to formally introduce the Alpha and Beta of each pack so that everyone knows without doubt who the leadership is."

My breath caught as Kyp stepped forward and my mate stepped forward on one side. He was Kyp's Beta?

My attention barely wavered as Dominic introduced Austin Thornehill and his daughter Sarah. Dark eyes fixated on mine in the middle of the crowd. I took a half step behind Cade.

"And our newest Alpha, Alexander Kypson, though he prefers Kyp, and his Beta, Bowen Oakes."

Bowen Oakes.

The name burned inside my brain.

"*That's* Bowen Oakes?" Cade whispered to himself. I nudged him. "He's a player. Basketball and with the ladies, I've heard."

Wonderful.

Jealousy and terror clashed and festered beneath my skin.

Chapter 4
Bowen

Pale Sunday afternoon sunlight filtered down through the branches and dappled the yard. I took a quick inhale of frigid air and swallowed hard. This was either a really smart idea or a really stupid one. Before I could lose my courage, I walked up the three steps to the Rivers' door and rang the bell before stepping back down onto the sidewalk. I'd pumped Kyp for any pertinent details about the Rivers before coming over.

I was hoping for Raven—just the thought of seeing her again made my blood race—but Cade opened the door. He shuddered with restrained fury as his fists clenched at his sides. He stepped out onto the landing, shutting the door behind him and towering over me as I stood on the sidewalk.

"What do you want? Come to try to finish the job?" He snarled through clenched teeth.

I tipped my head back, exposing all of my throat so Cade would know I came in peace. I hoped. I raised my hands up in surrender for good measure.

"I came to apologize." My voice cracked, and I could have died of mortification.

He raised an eyebrow and crossed his arms.

"Look. I…what I did wasn't my own doing."

"Seriously? You're making an excuse for what you did?"

19

This was not going well.

"I'm not trying to make excuses. I'm trying to explain what happened. I didn't *want* to kill you."

"I'm well aware of what happened. I was there. Just about had my tail handed to me on a platter. Remember that part?" he bit out.

"Dude. I came to tell you I'm sorry. I had no desire then, and have no desire now, to try and rip your throat out." I felt my wolf stirring, angry at Cade's accusations. I flexed my bicep where my brand-new tattoo rested, trying to calm my heart rate. I took another breath as Cade glared at me. "Victor," I ground out between my teeth. I seethed just thinking his name. "His will was exceptionally strong. He could compel me—the whole pack—more than the typical Alpha-control. It was like he wrapped his will around my wolf and squeezed until I couldn't breathe unless I obeyed. It was like that when I went after you. Direct command from my Alpha. Victor wanted to separate your Beta from you. He knew you guys were—are—a solid team together. You're his second. He wanted to break up your pack any way he could."

Cade's jaw flexed.

We stared each other down for a solid minute. Cade finally blew a hard breath out through his nose.

"Why else are you here, Bowen?"

My eyebrows shot up my forehead. He was perceptive. "You think I'm apologizing just to get in good with your sister." Realization dawned.

"I saw you watching her last night. A lot."

"I won't lie and tell you that I don't want to see her, but I came today to apologize to *you*. I hoped that was at least one wrong I could try to set right. If Raven will speak with me, I'd like to apologize to her as well."

"Good luck with that. She's even more angry with you than I am. Plus, she's my little sister. Keep your horny hands to yourself."

I winced while Wolf growled inside. Nothing could do about Raven's anger at the moment. Wolf whined. We'd see about the horny hands. I shoved them inside the pockets of my jeans.

"The last thing I wanted to tell you is that Coach asked me to join the basketball team when he saw that I transferred."

"And?"

"And I'll see you at practice tomorrow."

"No. No, no. You wait right here. I'm going to go get my shoes. We're going down to the court right now, and I'm going to see what you're made of. This is my team, and you are *not* going to come in and screw anyone out of their hard-earned position unless you deserve to."

I nodded. This would be interesting. I was sure Cade knew that I had moves. If my not-so-rosy reputation with the ladies had reached his ears, and it sounded like it had, he knew the reason why so many girls threw themselves at me. Back at Woodard High, I was a basketball god.

Chapter 5
Raven

He had sex appeal off the charts with his dark, devilishly good looks and brooding smirk. I hated myself for noticing and loathed the part of me that was attracted to him like a magnet. I knew he was my mate. Knew it down to my wolf's claws. And until now, I'd never questioned that mates should be together. This should have been the happily ever after every werewolf girl dreamed of. Not a waking nightmare.

I'd never heard of a mate pair breaking their bond before, but if there was any way under heaven that it could be done, I intended to find it. There was no way that I would be chained to a savage monster for the rest of my days. Visions of *Bowen* on top of Cade, poised to rip out his throat, crashed into my brain, and I shut my eyes against the onslaught. Swallowing did little to discourage the bile I felt rising in my stomach every time I thought of that horrible night.

I squinted through the window, sneaking another ashamed glance at Bowen Oakes as he and Cade talked. Mom ran the vacuum in the next room over, so I couldn't hear their words. But I could notice that his hair was dark, but not quite black like mine and Cade's. The sun caught it and brought out lighter pieces that whispered as the light breeze tugged on it. His jaw was square, casting a light V of shadow over his neck and chest where I could tell muscle lurked, even beneath his coat. I had no idea how old he was, though I guessed he couldn't be more than eighteen since Kyp had to be older than Bowen to assume Alpha. He looked like a fully grown man with wide shoulders, thick arms, and a broad chest. There was a hint of darkness over his jaw, suggesting that a full beard would grow willingly if given the chance. I was seventeen. Practically still a girl in some respects.

I resisted the urge to growl in frustration. My wolf sighed like a lovesick puppy. She was thoroughly besotted with him. But the human me felt differently. I would not allow myself to be bound to this...*dog*...for the rest of my life. Would *not* happen.

My lip curled in disdain once more as Wolf urged me to go out and bask in his presence.

This was the first time that the wolf and I had disagreed on something big. Not only did I both feel attraction and repulsion for the man on my front stoop, but I was at war with my own thoughts.

A good run would fix this. But first, I'd have to wait until he left. And make sure that he was far, far away.

Cade wheeled back inside the house right then, and I gasped, caught looking through the crack in the curtains. He raised his eyebrows at me as he jogged up the stairs. I glanced once more and saw Bowen looking hard in my direction and made a hasty retreat up the stairs to catch Cade.

"What are you doing?" I asked as I came to his doorway. He was bent over the side of his bed, tying on his tennis shoes. Dread pooled in my gut.

"I'm going to go see what he's made of."

"You're what?" I practically shrieked. "Are you out of your mind? You do realize that Friday night he tried to snap your neck with his incisors, don't you?" I was incensed. Red danced at the edges of my vision, and Wolf wriggled uncomfortably inside.

"Seriously. Rave. Calm down. We're supposed to be allies now. We don't all hold grudges forever. I might, but I'm going to give him the benefit of the doubt first. If I find out he's a terrible, horrible person, then I'll hang on to the grudge and make sure he never touches a single hair on your hide." He gave me a crooked grin, and I felt my stomach unclench a fraction of an inch. I was still ticked off, but I could appreciate his brotherliness. And the fact that he had no clue who Bowen and I were to each other.

"You're still an idiot for going with him."

"I'll call Sam. Don't worry. I'll be fine. I'll keep anybody who needs to be in the loop, in the loop."

He gave me a quick tweak on the shoulder and bounded out the door, hoodie slung over his arm.

Chapter 6
Bowen

It was an old court a few blocks from the Rivers'
house but still in the subdivision where I knew most of
their pack lived. It was a full court with two metal
hoops and a cement ledge on one side that butted up
against a grassy embankment. Faint lines traced the
weathered concrete at the free throw mark, and a faded
yellow arc sketched the three-point lines. I felt my
muscles thrum with the familiar excitement of the sport.
Basketball had been my release from my life with
Victor. It was the one thing I enjoyed; where I could be
free—savagery and frustration all channeled into the
game. It made me good. Nearly unstoppable. My genes
had seen to my size. I could move anyone around the
paint wherever I wanted them. I held the Woodard High
record for rebounds in a single game and a single
season. I knew Cade was captain of the team at my new
school and was a worthy point guard. Competitive to a
fault, I was glad we weren't vying for the same
position. That would not win me any points with Cade
or his sister if we had to compete for the same role on
the court.

Sam Wolfe, Beta of Cade's pack, waited for us,
sitting casually on the ledge with his legs crossed out in
front of him. His stance expressed a casual, relaxed
demeanor, but his eyes missed nothing.

"Let's see some ball, boys." He grinned, the smile not quite meeting his eyes. Great. Beta-Ref to make sure I kept my incisors inside my gums. I swallowed my irritation, reminding myself that two days ago, my teeth had been seconds away from killing the guy next to me. "Half court, first to twenty-one wins," Sam finished.

"You take first ball," I said as I wiggled out of my coat and tossed it up on the grass near Sam.

"You sure you wanna do that?" Cade taunted. "I don't miss."

I snorted. "Neither do I."

He bounced the ball to me from the three-point line, and I checked it back. Without a single dribble, he shot, and before I even turned to watch the ball, I heard the swish.

"That'd be points for Cade," Sam said evenly from his seat on the ledge.

I grinned. Two could play this game. I stepped back. Cade quirked an eyebrow as I bounced the ball back to him. He coiled to shoot again, and my muscles bunched in anticipation. As the ball rolled off his fingers, my feet left the ground. Two feet off the court, I caught the ball midair. I landed, pivoted, and with four dribbles down, one lunge up, I dunked the ball.

Cade cocked his head to the side, eyebrow going up once more.

"My ball," I said.

Cade passed it back. Hard. "So you always let your daddy tell you what to do?"

Red flashed across my vision as I gripped the ball so hard my knuckles popped. Breathing through my mouth, I forced myself to take a steadying breath. "You always end belly-up in a fight?"

Cade's eyes narrowed, and his jaw clenched. I might have pushed a little too far, but *nobody* told me what to do. Not anymore. My bicep flexed under my tattoo. I plowed straight ahead, bowling Cade over as I executed a perfect layup.

Another hard chest pass. This time, as I made to drive into him again, he anticipated and put his foot right where I bounced the ball. With experienced fingers, he snatched the ball as it bounded away. He was fast. Faster than me, but I was bigger and had a good twenty pounds or so of muscle on him.

The game progressed. The jabs got fiercer while tempers flared closer to the surface. I kept reminding myself that I was here to apologize, not to beat him to a bloody pulp. Raven was my mate. Cade was important to her. He would be my brother-in-law someday. Sweat dripped, and breathing became labored. Though we each had different strengths, we were a good match. He was a quick long shot, and I was tall and unstoppable with the ball in my possession.

"I hope you have a good excuse made up to tell Raven if you wanted to apologize to her." Dribbled through the legs, faked to the right. "I saw the *way* you watched her at the gathering."

"Pretty sure I've got a valid excuse." Mate and all—lunged left to guard.

"Please. It will take more than a pretty face to turn her head. Plus, you'll have to go through me." Swing wide to the right.

"I'm an expert at going *through*." I grunted as I elbowed him out of the way for a corner shot.

"Stay away from her, Bowen. She's not for you."

Right. That was definitely not an option.

"And if she doesn't want me to stay away?" I panted as I pivoted hard.

"You *will not* touch her." *Swish*. Suddenly this game had become more about Raven than the rivalry that might exist between Cade and I or that I'd tried to kill him.

"Why don't you let her figure that out." I snagged the ball from his shocked hands.

"I swear I *will* kill you."

"How'd that work out for you last time?" Elbow to the gut.

"When do you plan on trying to commit murder next?" Cade panted, blue eyes turning midnight as he dribbled topside.

"Sooner rather than later if you stand there stalling all day."

With a swoop, he turned, pivoting around me. I was ready and put a leg out, tripping him. In slow motion, I watched him fall, my mind seeing instead his wolf's form as it stumbled over the tree root. I felt the saliva pool in my mouth as shame and horror filled my gut. *I would have killed him.*

At the last second, he caught himself, but one look at my face, and he knew my thoughts. His face blackened as a snarl ripped from his throat.

"Are we ever going to be even?" I rasped. We were neck to neck, panting, and sweating. Ice crept down my back as I dreaded his answer.

So fast I had no hope of deflecting it, his knee connected to my groin. I dropped like a rock. Waves of nausea roiled through me as I gripped my crotch and fought to keep myself on my knees. I would not, *would not*, completely humiliate myself by puking and falling facedown in front of Cade.

Robbed of breath, my vision swam. I forced bile back down and swayed violently on my knees, my will the only thing keeping me from bending before Cade in pain.

Minutes passed. Hours passed. Days passed. I have no idea how long I sat there, fighting the agony pulsing through me. When I could force the tiniest bit of air into my lungs, I glared up, hoping lightning bolts would shoot from my eyes and incinerate Cade on the spot.

To my shock, he stood back two steps, arms crossed, cool expression on his face.

The words forced themselves out of my lips before I could stop them. "Raven is my mate."

Cade might as well have turned to stone. The blood drained from his face. Clearly, Raven had kept her silence. I knew Cade was replaying that night in the forest. She had been the one that distracted me from slicing open his jugular. If Raven had been any other wolf, Cade would be dead. Her pull was the only force strong enough to override Victor's control, and that had only lasted until Victor sensed he was in real trouble in his own fight and called me back.

Cade slammed the ball against the concrete, not caring when it bounced out into the field beside the court. Sam suddenly stood next to Cade, eyes pinning me to the ground as I rasped for air.

Chapter 7
Raven

"Raven!" Cade's angry voice boomed up the stairs to where I sat on my bed. The house rattled as the door slammed behind him.

Heart in my throat, I ran out of my room and met him at the top of the stairs.

"Cade?" Mom asked as she came out of the kitchen to see what the commotion was.

Cade's face was thunderous.

"Is Bowen your *mate*?" His voice carried throughout the house, and I heard the hurt in it. Mom gasped.

Wolf squirmed and thrashed. I closed my eyes and gritted my teeth as my heart pounded.

"Yes."

A frustrated noise ripped from Cade's throat.

The front door opened, and a gust of wind brought Bowen's scent straight up the stairs. I instinctively knew the musky smell of cedar and brown sugar belonged solely to him. My eyes dilated dangerously large as Wolf caught her mate's scent. My skin crawled. I wanted nothing to do with him. Sam closed the door quietly behind them.

"Raven?" Mom said on the main floor, her voice barely above a whisper.

I looked down the stairs at her and shrugged. I had

no words for the firestorm inside me.

"Why don't we all come sit in the living room and discuss this." It wasn't a suggestion. Mom wanted the full story. I sighed. She deserved the full story.

"I'm going to get your father." Two quick steps, and Mom was headed to the back door to call Dad in from the garage.

I felt Bowen's eyes on me the whole way down the stairs. Wolf wanted to run to him. I wanted to run *from* him. The hairs on the back of my neck stood on end as I slowly descended behind Cade.

Cade jerked his head for Bowen to follow him into the living room. I waited until Bowen's gaze left mine. He limped slightly, and I briefly wondered what had happened at the basketball court. Sam nodded to me before taking himself to a seat next to Bowen.

I wasn't sure what to make of that. Was Sam there on my behalf as my Beta or there on Bowen's behalf as a liaison with an allied pack?

My stomach tightened as I sank into the blue easy chair and clenched my hands in my lap. I refused to make eye contact with anyone.

Dad came in through the back door, and minutes later, everyone was seated, the tension mounting by the second.

"Why didn't you say something, Raven?" Cade finally broke the silence.

I swallowed. "Are you excited to hear that the wolf that nearly ended you is your sister's mate?" Wolf snapped inside me at my callous words. I could sense Bowen's discomfort across the room.

Cade blew a hard breath through his teeth.

"Let's back this up," Dad interjected. His eyebrows

drew together, and he braced his wide hands on his knees. "Bowen. Let's hear your side of the story first." Dad's voice was tight.

My belly churned, and I wanted the chair to open up and swallow me down.

Bowen nodded to Dad, then turned to my brother. "I never wanted to hurt you, Cade. If you believe nothing else, believe that. Victor—" His voice strangled over the name and memories of the fight chilled me to my toes. "—controlled his whole pack. Ordered me to target you specifically. I would have killed you and had no choice about it. But then Raven came. Her mate pull saved your life. And probably saved mine as well."

My head came up, and I finally met his gaze. Dark, intense, and riveted on me in a way that made me want to layer clothes on. It wasn't dirty, but it made me feel like every one of my secrets was exposed before him.

"Raven?" Dad nodded to me to pick up the story. My mouth was suddenly as dry as Aunt Georgia's baked chicken breast.

My mouth opened, but no sound came out.

"Is Bowen your mate?" Mom ask gently.

I nodded, my capacity for speech leaving as Wolf rubbed her head against me even as dread spiraled through my middle.

My parents looked at each other and smiled knowingly. They obviously missed the terror tripping up my spine.

"Then congratulations," Mom said quietly.

I risked another glance at Bowen. His eyes were still intense, but there was a new heat kindled in their brown depths that sent my heart lurching into my throat.

"When do you want to set the ceremony?" Dad asked.

All the blood drained from my face. I knew how rare a phenomenon it was to find a true mate. Wolf confirmed Bowen was mine. Pack tradition said true mates were widely and immediately celebrated—this was something for both our packs to rejoice over. Especially in light of the war we'd just fought. But while I'd always dreamed about finding my true mate like a human girl would dream of her fairy-tale prince, this was not it. I didn't want this. I didn't want to be Bowen's mate.

"Do we have to do it so soon?" My strangled words seemed to echo in the stillness of the room.

A flash of concern came over Mom's face. "Do you not want Bowen as your mate?"

Jealousy, hot and potent, reared up and gnashed its teeth, covering me in a pheromone-induced haze.

"No. He's mine." The words were out before I could stop them. I was such an oxymoron. I didn't want him, but the thought of anyone else having him was enough to rob me of breath and set Wolf brandishing her teeth. Wolf was close to panic at the thought of Bowen belonging to someone else.

Embarrassed heat crept into my cheeks, and as I ventured another glance at Bowen, I saw the corner of his mouth tipped ever so slightly at the corner.

"Do you want me to talk to Rev and Dad?" Sam offered, scrutinizing my reaction.

I was drowning. Once we were officially a mated pair, I belonged entirely to Bowen. He belonged entirely to me, too, but that was beside the point. I'd have to leave my pack and join his. Maybe not immediately, but it would happen. Dread took my heart down to the floor. Bowen terrified me. The raw power that came off him was both magnetic and repellent. His size was imposing, wide shoulders, arms corded with muscle. His wolf was massive. Part of my insides quaked. Wolf nudged me and whined inside. Bowen had Claimed me the night of the fight, but I hadn't Claimed him back. Wolf was dying inside because our mark wasn't all over him. It needed both parties to complete Claiming.

"Raven, we don't have to do anything quickly if you don't want to. Let's have the ceremony and take it a day at a time after that," Bowen offered, surprising me with the sincerity behind his words. Although I supposed it could have been an act. His wolf must want to finish our Claiming as badly as mine did. Based on his look, his human side was ready to finish things, too. I suppressed a shudder and bit the inside of my lip.

Cade smirked. "You won't be doing anything quick for a while."

Bowen shot him a look I couldn't interpret that bordered on murderous and amused.

Sam coughed.

"I don't think I'm ready to move out of my parents' house yet," I countered, ignoring whatever male sub-speech was going on.

I saw Mom's confused look in my periphery.

Bowen nodded.

I clenched my teeth. If I didn't Claim him, could someone else? He was my true mate. I realized that as much as I loathed him as a person, I couldn't live with the thought of someone else having him. Wolf would not allow that. I was a hot mess. "All right. Sam, when is a good time for a Claiming ceremony?"

"Since you're true mates," Mom interjected, "do you just want the Claiming ceremony, or do you want the full Ancient Marriage Rites of Mates?" Her eyes were encouraging.

The room was silent for a minute. Only true mates could have the Ancient Marriage Rites of Mates. I swallowed. As a girl, I'd dreamed about being able to complete the ceremony myself. True mates were rare enough that the ceremony was done maybe two or three times each century, at least in our pack history I was aware of. It was an honor. An honor I didn't want with Bowen, but the small wistful girl inside me still wanted it.

In for a penny. I glanced at Bowen. My stomach flipped at his hopeful look.

"Might as well do the whole thing."

****

"Rave, why didn't you tell me?" Cade asked me again later that night as he leaned against the doorjamb of my bedroom. He was hurt by my silence. We were close. We didn't have many secrets from the other. And certainly, something this big, I should have shared. I sighed, stopped folding my laundry, and plopped onto my bed.

"Like I said. How well did you like hearing my true mate is the same beast that tried to kill you?"

"Well, now that I've had time to cool off and think a bit more rationally, I guess it's cool."

"Cool?" I nearly shrieked. "How can you be *cool* about this?"

Cade shrugged. "He was forced to come after me. And it's wolf nature. Your wolf wouldn't recognize him as your mate unless he was a good guy somewhere underneath all his tough exterior. I mean, if he ever lays a claw on you against your will, I'll string him up by his entrails. But my wolf says he won't."

My brother's words should have reassured me. But all I felt was a cold pit in the middle of my stomach where there should have been butterflies.

"Hey." I looked up at him. "I'm here if you need me, yeah?" He gave me a crooked smile.

I nodded. Cade always had my back. He tipped his head to me and walked down the hallway.

I absently folded a few pairs of socks, my anxiety ratcheting higher.

A soft knock at the door found my mom waiting in the hallway, a soft smile on her face.

"Can I come in?"

"Always," I answered, knowing I could use some motherly advice. I moved the laundry basket to the floor.

She came in and settled on the bed next to me.

"You all right?" She looked me in the eye. Her pale, white-blonde hair fell over her shoulder. I glanced down and pulled my long dark ponytail over my shoulder, fiddling with the ends.

"I don't know," I replied honestly.

"What are you worrying about?"

"I guess all of it," I said with a heavy sigh. "Honestly." I met her gaze. "I don't *want* to be Bowen's mate."

Her forehead wrinkled as her eyebrows nearly met. "Well, I can't say I've ever heard of a case of true mates not wanting each other."

I cringed. It wasn't that I didn't *want* him. My wolf

did. Wanted him desperately. It was the human half of me that wanted nothing to do with him.

"Wolf does. Wolf tells me he is my mate. I…the rest of me just hasn't caught up yet, I guess."

"It's not how you dreamed as a girl that you might find a mate?" Mom guessed correctly.

"Probably." I wouldn't admit how much he scared me. My fingers twisted my hair around.

"I think once the two of you get to know each other better, you'll feel differently." Mom patted my hand. "You'll still find your fairy tale; it'll just be more mundane than what happens in the stories." She winked, then thoughtfully pursed her lips. "Raven, I know we've talked about mates and things, but you know you can ask me any questions about the physical side of mating, right? If you have questions?"

I cringed again. "Ew. Yes. Thank you."

Mom chuckled. "I won't say more on the topic. Just know that true mates sometimes feel physical urges more adamantly than other pairs. It can take you by surprise."

"Mom," I stopped. Did I really want to go there? I grit my teeth. "Were—are—you and Dad true mates?"

"Yes." Her eyes lit up like stars in a night sky.

"Okay. Thanks. I don't think I need to know anything else right now."

She laughed and squeezed my shoulder as she rose to leave.

"Try not to worry too much. The wolf is always right in matters of the heart. It's something innate in the werewolf psyche. Other creatures can't recognize a true mate like we do. It's okay to be excited about it, even if you're unsure." She smiled warmly at me. "Oh, before I forget to tell you, I've invited Bowen for dinner Monday night. I thought it might be good for you all to get to know each other—and for us to get to know him, too—at least a little more before the ceremony next weekend."

Great.

****

Second week of December

School Monday morning was just odd. As soon as Bowen was seen in the office getting his schedule, gossip lit the halls like wildfire.

Aria, my best human friend, sidled up to my locker. "Rave, did you see that yummy piece of senior who just transferred?"

My cheeks flushed as Wolf growled inside me. "I saw him." Saw him and immediately did an about-face and took the long way to my locker.

"You saw him? That's it? Girl, you gotta get your eyes checked." She leaned against the bank of lockers and looked down the hall and smoothed a piece of tawny hair. "Skylar just texted one of her friends from cheerleading camp. Turns out he's Bowen Oakes. Like, *the* basketball star from Woodard. I wonder what he's doing here? Weird time to move, in the middle of your senior year? Anyway, I heard he parties a lot, too. Skylar won't wait long to try to get him to one, I bet. Her friend said he has *the moves*, if you know what I mean." She winked at me as my stomach turned to lead and fell somewhere down around my toes.

I tried to ignore the buzz flitting through the school about Bowen and his many conquests and his great prowess—on and off the court. It made me literally sick to think about it. I had to take deep breaths through my nose more than once to quell the rising nausea. What was so different about me that anything he did with me would be special? It hardened my resolve to keep my distance.

It would have worked better if Bowen hadn't been unexpectedly in my science class. He'd probably failed Junior Science and had to retake it. It was an excruciating hour of doing my best not to look at him but being utterly aware of him and the way his eyes were burning a hole in the back of my head.

It was a relief when the bell rang and I could escape. Even though he wasn't sitting behind me in last period, I could still feel the hole his eyes seemed to have carved in the back of my skull. Tension crawled over my scalp.

I wasn't feeling so hot by the time cheerleading practice rolled around, and things were only worse when Skylar, captain of the cheerleading squad, was dishing to someone about sitting next to the new guy in her last period class and how they'd flirted the whole time. Wolf wanted to go straight for her jugular. The human half wondered how much of what she said was true. Surely, he felt at least a fraction of the jealousy I did. Wouldn't that prevent him from going after other girls? But if he'd already been with who-knows-how-many other girls…would one more make a difference to him? Even knowing I was his mate? I swallowed thickly and put a hand over my achy stomach.

"Raven, are you sick?" one of the cheerleaders asked.

"Probably something I ate. I may see if I can sit this one out today."

Aria frowned and nodded sympathetically in my direction, overhearing. Her eyes were a little unfocused. I looked harder at her. I might not be the only one feeling sick. Aria looked pale.

"Let's hustle up, ladies!" Mrs. Johnston called us from the locker room.

I'd done gymnastics since I was little and was an excellent tumbler. I was always on time, never rocked the boat. I decided to use the sick card today.

"Mrs. Johnston, I'm really feeling awful today. Can I watch from the sidelines for a while?"

Mrs. Johnston gave me a once-over as her eyebrow raised. "Sure, Raven. Just watch. Sip some water."

The problem was that sitting on the sidelines gave me not only a view of my fellow cheerleaders and the routines we were supposed to be learning but also of the boys' varsity practice going on at the other end of the gym.

Bowen was here, too. My stomach churned.

I planned to flee the second practice was over.

Chapter 8
Bowen

I could feel her. The second I came out of the guys'
locker room, the hairs on the back of my neck stood up,
and Wolf lunged toward Raven, sitting against the wall
near the stage, watching a group of brightly dressed
girls. Our eyes met, and my heart stuttered. I gave her a
brief nod before forcing myself to turn back to my
practice.

Coach Watson blew a quick blast into his whistle,
and we rounded up. He started without any preamble.
"Boys, we have a new forward. Bowen Oakes. He'll be
starting first string."

My shoulders tensed as a few grunts and irritated
throat-clearings echoed around the circle of guys. My
eyes swung to Cade.

He clapped the tall boy beside him on the shoulder
and squeezed lightly. The tall boy's eyes were dejected,
his mouth a downward slash across his face. That must
be who I just replaced.

Coach said something else, and I tuned back in
only to hear him say, "Go take warmup shots. Five
minutes." The whistle shrilled again, and Wolf recoiled
at the high pitch.

Moving with the herd to the ball rack, I snagged a
ball, the feel of the tiny bumps in the leather against my
fingers bringing instant relief to the tight muscles in my

shoulders.

I was king here in this sanctuary of the basketball court. My bicep flexed, and I reminded myself that Victor had no power over me here or anywhere else. Never again.

Cade bumped my shoulder as he reached across me for a ball.

"We're *all* a team here. We help each other. Yeah?" His words were soft, meant only for me, gauging my reaction. His blue eyes were narrowed.

"I'm a team player. Packs and teams have to work together. You're the captain here." I outranked him in pack hierarchy. Though we were in different packs, I still held more dominance. But here, this team of humans and the two of us, this was Cade's pack. He knew their strengths and weaknesses. I didn't. Yet. I acknowledged he called the shots here with a slight tip of my chin.

Cade nodded, satisfied with my answer. His quick slap to my back both startled and pleased me. "Then let's play ball."

"Let's play ball," I echoed quietly. I glanced once more at Raven, who still sat against the wall, sipping from a water bottle. She wasn't participating with the others. I wondered why. A muscle in her jaw twitched as her eyes stayed riveted on her squad.

With a sigh, I dribbled twice and sank a three-pointer.

****

Practice was good for my focus and my muscles. I was lathered in sweat once we were finished. Wolf's tongue flopped around, happy with the exercise.

Putting my ball back on the rack, I caught Raven's

stiff retreat out the double doors of the gym. My fist clenched. I wasn't sure how to make things better with Raven if she wouldn't even speak to me. Wolf whined inside.

"Hey, see you at the house?" Cade called as he headed to the locker room.

"Yeah. I'm going to shower and head over."

"See ya there." Cade waved.

Dinner. With Raven's parents. Unease slithered inside me.

The unease was momentarily replaced by annoyance as Skylar, the blonde who'd given me at least a dozen flirtatious looks during the last hour, waited for me as I left the locker room.

"Bowen! I thought you were never coming out!" She latched onto my arm, and Wolf bared his teeth. She must have just doused herself in perfume. It was potent. Her long lashes batted against her smooth skin as her springy ponytail swished against her shoulders. Victor's preferred type for me. I fought the sudden reaction to smile and flirt with her. I didn't need to do that anymore. Victor no longer watched my every move.

Feeling a deep sense of freedom, I shook her off.

"Sorry. I'm on my way to have dinner with some friends."

"Oh. Well, did you hear about the party this Friday night? I know you're new, and I wanted to make sure you were invited. It's at Darnell Thompson's house. His parties are epic. We could maybe go together?"

I resisted the urge to shudder. I'd been to more parties than I could count in the past four years.

"Maybe some other time." I smiled politely and walked toward my car.

Relief bloomed inside my chest. I hadn't been at liberty to say no to a girl like that since I'd become a member of Victor's pack.

The relief was short lived as I turned out of the parking lot.

Dinner.

****

Nervously, I cleared my throat before leaving my car. I was parked at the Rivers' house, showered, changed, and ready to go in for a nice family dinner with my intended.

I didn't know how to do a nice family dinner.

Victor had taken me from my mom when I was fourteen, and there certainly hadn't been any cozy family dinners with him. Family dinner with Victor involved blood loss, mangling, and varying degrees of hatred.

I took another breath and opened the car door. Cold November air rushed to greet me, my breath plumed, and my hair crisped, still damp from my hurried shower at school after practice. Everything smelled clean here. And held traces of Raven's cinnamon and plum smell. The barest hint of her caught on the wind and sent my blood racing.

"Come on in, Bowen!" Mr. Rivers called as he opened the door.

"Thank you, sir." I walked into the heat of the entryway.

"No need for the sir. Steve is fine."

I smiled tightly and nodded. I had charm in spades that I could turn on at a second's notice. Girls like Skylar fell all over me when I used it. But charming a future father-in-law? I'd never crossed this bridge. I flexed my bicep under my tattoo, reminding myself I didn't have to play anyone's game anymore. I didn't have to bring the charm. I just had to bring myself. Which was equally terrifying. I wasn't even sure who I was after the past four years with Victor. But I knew who I wanted to be.

My mouth watered as smells from the kitchen wafted into the living room. Home-cooked meals had been scarce in my recent history.

"Hey, Bowen," Cade said as he crossed through the room in socked feet, his hair wet from a quick shower, too. My muscles tensed hearing him, still unsure where we were while on his territory, but not on the court. "Nice job at practice today." He nodded, a dark piece of hair falling over his forehead. His eyes were steady, and I realized Cade and I were on more solid footing than Raven and I were.

I nodded back. We were good.

"Raven's upstairs." Cade shrugged apologetically and turned to go into the kitchen. I shoved my hands into my pockets uncomfortably.

"Can I get you something to drink?" Steve asked politely. His eyes were kind, but they missed nothing. Not the nervous swallow, not my stiff posture.

"Water would be great," I croaked.

****

Dinner was delicious, and Steve, Amalie, and Cade were all welcoming enough. Raven sat next to me, her back ramrod straight. She didn't do much besides push her food around on her plate. She remained silent throughout the entire meal unless someone asked her a direct question. And even then, she only gave the barest answers possible.

Dinner would have been pleasant if my stomach hadn't been tied up in so many knots and Wolf hadn't paced the whole time. I was so close to Raven. So close to my mate. But as far away as I'd ever been. Part of me wanted to howl in frustration, while the other part of me was insatiably curious.

I cleared my throat. "Raven, would you pass the rolls?"

Wordlessly, she snatched the basket and handed it to me. Reaching out, I took the basket, and our fingers grazed. A shock like a lightning bolt shot up my arm, and I nearly dropped the basket.

Raven gasped, her wide eyes flying to my face.

"I'm sorry. I need to be excused." Her voice was breathless, color rising in her cheeks as she threw her napkin on the table and fled the room. Her footsteps echoed lightly as she ran upstairs.

I sat frozen, my arm extended, still holding the rolls. Silence held the room.

"Are you all right?" Amalie finally broke the quiet.

I cleared my throat again. "Yeah. Yeah, I'm fine." Maybe. My arm still tingled.

"I think this is going to take some getting used to," Steve said with a chagrined smile. I nodded back, still a little dazed.

Chapter 9
Raven

I sprinted to my room. My heart pounded, my fingers still prickled where he'd touched me, and Wolf was nearly having convulsions in agitation.

He smelled like Skylar.

Why did he smell like her?

Why did I react to his touch like that?

Why did I even care?

I jammed my fist to my mouth, pressing my lips tight against it so I wouldn't scream my frustration out loud.

Emotions, thick, virulent, and heavy, twisted in my gut, bringing the nausea I'd felt all day to a head.

Yanking open the door to the Jack and Jill bathroom Cade and I shared, I heaved what little I'd eaten at dinner into the toilet. I wretched until nothing came up, then I flushed down the physical evidence of my inner turmoil.

I washed my hands and rinsed my mouth out several times before taking a couple big gulps of water straight from the faucet.

Even Wolf was in misery, wondering why the scent of Skylar's body spray had been all over Bowen. Despite that, Wolf still longed for him. He was ours. Wolf gnashed her teeth. We needed to finish the Claiming. Surely our bond would be strong enough after both parties were properly Claimed. Strong enough that Skylar would have no hold on him.

I sank into my desk chair and put my face in my hands, scrubbing them over my cheeks.

This was an impossible situation.

How could I want someone to be mine this much with one breath and feel nothing but revulsion and detestation for them the next?

And then there was my fear.

Bowen terrified me. I couldn't look at him without remembering the way his saliva had dripped down his canines, tinged red with Cade's blood. The way his muscles bunched and corded as he fought. The manic look in his eyes the first time our gaze connected.

My stomach threatened to revolt again. I took a few more deep breaths, and the wave of nausea passed.

Of two things I was very certain. I loathed Bowen Oakes. And I needed to Claim him.

Because he was mine.

****

Tuesday, more rumors whispered down the hallways. I shut my eyes and turned deaf ears when I could. But nothing I heard quelled the uneasy roiling in my gut.

I didn't think Coach would let me sit out two days in a row without a major excuse, and I couldn't very well tell her my wolf and I were at serious odds because Bowen Oakes was my mate. Really, it would just take too long to explain. Also, Coach was a human and blissfully unaware of the existence of werewolves.

So I changed into my T-shirt and shorts and met the rest of the squad in our corner of the gym. The curtains were drawn across the stage. Rachel and the rest of the drama club were putting on the finishing touches on things and having last-minute checks. All the cast members had been allowed to skip their classes that afternoon so they could do a dress rehearsal. From the sounds of things, there were a few minor issues.

"No! You have to swoon like this!" Rachel's voice sounded close to the curtain, followed by a loud thump.

"Rachel, I'm not going down like that. I'll bust my chin open!"

"Ugh, I think I just did." Rachel's voice was chagrined.

I smiled. I looked forward to going to the play tomorrow to support my friend's directorial debut.

"Girls!" Skylar called us in for a huddle, bringing my attention back to the group even as Wolf seethed. All focus was lost again as the boys spilled from the locker room. They must have had some sort of talk before practice to make them this late entering the gym.

My heart kicked up as Bowen came into view. Just like yesterday, his eyes locked onto mine as he began his warmup lap. A quick nod, then he fell into step next to Cade.

Cade, cheerfully oblivious, or maybe just cheerfully obnoxious, gave me a quick smile and a wave before they turned the corner and continued running.

"Mmm. I would love to tap that." Skylar rubbed her finger against her bottom lip as she openly stared at Bowen's jogging backside.

Wolf growled inside me, my internal storm momentarily overridden with white-hot jealousy.

"Told you she'd already set her sights on him," Aria whispered as she came up beside me. Her eyes were bloodshot. Concern immediately tripped up my spine.

"Aria, are you okay?"

She shrugged, her nonchalance not making it to her eyes. "Yeah. Didn't sleep much last night."

I was about to say more when Coach blasted in from outside. "Sorry, girls." She was slightly out of breath, her short curls fanning out like a halo. "I had a quick errand I had to run right after school and got caught in some traffic. Skylar, have you led stretches yet?"

"We were just getting ready to."

Coach nodded, then practice was underway.

****

Mom had invited Bowen again for dinner since last night had ended so fantastically. I couldn't decide if I was surprised or not that he'd taken her up on the offer.

I gave myself a stern lecture in my bedroom mirror when I got home. Cade hogged the shower. He needed it. He smelled like unwashed dog after practice. We hadn't done much strenuous work at cheer practice tonight, so I hadn't sweat.

But my palms were already slick with anxiety, waiting for Bowen to show up at my doorstep again.

"You can do this," I told myself. "You are Raven Rivers. Bowen is your mate. There is no reason for you to be nervous." Or to be afraid. I shuddered again as memories laced with the terror of war popped into my brain. I abandoned the mirror pep talk but did resolve to get a grip on my emotions and at least make it through dinner.

"Raven! Bowen's here! Come on down for dinner," Mom called up the stairs.

Swallowing hard once more at my reflection, I steeled my nerves and went downstairs.

There he was. The whole stairway reeked of cedar and brown sugar. I hated that my heart rate picked up—both from his scent and the fear that spiked adrenaline through my limbs.

He can't do anything to you here, I reminded myself. Mom, Dad, and Cade were all in the house with me.

"Hi, Raven." His deep voice wrapped around me like velvet.

I managed a tight nod and a hard swallow, then slipped into the dining room. Mom had the table all set but was still bringing in dishes from the kitchen.

"I'll get the salad," I blurted and dashed through to the kitchen. Admitting to myself that I was a coward, I stayed in the kitchen, gripping the wooden bowl of salad until chairs started scraping in the dining room.

Bringing in the salad, I exhaled as I noted an empty chair on the opposite side of the table from Bowen. Plunking the salad unceremoniously on the table, I scurried to the vacant seat just as Cade came in from the living room. He quirked an eyebrow but took the open seat next to Bowen.

It was awkward. Painfully so. But I managed. It was easier sitting where I didn't have to touch him or look directly at him. I even achieved a few words of conversation. I counted that as a win.

I was looking forward to Rachel's play tomorrow, if only so I didn't have to suffer through another awkward dinner.

****

Soft music flitted through the gym, echoing oddly

in the corners where the acoustics were beyond pitiful. There was a general hum of conversation as people filed in and settled in the bleachers and in the chairs set up on the gymnasium floor.

"Hey!" Kyp waved when he saw Cade and me entering through one of the side doors.

"Kyp," Cade called back. I smiled.

"Rachel had me reserve two rows for everyone. Her parents will be here"—he pointed to two empty chairs—"but the rest of this row and the one behind are for special friends." He winked. There were members of three different werewolf packs coming to support Rachel. Anxiety made a sudden appearance. Surely Bowen wouldn't come. He hardly even knew Rachel. Although she was Kyp's mate. I mentally shook my head. He wasn't here now. There was no reason to think he'd show up later.

Seconds later, Mr. and Mrs. Crumb arrived. I knew who they were, but I'd never been introduced to them.

"I see Sarah. I'm going to go say hi," Cade whispered nervously as Mrs. Crumb gave Kyp a warm hug. I glanced at Cade.

"Cade?" I wasn't sure Sarah Thornehill was in my brother's league. Not because I didn't think he wasn't good enough for her or anything, but she was Beta of her pack. She'd be expected to marry an Alpha or a Beta someday. Cade was high up the pecking order in the pack hierarchy, but he wasn't that high.

"I'm just going over to say hi. Nothing wrong with being friendly."

"Are you trying to convince me or you?" I whispered back.

He gave me a scathing look. Tapping my elbow

once, he turned and walked in her direction. I watched with interest as her whole face seemed to perk up when her gaze landed on Cade. They stood a little way apart; Cade made no move to touch her. He said something, and then they smiled and walked back into the hallway together.

Oh, yeah. He was definitely getting in over his head.

"Raven, have you met Rachel's parents?" Kyp asked.

I quickly turned with a smile on my face to formally meet Mr. and Mrs. Crumb.

Megan and Sam sauntered in just a few minutes later as the Crumbs and I were discussing the baking business Rachel and Megan were creating and that I sometimes decorated cookies for.

"Sam, Megan!" Mrs. Crumb said happily as Meg hugged Mrs. and then Mr. Crumb before sitting in the seat next to me.

"Hey, Raven. Where's everyone else?" Megan nodded toward the rest of the empty row of seats.

Sam popped into the aisle side seat next to Meg. "I thought Cade said he was coming with you?"

"Oh, he did. Last I saw he was following Sarah Thornehill into the hallway."

A grin tickled the side of Sam's mouth.

"I see," Megan quipped, her eyes sparkling. I rolled mine.

Not three minutes later, the hair on the back of my neck stood straight up. I didn't have time to respond before Bowen slid into the seat next to me, followed by Cade, and then Sarah. Jake and Cindy, two others from my pack, finished off the train of werewolves.

He was so close I could hardly breathe. I scrunched to the far side of my seat, afraid of what might happen if his leg brushed against mine.

Before anyone even had time to wave or say hello, the scent of Skylar's perfume infiltrated the space, and Wolf's hackles rose to new heights.

"Hey, guys! Bowen, there's a group of us sitting up in the bleachers. Do you want to come? Cade, some of the team is there, too."

She gave me a fake smile. "Hey, Raven." I was on the squad after all. My teeth ground together.

"I'm good here." His deep voice rolled over me like music. Wolf's tight muscles relaxed while the human part of me held rigid in my chair.

"If you're sure. We're right there if you change your mind." She winked at him, then pointed up the bleachers. "Cade?" she asked.

"Better view here," he answered with a touch of saccharine sweetness.

"All right. See you all around then." She looked at me, glanced at Bowen, then smirked to herself, and flounced toward the stairs to the bleachers. I shoved a growl back behind my teeth.

Cade waited only until she was barely out of earshot before snickering loudly, covering his mouth with his hand, and elbowing Bowen.

"Dude," Cade started.

Bowen grunted and flicked Cade in the back of his head. My mouth almost fell open in shock. When did they become best friends?

Kyp turned around from the row in front of us as Sam leaned down to see the two of them. "Boys," he said with mocking authority.

We were saved from further antics as the lights dimmed and Rachel's voice boomed a thank you for coming to the audience and a reminder to please silence all cell phones.

"Relax. I won't bite." His whispered words sent little shivers rippling over my skin, and the hush of his breath near my ear had Wolf's hackles lying flat. I couldn't help but hear the difference between *won't* and *don't*. I shuddered. I couldn't make my muscles unclench.

The heavy velvet curtains drew back, and I swallowed. *The Elf King and His Horse, Tremaine* commenced. Bowen shifted, intentionally bringing his leg closer to my space. Wolf rammed me hard from the inside, her desires clear. Compromise was in order. Bowen made the first move. She insisted we reciprocate. Screwing my eyes shut while my heart thundered, I forced my leg to move, bringing it a hair's breadth from Bowen. I didn't want to touch him. But Wolf was insistent.

He shifted again, and his thigh brushed lightly against mine. Instead of rocketing bolts of lightning, this time the contact made pleasant heat rush through me. And even more surprising, it took some of my tension.

The play continued, but I didn't follow much of it. I was both confused and hyper-aware of the feelings coursing through me in reaction to the man sitting next to me.

Chapter 10
Bowen

I thought Saturday and the ceremony would never come. It wasn't like I didn't have anything to keep me busy. I was still getting to know the guys on the basketball team—making myself one of them and not an outsider who had come in and stolen Jamie Dayton's place as forward. The pack was still finding its footing with Kyp as the new Alpha, and I was doing everything I could to make that transition work. Kyp and I were still trying to figure out what he wanted and needed from me as his Beta. Fortunately, with the holidays coming up, there wasn't anything super strenuous at school. Finals wouldn't be until after Christmas break. And then there was Raven.

Thoughts of her consumed me. The fact she seemed determined to do everything she could to stay away from me both hurt and confused me. How could she not want to be near me? I wanted to spend every single second with her. Wasn't that a mate thing?

I was trying to give her space.

I thought it might kill me in the process.

****

"Bowen, your wolf is practically frothing through your skin," Kyp commented Saturday afternoon. I'd come over to his house so we could discuss a few pack members who were having some difficulty acclimating to life without a sadistic control freak as their Alpha. They were deeply scarred, and rightly so. Jennifer had some good counseling ideas we planned to put into place.

"Sorry. I don't guess my head is exactly where it should be for pack matters."

"I can't say I blame you." My brother smiled at me.

We didn't know each other well, but tragedy and a shared parent had bonded us and cemented our relationship within the pack. "At least you know what it's like," I commented dryly.

"I do. But Rachel was far more receptive than Raven is toward you."

I glanced at him and lifted an eyebrow. "Yeah." I wasn't sure what else to say.

"Maybe your mate bond will make her feel differently. There's something solid and unbreakable once you're Claimed."

"Maybe that's the problem. I Claimed her, but she hasn't Claimed me back." I ran my hands through my hair in frustrated anticipation.

Turning back to pack matters, we were able to schedule several pack members into different therapy sessions.

"Go, Bowen. I'll finish this. You can't sit still. Go shower, or go for a run, whatever you need to do. I'll meet you back here when it's time to go." Kyp smiled. "And I'm happy for you. Really happy." His eyes—so similar to mine—gentled and took on the look of an older brother. Though we were barely a month apart in age, in that moment, my mind was at rest, knowing that I wasn't alone. And soon, I'd be Claimed. Wolf shook with anticipation.

****

The sun was about to set. Long fingering shadows streaked the cold ground as purple and gold flamed behind the trees. It was time.

We had decided to have our Claiming and the Ancient Marriage Rites of Mates at the communal fire pit out behind Sam and Megan's cabin. Heat filled my chest as I thought about it. I was about the most unworthy wolf in the history of werewolves to have the honor of finding a true mate. But I was grateful. I wouldn't waste this.

Wanting a moment's privacy, I took myself into the tree line and watched with my human eyes for a few minutes. Wolves were gathering. Shades of brown, gray, black, and auburn dotted the landscape and blended into the shadows.

I stripped out of my clothes and shut my eyes. Holding my arms out to my sides, I let myself feel every part of my shift. Possibly the most significant shift of my life.

Black fur whispered through my skin, the fur above my heart a patch of silver, as my claws replaced my fingernails, pushing out sharp and shiny. My back twisted and elongated as my tail separated from my backbone. Curved canines jutted through my gums as my face melted, rearranging itself into my wolf's muzzle. Whiskers danced gently in the breeze as my ears pushed through my scalp. Falling to the forest floor on all fours, I gave a tremendous shake and let the chill November wind whip through my ruff.

Scents of the woods and of the gathered wolves blasted into my nose, and I inhaled, trying to remember everything about this moment. This moment of anticipation. This moment that would define me for the rest of my life.

Chapter 11
Raven

Rev—Reverend Daniel Butterfield—an old family friend and basically our pack chaplain, stood on the stump by the fire ring. The only wolf in skin with only two other humans present. Everyone else wore fur. Jennifer Kypson sat next to Megan's grandpa, George Carmichael, in a pair of chairs set up on the side.

Wind whistled through the last of the leaves clinging to the trees and rustled them. I shivered. Not from the cold. I was plenty warm with my sleek black fur wrapped snugly over my body. I shivered from something much more sinister.

I stood, waiting, my paws feeling heavy even though Wolf was elated. Megan and Rachel were standing as my attendees. There were girls in the pack I'd known longer, but it somehow felt right to have them here. Two girls who had recently been changed into werewolves, taking part in the oldest and most revered of our pack rituals. The old and the new coming together.

Trying to relax my muscles, I told myself this was a good thing. Wolves didn't make mistakes about their true mates. Even though I was still plenty unsure of Bowen. Still, I knew in my heart that we would someday be together. Once I got over several different aversions to him…and my fear of him.

Rev's chocolatey skin and frizzy gray hair glowed orange in the firelight. He smiled and motioned for me to come forward.

Megan nudged me with her nose on my right while Rachel brushed her tail over my left flank.

This was it.

Slowly I made my way to the center of the ring, walking through an honor guard of wolves that felt like a gauntlet. Meg and Rachel melted into the pack, and I was left standing alone by the fire.

The breath caught in my lungs as Rev motioned to the other side of the clearing, and Bowen stepped out. Kyp trailed him.

It wasn't terror that flashed over my skin as I expected. There was heat, sudden and swelling in my chest. He was regal. His head high, chest out, silvery-white patch shining in the darkening evening. His steps were measured but not arrogant. He exuded confidence, and even the human part of me admired the animalistic grace and poise with which he carried himself. There was no doubt he was a dominant Beta. I allowed myself a moment of appreciation before letting my anxiety take over again.

The breeze changed direction, and I caught a whiff of my family. They were all clustered at the front of the gathering, not far behind me. Mom, Dad, Cade. My personal cheer squad and my supports.

Wolf swallowed as Bowen stepped into the ring of the firelight. His gaze met mine. Excitement danced in their brown depths. Not soulless now, but deep and searching in a way that kindled a fire in my belly and filled me with confidence enough to hold his gaze.

He stopped in front of me, and his scent of cedar

and brown sugar enveloped me in a musky haze that went straight to my head.

Before I could stop her, Wolf leaned forward and scented him, burying our nose in the silky fur of his neck and running up to the back of his jaw.

Mortified, I tried to jerk back, but Bowen stopped me as he leaned his massive head down and scented me, too.

Every hair on my hide stood at attention as his nose skimmed over my neck and lingered near my jaw.

If I'd been in my human skin, I'd have resembled a tomato.

"Blessings have fallen upon us," Rev intoned with a smile. Bowen and I broke apart, although not far as Rev began the ceremony.

The ceremony itself was everything I'd ever dreamed it might have been as a girl. Although my choice of mate would have been different.

But as it was, I still felt some of my lingering fears as Rev raised his hands. A shower of sparks burst upward at just the right moment, illuminating his gesture and wreathing Bowen and me in a glowing halo.

"You may now present your Claim." Rev's voice was full of reverence.

Bowen stepped forward, a mere hairsbreadth away from me. He nudged me gently once with his nose before opening his mouth.

Moonlight streamed onto his white incisors. I locked my legs in place, fearful they'd tremble.

Gently, more gently than I'd thought him capable, he closed his mouth over my muzzle, biting down just enough that I felt it.

Fissures of heat and something akin to sparkles raced through my veins this time. He let me go and stepped back, looking down at me with...adoration?

It was my turn.

My heart thundered, my focus sharpening like laser beams as I let my wolf eyes dilate further. He was tall enough as his wolf that I'd have to perch on my back legs to reach him.

As my thighs bunched to spring up, he surprised me again and bowed his head to me in an unexpected display of humility and kindness that showed his attentiveness to my needs. Not something I'd anticipated from him given his reputation.

Stilling my trembling nerves, I reached up and opened my mouth, fitting it over his muzzle. I bit down, a little too hard in my nervousness. He winced, and I immediately released and backed away.

Stunned, I felt mental tethers forming, braiding themselves into an intricate pattern with Bowen's.

Raven, his voice echoed softly in my mind.

Bowen, I replied, my own mental voice shaky and unsure.

His wolf smiled down at me, and perhaps the most shocking thing of all, I felt my fear and dread of him lift.

And that was it. I was a Claimed, married werewolf.

After, we went for a run, the three packs of us together, and it was one of the most freeing moments of my life. I wasn't ready to live with Bowen, or do anything else with Bowen, but the terror I'd worn like a cloak since the battle had gone. I was still wary, but I was mostly at peace.

****

Winter break started with fresh snowfall. It was delightful to romp in fur through the powder. Kyp, Bowen, and a few of the younger wolves from their pack came to Wolfe land, where we all played for hours. It was surprisingly good bonding between packs, though I still didn't let myself get too close to Bowen. I still needed to ease into this transition.

Mom seemed to realize this best, and she invited Bowen over for dinner every night. Without fail, he came. Now that the choking fear was gone, we could have some basic conversations without me needing to throw up afterward.

He became a fixture in my periphery, and I slowly started to thaw toward him.

Christmas Day was a bustle of activity at our house. We had our own family Christmas that morning, but then it was a flurry of motion to get things in order and start the meal. Kyp, Jennifer, Jonathan Stone—a wolf from my pack who had recently started dating Jennifer—and Kyp, Rachel, Dominic and Mary Wolfe, Sam and Meg, and Austin and Sarah Thornehill were all coming over that night for a Christmas party. And Bowen.

"Raven, would you check the rolls to make sure they're rising?"

"Sure, Mom." I stepped into the laundry room off the kitchen. A lot of heat got trapped back here when the oven was on.

"They're looking nice and fluffy," I told her.

"Good. Can you make cranberry sauce? I should have made it yesterday. I hope it has time to chill all the way. Where is your brother?"

"I'll make the cranberry sauce." It was a pretty foolproof recipe, which is why Mom handed that one over to me. Great chef I was not. "Cade is shoveling the driveway."

"Right. The casserole! I need to get the sweet potatoes going!"

I smiled to myself. Mom was frazzled, but she was loving it.

By the time everyone arrived that night, everything was ready, but I was exhausted. I was happy to see my friends and even admitted to myself that it was nice to see Bowen. But about an hour after dinner, I just needed a minute.

I slipped unnoticed out of the commotion and snuck upstairs to my bedroom. Shutting the door softly, I went and sat on the edge of my bed. The din of games and laughter wafted up from downstairs, but it was a relief to have most of it blocked out.

I took a few breaths, calming myself and recharging a minute. A light tap at my door startled me from my self-centered thoughts.

"Raven?" It was Bowen.

My cheeks heated, and my heart picked up. I wasn't sure how I felt about the two of us being alone in my bedroom.

"Hi," I said shyly as I opened the door. I cleared my throat. "I just needed a minute of quiet."

He nodded, looking slightly uncomfortable himself. "Um, I actually wondered if I could give you your Christmas present. You know, without everyone else watching."

My eyebrows lifted. "Oh." Guilt swamped me. "I, I didn't get you anything. Sorry."

"I didn't expect you to." His grin was easy, and I felt compelled to open the door and let him in. I didn't shut it all the way behind him, but enough that most of the noise was muted.

Chapter 12
Bowen

I was surprised when Raven opened the door and let me into her room. This was an intimate piece of her I hadn't yet been privy to. Her room was simple, tastefully done in shades of blues with a computer desk and a thick stack of graphic design and artistry books stacked on one side across the room. A cozy chair with a small table and lamp was against the wall opposite the bed. A dresser hugged the wall just inside the door, and that's where I put the little black box I'd been so nervously rubbing my fingers over all night.

Clearing my throat, I nodded to the box. "It's probably still premature, but I wanted you to have it."

She turned her clear blue eyes on me, wide with trepidation. My gut clenched. Was she so scared of my gift as all that?

She swallowed and reached out, cupping the box in her hands. Hesitating a moment, she cracked the lid back.

I found myself holding my breath as she looked down at the ring I'd had made. It was a simple gold band etched with tiny waves that wrapped around the finger but ended in an oak leaf set with a diamond in the middle. Her face softened, and air entered my lungs again.

"It's beautiful." Her eyes were sincere, even

though her words were hushed.

So are you, I wanted to say. She was like a skittish kitten. I didn't want to say the wrong thing. Wolf nudged me. She liked the ring. I could tell.

"Thank you."

"You're welcome."

Raven opened her mouth to say something when a chime cut her off. "Oh, it's Aria. I've texted her three or four times, and she hasn't responded. I'm a little worried about her."

"How come?" I was pleased she'd told me that much.

"She started acting a little spacey and kind of weird before break. I've been trying to figure out what's bugging her, but she's been going days between texting me back and hasn't taken any of my calls. I know her extended family is in town, so maybe that's keeping her busy." Her eyebrows drew together.

I could tell she didn't think that was the case, but I didn't feel it was my job to point it out.

Raven tucked her bottom lip between her teeth in a way that sent Wolf shooting thoughts through my head that were better left undisturbed for the time being. Fascinated, I watched her carefully lift the ring from the box and admire it.

"Is it all right if I wear it on my right hand for now?" Her voice was tiny, unsure. My heart clenched a little at her words. It was a wedding ring. She knew that. But at least she was willing to wear it—which was honestly more than I'd hoped for at our current stage.

"That's fine." It wasn't entirely fine, but it would do. And I liked the thought that she'd be wearing something significant that marked her as mine.

She slipped it onto her finger, and the diamond caught the lamplight, refracting little spangles on the wall. She smiled up at me and my lips curved in response.

"Thanks. And thanks for letting me…for taking things slow."

I nodded, wishing we weren't taking things quite this slow. "Are you ready to go back down, or do you need me to give you another minute?"

She searched my face for a minute and ran her finger over her ring. "I think I'm good."

I offered her my arm with a cheeky grin, half afraid she'd run from me.

Tentatively, she lightly touched her fingers to the inside of my arm. Just her featherlight touch made my heart kick up a notch.

"Merry Christmas, Raven."

"Merry Christmas, Bowen."

****

It was New Year's Eve, and the packs were all gathered on Kypson territory this time. It was strange to have so many wolves on the land where Victor had set up camp. It was understood that the general area was unofficially Kyp's land now.

There were a lot of bad memories here, but slowly, they were being replaced with good ones. Kyp really cared about his pack, and so did I. I wanted to fix the things Victor left broken, that he'd made me party to as his Beta. With Kyp, I had a chance to right some of those wrongs.

"Bowen, I think Raven just got here." Kyp nudged me with a smile. My head jerked around to where her car was just pulling in. "Before you go to her, sometime this week, I'd like us to talk more about how the counseling is going for a couple of our wolves."

I turned back to Kyp. "I think it's helping. Jim's nightmares have decreased. Lucy told me just this evening that she is willing to talk with a counselor now, too. New year, new leaf. Do you think your mom can set that up?"

Kyp nodded. "Good. And I'll speak with either her or the counselor directly. Keep an eye on Jim. I think he feels more connected to you since you suffered along with him. I'm still too new."

"I will."

The moon was high and nearly full in the clear winter night. I watched as it flitted white light down on Raven's shiny dark hair. I was a little disappointed when she reached back in her car and put a hat on. It *was* cold, though.

Tucking an errant piece of hair behind her ear, she scanned the crowd until she found me. Anticipation tightened my gut, and Wolf yipped inside me. I smiled widely at her, pleased she'd sought me out.

It was nearly midnight, and people were gathering around. Someone was passing out sparklers. Raven shoved her hands in her coat pockets and slowly started toward me. I met her halfway. I wanted to hug her, but her back was straight, her eyes wide like prey smelling a predator.

"Hey," I said softly.

"Hey."

There was a *boom*, and we turned to watch a small firework shoot up and burst into a riot of color in the black sky dotted with stars.

The countdown started, but I only had eyes for

Raven, standing stiffly beside me. Her back was poker straight, her arms clasped securely about her middle while her mouth was a tight line across her face.

"Ten, nine, eight, seven—"

Raven turned wide eyes to me, meeting mine in the firelight. I wanted to touch her.

"One!"

More fireworks exploded, lighting her face in a wash of blue and white light. Without meaning to, my head dipped just slightly toward her.

Her eyes darted to my lips and back to my eyes. Hers were huge pale orbs in her face, wild like a spooked horse.

She turned on her heel and sprinted back to her car while cheers and shouts rose into the dark night.

My chest seized, and the breath froze in my lungs.

Raven—my mate—was terrified.

Of me.

Chapter 13
Raven

I dove into my car, slamming the locks down as I engaged the engine. Speeding down the gravel path away from Kyp's pack lands, I didn't allow myself to think, to feel.

It wasn't until I threw the car in park in my own driveway and had locked the front door behind me and bounded up the stairs to my own room, that I let myself take large shuddering breaths.

I curled up on the floor beside my bed, knees to my chest, arms holding them tightly against me. Wolf wiggled inside me, distraught with me. I was distraught with Bowen. He'd been about to kiss me. Wolf longed for it with the same fervor I recoiled from it. His lips had been on countless other girls. The thought turned my stomach.

Literally. I jumped up and ran to the bathroom and emptied my stomach into the toilet. I flushed the nasty stuff down and slumped to the floor.

I needed to get over this aversion to his past. If I couldn't, we wouldn't have a future. And that was unacceptable. He was mine. But I had no idea how to be his.

I wondered if I should text him. I did feel bad for leaving like that. I just got so tied up in knots around him. I didn't know how to behave. I didn't know how he expected me to behave. I'd never dated, never had this kind of male attention, and I didn't know what to do with it.

There on the bathroom floor, I dug out my phone. Bowen had already texted me.

—*Happy New Year. You okay?*—

I sighed. I wanted to be okay. I wasn't there yet.

Ripping my glove off with my teeth, I answered him back.

—*Sorry I left like that. Happy New Year.*—

—*Anything I can do?*—

—*Not right now. But thanks.*—

****

It was almost a relief when school started again. New Year's Day had fallen on a Sunday, so Monday morning, bright and early, I was back on my way to school. The sun glinted off the small layer of snow, and the branches creaked under their stunning layer of ice.

I was happy to be going back to a routine, but there was a knot in my stomach when I thought about Bowen. How did what happened to us over break translate back into our regular human world of school?

I should have asked him. But I hadn't because I already knew he was ready for a public relationship. My finger grazed over his ring still on my right hand. I wasn't sure what I was ready for.

"Hey, Raven," Skylar said. She sauntered by my locker as I got books out for first period.

"Oh, hey, Skylar. Did you have a good break?"

"I did. Hey. So like, are Bowen and your brother friends now?"

I was momentarily taken aback. "Yeah, I guess so." Wolf raised her head, eyes narrowing at Skylar. I had not forgotten the way Bowen had come to dinner, smelling like her.

"Hmm. I was trying to get in touch with Bowen. There's a huge first party of the new year this Friday. I want to take him." She smiled, her eyes predatory. Wolf's hackles rose. I shushed her before I growled outright.

"Um, I'm not actually sure he's on the market anymore." I desperately hoped that was true. I thought our bond would prevent his desire for other…companionship…but I wasn't absolutely certain.

Skylar snorted. "Please. I've talked to some of my friends at his old school. He's not the settling type. He wouldn't go for just one girl. No, he's a player. And I want him to *play me*." She smacked her lips, and Wolf about went for her throat.

Nausea churned in my gut. Skylar wouldn't put up any resistance. Bowen could take what he wanted from her without any fight. Bile crept into the back of my throat. Painfully, I swallowed it down.

"Anyway, thanks for the tip. See you at practice."

She strolled down the hall, leaving me alone and questioning my non-relationship with Bowen.

Chapter 14
Bowen

The school hallways teemed with emotions. I could smell the hope, the disappointment, the newness of a fresh year. Wolf puffed inside me. This year would be different for me, too. This year I had Raven. I had Kyp. I had a pack. And I no longer had Victor.

I resisted the urge to groan when Skylar saw me and loped down the hallway toward me.

"Happy New Year, Bowen!" she chirped.

"Happy New Year, Skylar," I dutifully replied. I shifted my backpack up higher on my shoulders, looping both hands around the straps so they weren't dangling at my side where Skylar could snatch one.

"Have you heard about the party on Friday? It's a huge bash to officially bring in the New Year—a week late this year—but we have one every year. Down by the river out at Power Peak. Have you been there?"

"I don't think so."

"It's out by the original Rock Falls the town is named for. You really should get to know your new area. I could show you." She smiled and batted her eyelashes. Victor would have beat me senseless if I'd had this kind of girly attention and hadn't capitalized on it. I swallowed hard.

"Thanks. I'm pretty busy with school and basketball and stuff, though."

"Well, will you at least come to the party Friday night?" It didn't matter that my hands were tangled in my backpack straps. She wrapped her tentacle-like fingers around my forearm anyway. Wolf snarled inside.

Suddenly, plum and cinnamon drifted down the hall, and Wolf's attention was immediately taken with Raven. What I saw dropped my stomach like lead. Her eyes were huge in her face, her lips a flat line. Her wolf stared reproachfully at me through her human eyes.

"Thanks, but I'm good. Have a nice day," I said brusquely to Skylar. I pivoted to see Raven turn on her heel and stalk the opposite way down the hall. This was not good.

"But Bowen," Skylar nearly whined. "I really want to go to the party. With you. I'll make it worth your while." She let her chest graze my arm, and I backed up in alarm, jerking her off balance in the process.

"Skylar, I'm good. I've got to go." I shook her off. Ugh. She clung like a second skin. I didn't care that I left her stuttering in the hall. I had to find Raven. She was far enough down the hallway I couldn't see her from where I was.

I jogged after her. Something I wouldn't have abased myself to do while still under Victor's control.

"Raven," I called her name as I found her. There weren't a lot of people in this part of the school at this hour, and I was grateful.

She turned, her expression wary.

"Hi, Bowen." Her voice was like ice.

"Look. She came onto me. I don't want anything to do with her."

Her eyes darted to my face and then the ground. I

ran a hand through my hair.

"You smell like her."

Her words felt like a punch in the gut. "I'm sorry. Like I said, she came up to me. I wasn't looking for her." I dropped my voice. "I don't even like her."

"That's a relief." I didn't miss the sarcasm in her tone. Dread writhed in my middle. The rumors. Of course she was concerned about the rumors she had to have heard. They painted me as a callous dog who screwed anything chesty or leggy. I swallowed on a dry mouth. This wasn't the time.

"Raven, look at me." I had to do what I could to set the record straight for the moment. There'd be time enough later to sort out my checkered past.

With a sigh through her nose, she raised her eyes.

"I am *only* interested in you." I wanted to touch her. Wrap my arms around her, and kiss her until she knew I was serious. Instead, I let my finger graze her wrist where her hands were clasped tightly in front of her. She still had my ring on. "*Only you.*"

She finally met my gaze.

"Do you believe me?" I asked her quietly. I desperately needed her to believe me when I said I only wanted her.

Her shoulders sagged, and I let out a breath.

"I think so."

I lifted an eyebrow. "No. I need you to know. You are the only one I'm ever going to want. Okay?"

Mate, I sent to her over our link. We had yet to use our link since the night of our Claiming.

She gasped as her gaze flew to mine. We held each other's gaze for several agonizing seconds before she slowly nodded.

Mate, she sent back.

Relief swept over me. "We're okay for now?"

"We're okay for now."

Chapter 15
Raven

I was somewhat unfocused the rest of the morning. Wolf lapped up Bowen's confirmation and declaration of matehood. The human part of me strangely reveled in it, too. I did believe him when he said he only wanted me. At least, for the moment. I still wasn't convinced I was ready to move forward with him. I was still processing his past and trying to reconcile it to my present.

I was still distracted when I went into the bathroom before lunch.

"Aria!"

My friend looked at me in the mirror where she applied lip balm to her dry mouth. Her eyes were red.

"Heyraven." Her words ran together.

"Aria? What's wrong?"

"S'fine."

"Aria. You aren't fine." My nose twitched. She didn't smell as fresh as she should have. Like she hadn't showered in a day or two. She didn't stink, but there was a layer of scent to her not normally present. Her hair was up in a messy bun. A contrast to how she usually wore it down.

Her eyes closed, and she braced her hands on the sink.

"Aria, tell me what's wrong." I rubbed a soothing

hand down her back. Wolf whimpered inside me. Something wasn't right.

"My dad left us, okay?" Her biting words stung.

My mouth hung open. "Your dad *left*?"

"That's what I said, isn't it?" Her voice cracked.

"Oh, Aria, I'm so sorry." I wrapped my arms around her in a tight hug. "When?"

"About a month ago. I thought he was coming back. I thought…he wouldn't leave *me*."

My heart squeezed painfully in my chest. The betrayal she must feel. Betrayal from the one person who should have always stood by her.

She disentangled herself from my arms and swiped under her eyes. "I mean, whatever."

"No. Not whatever. That sucks. Majorly."

Her chin wobbled before she clenched her jaw and smoothed her features. "It's fine. He can leave and go do whatever. I will be just fine without him." She unscrewed the lid from a bottle of juice and took a hefty swig. "I'll be just fine," she repeated, looking at her pale reflection in the mirror.

****

I was even more worried when Aria skipped cheerleading practice. I was so wrapped up in my concern I missed a step and nearly brought down the three girls next to me. I pulled my mind together and did my best to pay better attention.

It didn't help when I caught Bowen watching me from his side of the gym. He gave me a little half smile and tipped his head to me.

"Raven." Skylar snapped her fingers as her voice raked over my skin like claws. My eyes jerked to her and took in her flushed cheeks. "Focus here. Seriously.

80

Wipe the drool off and get with the program." My own cheeks heated. But like Skylar had room to talk. Wolf chuffed.

Coach called me over after practice ended. "Raven, may I speak with you a moment?"

"Sure, Coach. What's up?"

Coach waved to the other girls as they scattered either to the locker room or their cars. "You were particularly distracted today. Are you okay? Is everything else okay?"

My thoughts took a quick downward spiral as I thought of Aria. It must have shown on my face.

"Raven?"

"I," I started. I wanted to help Aria, but I wasn't sure this was the best way to go about it right now. I wanted to talk to my mom first. "I'm concerned about…a friend."

"You want to share? You know I'm a safe person to talk to, right?" Her green eyes were kind.

"I know, Coach. But I think I'm not ready to say anything yet."

"All right. I'll respect that. But if you find a problem, you will come to me, won't you?"

I nodded, not exactly lying to her, as she wouldn't be my first choice to confide something in, but I would tell my mom. "Have a good evening then. I'll see you tomorrow."

"Thanks, Coach. You, too."

Chapter 16
Bowen

Tuesday morning was better. I kept my nose and eyes out for Skylar and was able to give her a wide berth. Raven even let me walk with her down the hallway without flinching.

"Are you excited about Thursday's away game?" she asked as we rounded a corner and headed to our joint science class.

"I'm always excited for games."

She smiled, and my breath caught. "Cade is the same way. This will be your first game with Rock Falls High. Will it be weird?"

"I don't think so. Practices have gone really well. Cade has been great in helping me with the team and getting them to accept me." Truthfully, Cade had made this one of the best basketball experiences it could have been. If Cade had been set against me, playing with this team would have been horrible. Impossible, even. They all followed his lead. He really was the Alpha of the basketball team.

"Cade is pretty awesome like that." I heard the love she held for her brother in her tone.

We were at science. I tipped my head for her to enter first. She blushed prettily. I wasn't sure why. I didn't stop myself from watching her hips as she went back to her desk and slid in. Perfect amount of curve.

Wolf agreed. I told him to stuff his tongue back in his mouth.

Mr. Shaver brought the class to attention as soon as the bell rang. "We'll be starting a new unit today. We're going to go over the general outline of what we'll be doing in the coming weeks, and here's the really exciting part"—he gave us a teacherly look that spelled destruction for some and fun for others—"this will be culminating in a group project that will account for a large chunk of your grade." There were a few groans. "Now, before you all bemoan the hand Fate has dealt you and plan ways to set fire to my hair or whatever in vengeance, there will be surveys at the end of the project. You'll be anonymously telling me who did the work on the project and who slacked and left the work for others. Keep in mind, I am very observant, and I assure you, each student in here has his or her own flavor to the work they submit." He stopped talking and waggled a finger in the class's general direction.

A girl raised her hand a few tables over. "Yes, Taylor?"

"Will we get to pick our partners for this?"

"That's the plan."

I smiled to myself. I was going to convince Raven to be my partner. We'd be forced to spend time together.

As if hearing my thoughts, Raven shyly glanced back at me from under her lashes. She quickly turned around again, but I could hear her heartbeat accelerate. Wolf sat on his haunches proudly. We were making progress.

Very, very slow progress.

Chapter 17
Raven

I found Aria in the hallway right after last bell. She looked awful. Her eyes were still bloodshot, her hair was still in its top knot, and her clothes were wrinkled more than they should have been for the end of the school day. I'd told Mom about Aria's dad. Mom had called to check on Aria's mother, but I wasn't sure what had come of the conversation.

"Hey," I greeted my friend quietly.

"Hey," she mumbled back.

"Come on. Let's go to practice." I looped an arm through hers and tugged her down the hallway.

"I think I might skip."

"You already skipped yesterday. Coach won't be pleased. Besides, you love cheerleading. Your dream since middle school has been to make the varsity cheer squad. You, my friend, have arrived."

She smiled wanly and let me lead her into the gym. We changed quickly, the girls around us buzzing about the coming away game. Away games always seemed like some grand adventure. I usually went to watch Cade regardless, but since I was on the squad this year, I'd be on the bus with the team and the rest of the squad. It made me feel very grown up in a childish sort of way that wrung a grin from my lips.

"Ladies, change in routine," Coach announced as

she came into the locker room with a box balanced on her hip. "It's mandatory and comes down from on high. We'll go in alphabetical order. Aria Alcote, you're up first, my dear." Coach dug into the box and handed Aria a little plastic cup with a white screw-on lid. "We'll go one at a time. We learned that lesson last year when the girls' basketball team got all their urine samples mixed up. The rest of you can wait out in the gym. Do some stretches and warmups. This shouldn't take too long. Aria?"

Aria's face was gray. Her eyes grew large in her face, and she swung her gaze wildly to me. I shrugged. We all knew there would be a random drug test at some point during the year.

I'll wait outside, I mouthed.

"I think I need to go home," Aria stammered. Unease trickled down my spine.

"Oh, come on. This will just take a sec." Coach handed her the cup and gently ushered her into a bathroom stall at the back of the locker room.

I went out with the other girls and started stretching. Bowen caught my eye and winked at me. He sank a three-pointer while he knew I watched. It gave me a curious tickly sensation in my belly to know he was showing off for me.

Smiling, I turned back to my leg stretch before the other girls noticed me watching the boys. I needed to let Wolf out to run tonight. My muscles were tighter than usual.

Aria stumbled out of the locker room. "Miranda, you're up."

"Hey, are you sure you're okay?" I got up and went to my friend.

"I'm going home." She left. She said no more, gave no explanation, just left the gym as I watched her go, shocked and confused.

Chapter 18
Bowen

Thursday morning, I woke full of energy. There was a forty-five-minute bus ride to the school we'd be playing tonight, and I was plotting ways to get Raven to sit with me or to let me sit with her.

I pulled up short when my phone dinged. Text from Cade.

—*Think I've got strep. Mom won't let me out of the house. You have to carry the team tonight.*—

Unease coiled in my belly. No Cade at the game? I wasn't worried we couldn't win; I was worried we wouldn't work together as a team without him.

—*It's your pack tonight. Bring the Beta.*—

I smiled. I did know how to do that. I knew how to lead. If the team would let me.

—*Feel better.*—I texted back.

He sent me a thumbs up.

****

At lunch, I went through the line as usual and got a tray full of stuff that passed as food. That morning I made sure I had some jerky and an apple in my bag, too. Needed good protein and some sugar to play well. The school would provide dinner before we left since it was a long drive over, but it was anyone's guess as to what it would be.

"Hey, Bowen," Jamie said as I put my tray down

next to his. He still wasn't happy I'd replaced him as starter, but we'd developed a healthy respect for each other.

"Ready for tonight's game?" I asked as my long legs found a spot under the cafeteria table. I glanced across the room where Raven sat with Sam, Meg, Kyp, Rachel, Sarah, and some of their friends. I'd wanted to sit with her from the beginning, but Cade had cautioned me against it. He'd made the point that it was important for me to be with my team and to also let Raven come to me on her own terms. So I'd bitten my tongue and sat with the team and Cade but spent most of my lunch periods trying to steal glances of my mate. Cade assured me that after the season ended, there would be a readjustment of seating, and he'd move to Sam's table. He made it a priority to keep the team together during the season as much as possible. I admired him for it. It seemed to work. Rock Falls High's basketball team was a tight-knit group.

"Did you hear about the cheerleaders?" I caught the words from farther down the table. I thought the girl might have been the sister of one of the girls' basketball players.

"Didn't they just get drug tested?"

"Yeah. And one of them got *busted*."

Blood pumped a little harder, a little colder through my veins. Not because I was worried it was Raven, but because whoever it was would probably have an impact on her.

Before any more gossip could float around, the side door to the cafeteria slammed open, and the hairs stood up on the back of Wolf's neck.

"Raven! How could you?" The shrieking wail

pierced the atmosphere. All eating stopped. Every eye riveted onto the spectacle unfolding. I was out of my seat before I knew what I was doing. My actions must have spurred others because suddenly there was a crowd of people ringed around Raven's lunch table. I was about to vault myself over them all, but I hesitated when Sam and Kyp both stood as Raven's mouth hung open. Her friend Aria stalked to her, and even from across the room, I could see her shaking.

"You were my friend! How could you betray me like that! Haven't I had enough betrayal? Haven't I been through enough? Have I not suffered enough? Cheerleading is the one thing I wanted. You took it away from me! I know you talked to Coach! They saw you talking to her! I never want to see you again! I hate you! *I hate you!*"

Aria's screams had drawn several teachers who came running. Aria sprinted through the door while two teachers went after her, and the rest of them herded us back to our places.

I was caught in the crush and couldn't follow, only watch helplessly as Raven bolted out the door, Megan and Rachel close behind.

The prospect of the game had lost some of its appeal as I wondered what was going on and how Raven was doing in light of Aria's accusations. I finally caught Raven on the way to science.

"Raven, are you all right?"

"Just leave it, Bowen." Her voice was tired, old, brittle sounding. My eyebrows drew together, unsure how to give her what she needed. I skimmed my fingers over her elbow as she walked into the room and sank wearily into her seat.

****

As it turned out, I didn't get to sit with Raven on the way over. I tried, but that barely perceptible shake of her head let me know she didn't want me. I ached to make things right for her. I wasn't sure what I could do but trying would be better than her freezing me out like this. Wolf paced.

The game was good. We all missed Cade, and it was obvious, but the team somehow subconsciously let me step into his shoes in his absence.

We won seventy-eight to sixty-two.

****

"Bowen, nice job passing that last one off to Zack!" Jamie clapped me on the back, pleased we'd won, still smarting that he hadn't played much, but making the best of it.

"Thanks." I wiped sweat off my forehead with the front of my jersey. I wondered if I had time for a brief shower.

"I'm texting Cade we won!" someone else hollered. I smiled. This was beginning to feel like an extended family.

"Bus leaves in ten!" Coach Watson shouted from the door of the locker room. That would be a no on the shower. I sighed. I hoped Raven would relent and let me sit with her on the way back, but she probably didn't want wet, sweaty mongrel wafting around. I snagged a towel and at least wiped the sweat off me before downing a bottle of water. Applying some fresh deodorant, I grabbed my bag and was one of the last out of the locker room.

Chapter 19
Raven

I crawled onto the bus and sat in my usual seat about halfway back, facing the cold window, dying a little inside, wishing Aria were here to sit beside me. Since her drug test popped, she'd been suspended from the team indefinitely. My stomach twisted.

A few of the boys got on and headed to the back. Then the bulk of the cheerleaders climbed aboard *en masse*.

Skylar zeroed in on me the second her blonde ponytail swished through the doors.

"Hey, look, ya'all," she said with a forced Southern twang that had Wolf alerting her ears. "It's the snitch-bi—" The last part of her sentence disappeared into Eric Kawoski's sneeze, but it didn't take a rocket scientist to figure it out. Skylar glared at Eric, then pointed a long, manicured finger at me. I simultaneously wanted to rip her face off, disappear into the air, and sob uncontrollably. Wolf growled, baring her teeth at Skylar. Everyone laughed. *Everyone*—all the guys, all the girls. Why did the coaches never get on the bus with the kids? My insides withered.

I set my jaw, clenched my teeth, and tried to ignore her.

"Oh, I better not say too much. You'll go and tell

on me," Skylar shot. I remained silent. "Ooh, sure. Now you have nothing to say."

More of the team got on the bus, but still no coaches. If Cade had been there, Skylar wouldn't have been so brave. Cade would have ripped her a new one for looking at me sideways. But Cade was not here. It was just me. And I was alone. No big brother, no best friend, no pack to back me up. I wasn't sure it was worth it to try to defend myself. I probably *had* inadvertently turned Aria in and gotten her busted. It was probably my veiled conversation with Coach that resulted in the timing of the drug test.

Skylar dropped her bag into a seat not far up from mine and leaned against the back, facing the crowd, who now hung on her every word.

"Don't you know you're not supposed to rat out your teammates? You know—people who are supposed to be your *friends*?" She glanced around, hand on her hip, making sure people were still paying attention. Of course they were. She opened her mouth to say more when Bowen stepped onto the bus.

His dark hair, still damp from the game, emerged first, followed by his chiseled jaw, clamped tight. His scent of cedar and brown sugar mixed with the musky smell of wolf that lingered in his sweat hit me full force. Skylar wiggled toward him as he came down the aisle. Wolf growled inside me.

"Hey! Great game tonight, Bo-Man!" She reached out to brush his arm as he passed, and Wolf bristled even more.

He nodded to her, caught my eye, and without waiting for my permission, plopped himself down into the seat beside me. I held my breath as my heart picked up.

"NnMm, I wouldn't sit there if I were you, Bowen." Someone coughed my new nickname surreptitiously from the back of the bus. Skylar grinned wickedly. "Yep, you heard right. She might tattle on you."

I felt my face heating as she called me out in front of Bowen. As if his opinion mattered to me.

"I'll take my chances," he replied. Skylar pursed her lips.

"Don't say I didn't warn you. She catches wind you did a little pot, drank a little beer at a party, she'll turn you in and get you kicked off the team."

My heart pounded painfully in my chest, waiting for Bowen's response. His reputation said he partied hard, although I didn't think he'd been to one since he'd transferred. But what could he say to that?

"Some people are worth the risk."

Skylar seemed to do a double take. He stared her down, unflinching, unmoving as a mountain of granite. His solid presence beside me suddenly became a welcome haven. He stood up for me. In front of the whole team.

"Fine. But don't expect sticking up for the Ice Queen to get you any. It won't." Skylar huffed and flounced past our seats to the back of the bus as the coaches finally climbed aboard along with our driver. I wanted to melt into the floorboards.

The bus pulled out, and the cabin lights went off, leaving us in darkness. My wolf's ears could still hear snickers and whispers about me along with the repetition of Skylar's rhyming prowess, and I knew the rumor wouldn't be dying on the bus ride home. I knew

Bowen could hear them, too. I wanted to tell him something—say anything to make him understand I had only been trying to look out for Aria, but the words stuck in my throat.

I leaned my head against the cold pane of the glass and shut my eyes. Heat enveloped my hand as Bowen gently covered it with his own. My eyes flew open and met his, shadowed in the dark. He nodded at me once, squeezing my hand, but said nothing.

****

Forty-five minutes later, we finally pulled into the school parking lot. I had never been so relieved to be back from a game. Bowen squeezed my hand again in the dark, then released it as the lights came on. We all piled off the bus, and I wasted no time in hightailing it to my car.

The rich smell of wolf, forest, and leather soothed some of the tension riding in my shoulders as I sank down into the seat. I stuck my key in the ignition to bring the car to life.

I nearly howled in frustration as I turned the key over and nothing happened. No spark, no sputter, no nothing. I slammed my palms against the steering wheel and let my head sink back to the headrest while I clenched my teeth to keep the tears at bay.

A light tap on my window startled me, and I glanced up into Bowen's concerned face.

Reluctantly, I cracked the door, since my window wouldn't roll down with the car dead.

"Won't start?"

Way to go, Captain Obvious. But he'd actually been kind of awesome tonight, so I kept my sarcasm to myself. I nodded.

"Pop the hood. I'll take a look."

I did and then got out of the car to look with him.

"When was the last time you had your oil checked?"

"Um…"

He glanced up at me, a cheeky grin hiding at the corner of his mouth.

"That's more of a Dad and Cade thing."

He smiled as he went back to examining my engine. "Looks like some of the teeth on your flywheel aren't in great shape. I'm not a mechanic, but that's my best guess."

He might as well have been speaking a foreign language.

"So…will my car start?"

He grimaced. "Probably not tonight."

"Brilliant." I closed my eyes and pinched the bridge of my nose. Of all nights for Cade not to be here. I could either call and then wait for my parents, or wait for everyone to leave, shift, and run home. Wolf was nearly as tired as I was. I didn't really want to wait another half hour for Mom or Dad, and I wasn't sure I had the energy to run. I was emotionally wrung out.

"Hey." He brushed my arm with his hand and sent little tingles rushing to my fingers. "You've had a crap night. I've got a hot tub. Let me take you back to my place. You can soak out some of the frustration. I won't even join you if you don't want me to." He held his hands up in surrender as I stabbed him with a look. "I'll take you back home whenever you want."

A sigh heaved my chest up and down. I didn't want to admit how awesome a soak in a jet-filled pool by myself sounded. I was tense. Tense like my muscles might snap in two.

I looked him over, judging how sincere he was about not joining me if I didn't want him to. Part of me just wanted to be alone, to lick my wounds and grieve what was probably the end of my friendship with Aria. The other part wanted Bowen to hold me. I shook my head, trying to clear that last thought.

"I can have the whole hot tub to myself?"

He nodded. "The whole thing." I hesitated still. "It has five different jet settings," he offered.

I pursed my lips. I was nearly persuaded when I realized I had no swimsuit.

"Does your hot tub come with swimwear?"

He squinted an eye. "Well, you can either borrow a shirt, or I think there's some of Shelby's stuff around, if that's not weird."

He didn't expect me to skinny dip in his hot tub. That was a good sign. I wavered.

"Hey, Oakes!" someone hollered from across the parking lot. "Everything cool?"

Bowen glanced at me.

"Yeah. Just some engine trouble," he shouted back. That attracted the attention of one of the coaches who jogged his way over to us.

"Your car won't start, Raven?" he asked. Because I randomly left the hood of my car up.

"Doesn't look like it."

Coach looked uncomfortable. "Well, let me just call my wife and let her know I'll be late. Do you need to borrow a phone to call your parents?"

I took pity on him and decided on the hot tub.

"It's no worry," I said. "Bowen just offered me a ride. I'm sure my parents won't mind."

A frown appeared between Coach's eyebrows.

"I'll have to speak to your parents. I can't actually let you go with Mr. Oakes here unless I speak with your guardian."

"No problem," I said and snagged my phone out of my purse.

Mom picked up on the third ring.

"Hey, Mom."

"Hey, Sweetie. You back at school?"

"Yeah. And my car won't start."

"Oh no!"

"Yeah, um, Bowen said he'd give me a ride, but Coach needs to hear it from you that it's all right."

"Of course." I heard the surprise in her voice. I passed the phone to Coach.

"Yes, Mrs. Rivers, this is Coach Watson. Mr. Oakes is a fine young man, but I do need your permission to let him take Raven home." His face broke into a grin. "Yes, ma'am. That's right. All right then. You folks have a great night, too. Tell Cade we all miss him. I'll pass you back over to Raven."

Coach handed the phone back to me with a smile and a nod to Bowen and started back across the lot.

"Hey, I'm back," I said as Coach's back retreated and Bowen closed the hood of my car. "Actually, I think I'm going to go over to Bowen's house, if it's cool. He has a hot tub, and it's been a really long day."

"Oh." Her surprise nearly leaped out of the phone. "That's fine. Do you have condoms? You know, in case you need them?"

"*Mom!*" I screeched.

"What?" She sounded slightly defensive. "You are mates. Things are bound to happen at some point. And that's fine," she clarified quickly. "I just want to make sure you're prepared."

"I'm just fine, thanks," I said, gritting the words between my clenched teeth.

"All right. Be safe." She giggled at her pun. I rolled my eyes. "I'll see you when you get home. Love you."

"Love you, too." I punched the end call button a little too forcefully and tried to swallow my mortification, praying Bowen hadn't been able to overhear our conversation.

"Everything okay?" he asked, his face giving nothing away.

"Yeah." My face heated just looking at him, and Wolf sighed in his direction. She was much more peaceable when I wasn't actively fighting the attraction to Bowen.

Mercifully he didn't press the issue, just grabbed his bag and mine and nodded his head at the black sports car a few aisles over. The parking lot was nearly empty, and those who were left were still giving me the cold shoulder, so it didn't take long for Bowen to put the bags in the back seat, and to my surprise, open my door.

"Thanks," I said and glanced up at him. His face was unreadable, but his eyes were kind. He nodded and shut the door behind me.

His engine started right up, and he quickly turned down the radio blasting '80s rock from the speakers.

"Sorry," he said sheepishly. A smile twitched the corners of my mouth. Not what I'd have pegged for Bowen's musical tastes.

I sank down into the dark gray leather and let my mind wander as Bowen pulled out and onto the main road out of town. I knew the general area where he lived, but I'd never been to the house he'd inherited. I was a little curious. And a little apprehensive.

I kept my hands in my lap so Bowen wouldn't be able to hold them again unless he was really obvious about it. The tension in my shoulders ratcheted up again as I thought about the bus ride back tonight. My skin crawled as I replayed Skylar's taunts. I shut it off, determined not to relive it again in front of Bowen. Time enough for that once I was alone in the hot tub. As if sensing the direction of my thoughts, Bowen broke the silence.

"So...I don't really know any of the surface stuff about you. What's your favorite flavor of ice cream?"

I nearly sighed in relief at his mundane question. It was just the sort of random conversation to take my mind from the dark thoughts for the next few miles of highway.

"I like pistachio," I answered.

"Pistachio. Unusual choice," he replied.

"Yeah. I had it for the first time when I was a little girl. We were at King's Island, and my dad brought it back to me as a special treat—something new to try—and it stuck. I think about that trip every time I eat it." The words tumbled from my lips, surprising me with the ease at which they came. "What's your favorite?" I figured I could at least be polite and return his question.

"I like peanut butter cup. No particular reason. I just like it."

I nodded. I wracked my brain for some other commonplace question to keep the conversation going, but my mind was a blank slate. Bowen came to the rescue again.

"Favorite color?"

"Um…turquoise, I think. You?"

"Blue. Boring blue. Do you have a favorite sports team?"

"Cade's team is always my favorite. I don't follow professional sports much."

He grinned. "Good. Then my team is your favorite, too." He winked at me, and my stomach clenched. "I'll spare my ego and not ask you who your favorite player is."

A smile twisted its way from my lips. Self-deprecating Bowen was something else I hadn't expected of him. His reputation painted him as a totally arrogant, self-absorbed playboy. Tonight had been a lesson for me.

"Do you play any other sports or just basketball?" I asked, willing my tongue to move and my brain to think.

A strange look crossed his face. "Just basketball. I like other sports, but basketball is the only one I've devoted much energy to. Do you play any other sports?" With appreciation, I noticed he skirted around the issue of being a cheerleader. It wasn't the most comfortable topic at the moment.

"I did gymnastics and tumbling when I was younger. I like swimming, but I've never done either competitively."

"Favorite food?" Bowen kept the conversation rolling.

"I like a lot of different foods, but Mexican is high on the list."

"Something we have in common."

I glanced at him as he turned onto a paved road,

nearly hidden by the trees lining the side of the lane. Conversation dropped off as I saw the outline of a huge house illuminated by porch lights.

My jaw hung open as Bowen pulled into a circular drive and then to a stop in front of a massive two-story Georgian-styled brick house. The shutters and front door were dark. I couldn't quite make out the color as night pressed in around us, but the doorframe was painted white and nestled comfortably right in the middle A brass doorknocker gleamed in the light coming from an iron lamppost stationed just beside the walkway to the door. Neatly manicured beds of bushes and what I assumed would be flowers in the spring lined the curving sidewalk.

"Wow."

"Yeah. It's a little pretentious. Especially for an eighteen-year-old guy who lives alone." I could hear the invitation to insinuation in his words but left it alone. "But if you think this is impressive, you should see the house Kyp chose. It's this three-story monstrosity. You could probably house half the pack comfortably in its basement. Actually, I think that's why he and Rachel picked that one. They wanted a place where pack members could stay if they needed to."

It sounded like something Rachel would do—especially since her sister was in rehab now, recovering from her drug addiction. It made sense that Rachel would want the ability to care for or help someone from their pack who might be struggling. With a startling revelation, I realized someday their pack would be mine, too. My stomach dropped. Quickly, I searched for something—anything—else mundane.

"So did you pick this one, or was this your only option?" I asked unsteadily as we got out of the car. Bowen grabbed both bags from the back and slung them both over his shoulder.

"Yeah." He unlocked the front door. "I picked it. It was actually the smallest of Victor's properties." His voice strained on the name. He cleared his throat. "This one is also the most secluded of the houses he owned. We're keeping one for official pack use and selling the other two and putting the profits into a pack fund like your Alpha does." That was another interesting surprise. It was a…*responsible* decision. Another thing his reputation didn't include. He flipped a light on, and my eyes adjusted and took in a surprisingly homey great room. The carpet was light, and the furniture was a soft brown leather with tasteful throw pillows, décor, and a brick feature wall with a huge stone fireplace. I noticed a pair of running shoes beside the door and a jacket thrown over an armchair. Otherwise, it looked pretty pristine.

"The hot tub is out on the back deck. Do you want me to get you a shirt, or did you want to see if any of Shelby's stuff is around? Or you, we…can hang out. Whatever," he finished awkwardly.

"Hot tub still sounds great. Um, I guess I'll borrow a shirt? And shorts?" I finished. I needed something to cover my rear under his shirt. I glanced at my bag by the door. I did have a pair of practice shorts in there. They needed to be washed, but that wouldn't matter if I was just going to go dunk in the tub anyway. "Actually, I have shorts in my bag. But a shirt would be fantastic." The only spare shirt I had was white.

He nodded. "Make yourself at home. Seriously.

You can come up and see the rest of the house if you want. The bedrooms are on the top floor."

The mention of bedrooms made my cheeks heat for no apparent reason. "I'm good. I'll just, um, wait here."

He lightly touched the small of my back, and my muscles froze while Wolf turned to jelly. "Kitchen is through there and to the left if you want anything. Be back in a second."

He went to the left and up a flight of steps with beautifully carved wooden rails. I grabbed my bag and went toward the kitchen. I stepped through an archway, found light switches, and instantly loved what I saw. To the left was a massive kitchen with warm-colored granite counters and amber-colored cabinets all over a rich hardwood floor. Double glass sliding doors leading to what had to be the back patio wedged themselves between the kitchen and the second living room. Separated by the back of another leather couch was a carpeted area with a huge TV and multiple seating areas. There was another fireplace, and everything about the space was set up to seduce you to sit down and relax. It felt warm. Something else I hadn't expected about Bowen's house. As I looked around, I smiled when I noticed a few candy wrappers and an empty soda can. Bowen liked this space, too. My smile fell as I looked around again, noticing that there were no personal touches on the walls. No family photos, nothing that spoke of happy memories here. It was a warm space. Designed to sell, I realized. This must have been a property Victor owned and had only planned on selling. It made me sad to think of Bowen living here, in a house, inviting enough, but not quite a home. Wolf nudged me, and I shushed her, shutting down that line of thinking before I wandered into its quagmire.

"Here you go." Bowen appeared through the archway and handed me a gray shirt.

"Thanks." I snagged the shirt.

"You can change in the bathroom, just back down the archway. I'll, um, leave you to it. I'll flip the jets on and get out of your way."

He really was going to just let me soak away in his hot tub. I was a little surprised. There was a large part of me that really thought he'd just used the pretense of the hot tub to get me alone in his house. Which we were. Very alone. Together. Wolf grinned. I gave her a silent lecture as I put Bowen's shirt on over my head. I wasn't immune to the whiff of his smell that lingered under the freshly laundered scent. It draped all the way to the bottom of my shorts. It was the perfect huge fit of a guy's shirt on a girl's body. I shut my eyes as images of me wearing Bowen's letter jacket flashed through my head. Nope. Not going there. Ever.

True to his word, Bowen was nowhere to be seen as I slid through the glass doors into the freezing air. My breath puffed in a white cloud as the bubbles in the hot tub gave off white clouds of their own. It was a big in-ground hot tub with lights inside. The decorative stone edges made it look like something straight out of a resort. I glanced over the back of the yard, and my eyebrows lifted when I saw the tarp covering a huge in-ground pool. The lights didn't go much farther, and I didn't use my wolf vision to see what else might be beyond the pool.

All other thoughts stopped as I sank down onto the ledge of seats running around the inside of the hot tub. I closed my eyes and finally let my muscles relax as the hot jet streams pounded against my shoulders, back, and legs. It was glorious.

For long minutes I just sat there in the heat, muscles releasing more and more tension. Eventually, my brain moved to the events of the day. Every bad moment started replaying. One horrible moment to the next. Tears left wet tracks down my cheeks as I thought about Aria. About what this might mean for her. I had enough sense to know she needed help, and that if Coach hadn't done the drug test—which might or might not have been prompted by my comments—Aria might not get that help. But sense didn't stop the hurt. The anguish of knowing my actions had sounded the death knell of our friendship twisted my insides up in painful knots.

The jets changed their pattern from the hard pounding to soft, quiet streams of bubbles. The glass doors slid open, and I bit my lip. I was an emotional mess. Of course, this was the time Bowen chose to come out.

"I didn't think to give you a towel earlier." My back was to him, and I didn't turn, embarrassed by my tears and silently cursing the part of me that wanted his comfort anyway.

"Thanks," I mumbled, a sniff following. My eyes opened as I heard a glass clink near my head and stared at a brown glass bottle. Bowen walked to the other side of the hot tub and sat down in trunks and a hoodie, his own glass bottle in his hand.

"Tell me that isn't beer."

"It is."

"Seriously?" My shoulders tensed. Wolves have a

very low tolerance to alcohol of any kind, and it affects us in unusual ways. It made me nervous. As a general pack rule, we all stayed away from it. But Bowen wasn't from my pack. And then there was his reputation…

"Relax. It's root beer." He raised his bottle to me and took a swig. "Cade already gave me the speech." He winked. "Don't worry. I don't drink. Ever. It only takes a few sips for me to feel out of control. And control is not something I'm willing to give up." His expression shuttered. I relaxed a measure and even enjoyed a sip of the root beer. It was good. The fizzy tanginess burned down my throat as the sweet flavor coated my mouth. We were quiet for a few minutes, and my mind drifted back to Aria.

"Do you care if I get in, too? I can stay on my side. Or I can go back in the house."

"Oh. Sorry. Yes." I'd kind of forgotten he was even over there, so consumed with my own thoughts. All those thoughts flew out of my head as Bowen stood and stripped off his hoodie, revealing well-defined abs and a slight trail of dark hair around his navel leading down to…I jerked my eyes away as heat rushed to my cheeks. I wanted to dissolve into the burbling water even as I felt a stirring deep in the pit of my stomach. I could have sworn a mass of butterflies was trying to escape. Wolf's tongue lolled out of her mouth. I couldn't look at him as he slid in on his side.

"Nothing feels better than a soak after a game."

I risked a peek. It had to be getting late. I knew I should think about getting home, but Bowen had just gotten in, and he had played a hard game tonight. And he'd stuck up for me when no one else had.

"Bowen."

His eyes fixed on me. They were warm and brown with little flecks of gold reflected up from the lights.

"Thank you. For tonight. On the bus." The words crept out of my mouth, hushed, like I was afraid to let him know I appreciated what he did. I cringed inwardly. I didn't want him to think I was ungrateful. Because I wasn't—I was *really* thankful he'd done what he did. "I mean it. I," I stopped, trying to collect my words. "What you did. No one else said anything. You did more just by sitting next to me and facing Skylar down than anyone else could have done. And—" I had to pause to swallow as emotion clogged my throat. "—I…thanks," I finished lamely, afraid if I continued the tears would start again.

"Do you want to talk about it?" he asked softly.

No. No, I really didn't want to talk about it, but it came out anyway. "Aria is my best friend—at least she was. We're as close as we can be without her being a wolf. And I feel like I just completely threw her under the bus. I didn't mean for things to come out like they did. I didn't tell Coach to do a drug test—I didn't really even tell her anything. And then she did the drug tests and, well, you know what happened after. I'm worried about Aria. Really worried. Especially after seeing Rachel's sister, Joanie. I mean, what if that happens to Aria? I can't sit and watch that happen—but I never intended for everything else to spiral out of control from it." I sniffed. Tears were coming anyway. I swiped at them with a wet hand, which did absolutely no good.

More and more just kept blurting out of my mouth. At some point, Bowen moved from his side to mine, just sitting next to me, his shoulder touching mine in a silent show of support. The entire story spilled out, and Bowen let me talk. When I finally had no words left, I leaned my head back against the cold stones behind me.

"I'm sorry. I didn't mean to dump all that on you."

"It's okay." I felt his fingers slide over mine on the seat of the hot tub. I glanced at him, curious but afraid of what I might find. His eyes were troubled, which pushed some of my own worries away. Wolf suddenly came to attention, afraid he'd push us away after my emotional outburst.

"You did the right thing." He squeezed my hand, and I let out some of the breath I'd subconsciously been holding. "What happened after sucks, but you did nothing wrong." He blew out a heavy sigh, and I studied him. His face was at an angle to me, giving me his profile. As even-minded as I tried to be, I was not impervious to his deliciously dark good looks. The steam from the water gave his hair a slight wave. My eyes trailed down to his shoulder, the top of his defined bicep poking out of the water. I swallowed.

"What does your tattoo mean?" I stared at the script going across the rounded muscle.

"*Mi voluntatis meae est*. My will is my own." His voice had gone husky. He didn't need to elaborate further. I knew as much as I needed to about Victor's control of Bowen's mind.

We were silent a minute.

"I almost threw Skylar off the bus tonight." He looked at me. "Literally."

A silver bell of laughter burst from my throat without my permission. One side of Bowen's mouth tipped up. I clapped a hand over my mouth as another ball of laughter worked its way out.

"If I'd known you'd appreciate it that much I'd have gone ahead and done it." Bowen's eyes were laughing with me. It really wasn't funny, but the laughter helped release the lingering stress.

"Probably best you didn't." I sighed, contented enough for the moment. My eyes closed, suddenly too tired to stay open. "What time is it?" I mumbled.

"Quarter to twelve."

"What?" I shot up with a gasp. "Oh, bad. It's like at least half an hour to my house from here. I'm so sorry. I had no idea it was so late. You won't get to bed before two. And you have a game tomorrow! Coach Watson will kill me if he finds out I'm the reason the star post falls asleep during the game." I felt like a horrible person. Bowen had been nothing but kind to me tonight. He'd been the hero and then the perfect gentleman, and I repaid him by keeping him up to all hours of the night.

"It's fine. I've gone with less sleep." He couldn't help the yawn. "Although, I am kinda tired tonight." I felt even worse. He looked at me with an appraising glance. "Don't take this the wrong way, but you know you're welcome to stay here."

Wolf immediately warmed to the idea while my human hackles raised to new heights. "Excuse me?" Surely, I didn't hear that correctly.

"And you took it the wrong way." He sighed.

"You just asked me to stay here. All night. With you."

"Raven." He started to sound exasperated. "I didn't ask you to sleep with *me*. I just asked if you wanted to stay in the guest room since it's late, and we're both tired." He released my hand under the water, and for some reason, it felt like a big deal. Had I hurt him? The idea seemed so impossible in one minute and so probable the next. I clenched my jaws. The only immediate way I saw to smooth this over was to take him up on his offer.

"Fine."

His eyebrows nearly disappeared into his hair. "Fine?"

"Fine. Yes. I'll stay. In the guest room."

"All right then. I'm going to head in. Do you want to stay out here longer, or are you ready, too?"

Air gusted between my teeth as I huffed. "I'm pooped."

Bowen hopped out, and I tried, I really tried, not to stare at his back as his shoulders flexed as he wrapped the towel around his middle. Shaking myself out of my stupor, I scrambled out of the hot tub and snatched the other towel, quickly wrapping it around my shoulders and chest. Cold air and hot skin together with a sports bra were not a girl's friends.

We dripped into the kitchen where Bowen toweled off a little more, and I followed suit, careful to keep as much of the water from his billowing shirt off the floor as I could.

"It's fine. It's just a little water." He caught me awkwardly trying to dry off with the towel around my waist. When I glanced up, he was looking at me, eyes wide, nostrils flared. My stomach scuttled to my toes as anxiety crept up my spine.

"What?"

He shook his head and turned toward the front of the house. "Bedrooms are upstairs."

"Bowen, what was that look you just gave me?"

"Do you shower at night or in the morning?"

"Night. Stop avoiding my question."

"There are towels under the sink in the main bathroom. You won't have to share. I've got an *en suite*."

"Bowen."

We'd reached the stairs. He turned to face me, one foot poised on the first step. His eyes raked over me, and I could have sworn his eyes dilated slightly. The look he gave me sent shivers rippling down my body that had nothing to do with the water dripping off me. He leaned in, just far enough he was in my space, and I had the urge both to flee and to meet him halfway.

"It means you look really hot, dripping wet in my shirt." His voice was low and rough and sexier than anything I'd ever heard. My mouth went dry, and my eyes probably rivaled dinner plates for size. That shut me up real quick. He glanced at my lips, then back to my eyes before wheeling around, snagging both the bags we'd brought in along with my purse, and legging it up the stairs at an impressive clip. It took me a few seconds to make my feet follow.

He quickly showed me the bathroom and the three guest bedrooms. He motioned to the last door.

"This one is mine. Let me know if you need anything. Seriously, make yourself at home. You can pick any of the rooms you like." He caught my eye and gave me a quick wink. "*Any* of them." His voice was dangerously low again with a sexy edge that had my toes curling and my brain screaming retreat.

"Right. Thanks. Um, good night."

"Night, Raven." He gave me one last lingering glance before disappearing into his bedroom, though he did not shut the door after him. I glanced around me in the hallway, realizing I had nothing to sleep in. I was not about to sleep in the nude in Bowen Oakes' house. Mate or no mate. And I wasn't sure it was wise to call him back out and borrow another shirt as the one I was wearing seemed to have quite the effect. I wandered into the guest room on the other side of Bowen's room. It looked like Shelby had used it. It was a little weird to think about wearing her clothes with her still laying comatose in a facility, but it would be better than nothing.

I found a text from Mom I'd missed while in the hot tub.

Hope all is going well!

She'd be thrilled to death I was staying over. Though not for the reasons she'd assume. I quickly texted her back and let her know I was staying the night and not to get her hopes up. I mentioned the hot tub was impressive.

She texted back a smiley face. I rolled my eyes and dropped the phone back in my purse.

Shelby did have a wide array of clothes left in the drawers and even a few hanging in the closet. There were pajamas, and I was happier than I could express when I saw a package of unopened bikini briefs in the top drawer of the white dresser.

All the furniture was white. There was a white metal bedframe with a white comforter sprinkled with large pale yellow flowers interspersed with gray geometric shapes. There were white curtains and yellow and gray pillows. It was a beautifully staged room with pale gray walls to set off all the white. The hardwood floor had a plush gray and yellow rug covering a large portion of the area, with a stylish white chair resting on its edge with a small table near the window.

I didn't look overly long as I felt my eyelids drooping. I snagged the borrowed pajamas and new underwear and quickly showered.

I refused to glance through the open door of Bowen's room as I nearly ran back to mine. I made sure the door was shut. I stopped myself just short of locking the door. The bed was soft, and despite my reluctance to stay the night alone with Bowen, I was asleep within minutes.

Chapter 20
Bowen

I was feeling tremendously proud of myself. Raven slept one room down the hall. Raven. In my house. In my bed. Even if it wasn't the bed I wanted her in. I probably should have taken her home. There was no way I would sleep with her just a few feet down the hall. The image of her in my shirt was burned into the back of my eyelids. It was the only thing I saw when I shut my eyes. Wolf whined. I was in total agreement with him. I wanted to go curl up next to Raven in bed and hold her all night. I did, however, value my life, so I resisted the urge.

Instead, I forced my mind to replay what had happened on the bus. Raven had been more upset than she let on. I wasn't sure why she hadn't fought back against Skylar's jabs, and I hadn't pushed her to answer. But she had talked to me some tonight. More than she ever had before. Maybe that was what we needed. We just needed to talk more. Cade was right. She needed to know *me*. Not the me everyone assumed I was, but the me I was trying to become. I cringed as my past mistakes flitted through my brain. I had no desire to tell her who I was. What I had become because of Victor. Although I probably would have been equally reprehensible to her if I'd gone my own way, too. Wolf growled at the thought. I knew I'd have to tell her what I'd done—the things that still haunted me—at some point. But I needed her to trust me first. Raven needed to know I wasn't that man anymore. My lips turned down. Raven would hate that part of me as much as I did. If I told her too soon, I'd lose her forever.

I was my own. I absently rubbed my hand across my tattoo. I was my own. I no longer belonged to Victor. My thoughts grew darker, thinking about Victor. I shook my head to free the images and focused again on Raven.

A date. We needed a nice, normal date.

With a smile, I tried to drift off, but thoughts and ideas of what to do for our first date made it hard. The only thing I'd need to do now was convince Raven to come with me.

****

Groaning, I lifted my arms above my head to work out the kinks. I'd eventually slept, but it was late when I finally fell asleep. I squinted at the alarm clock.

Swearing under my breath, I jumped out of bed. We needed to leave the house in twenty minutes to get to school on time. I headed for the shower, then paused as I stopped to listen. I didn't hear Raven up and around.

Cautiously I crept to her closed door. Putting an ear to the door, I waited, holding my breath. I could hear her deep, even breathing. She was still asleep. I cracked the door, and my lungs hitched as I looked at her. Her black hair fanned out behind her on the pillow, her arm tucked under her head. The blanket had shifted enough I could clearly see the outline of her hip and a smooth strip of skin where her shirt had come up. My mouth was suddenly dry as cotton. Wolf was not helping as he slammed up against me, urging me to go to her.

Quickly, I shut the door and took a calming breath. My blood raced. I cleared my throat and knocked on the door.

"Hmm?" she responded groggily, muffled through the door.

"Raven? It's Friday morning. We need to hurry. We're going to be late."

"What?"

"It's late. We need to leave for school in about fifteen minutes if we're going to make it on time."

"Oh crap!" There were some thuds as she jumped out of bed, and I heard a drawer slide out forcefully.

"You okay?"

"Fine," she retorted. She did not sound fine. Wolf paced inside.

"I'm going to go get ready. I'll meet you downstairs in a few."

She grunted. I figured that was as good as I was going to get.

****

It was a fifteen-minute ride to school. I debated bringing up our going on a date or waiting until later. With a deep breath, I decided to broach those turbulent waters. I cleared my throat.

"Did you sleep well?" My voice cracked. *My voice cracked?*

She glanced sideways at me. "Yes," she admitted grudgingly. She took a deep inhale. "Thanks for letting me stay."

"Anytime," I said, unable to help the smile creeping into my voice. I glanced over and saw a hint of a grin hiding at the corner of her mouth. I took it as a good omen and plunged in. "So I was thinking. Our—" I cleared my throat, "—*encounters* so far haven't exactly been the normal sort where people get to know each other, and I think maybe this—" I motioned between us, "—would be easier if we knew each other a little better." I glanced at her again and saw a slightly confused look on her face as she glanced back at me.

"What do you mean?"

"I want us to go on a date. A nice, normal date with no pressure, just go out somewhere and have some fun together."

She remained silent as anxiety climbed into the back of my throat.

"A date," she said, her voice emotionless.

"A date," I echoed, my voice confident.

"What exactly did you have in mind?" Was that a hint of fear in her eyes? What was she scared of? My shoulders drooped.

"Over in Centerville, there's this really cool carnival I've heard about. They've set up booths all over inside the mall there, and they've converted some of the parking lot into a space for rides. It looks pretty cool. I thought maybe we could just talk on the way over and then have some normal fun without any of the weirdness that seems to cling to everything around us." I looked over at her again and saw her chewing on her bottom lip, her eyes uncertain.

"Raven, I'm just asking to get to know you better. Don't you think that's fair?" I asked, uncertainty riddling holes in my gut the longer she was silent.

"No, it's more than fair." She was quiet again for a moment. "All right. A date."

"Really?" I couldn't stop the smile spreading across my face.

"Really," she replied with far less enthusiasm. "When did you want to go?"

"Let's go tomorrow. Pick you up about three? We can check stuff out and eat there?"

She took a big breath and let it out slowly. "Okay."

Chapter 21
Raven

A date. A date with Bowen Oakes. My stomach
tripped over the knots it was tied into. Part of me
thought it was a brilliant idea—getting to know Bowen
better might take some of the fear of unknown things
away and satisfy Wolf—but it also introduced a new
anxiety. Bowen was reported to be a ladies' man of epic
proportions. I'd never even been kissed. I didn't know
how to behave on a date, and I was nervous about what
would be expected of me. I wasn't sure I wanted him to
kiss me. Wolf wanted it, but my inexperience made me
shudder with crippling uncertainty. What if I did it all
wrong? What if I wasn't any good at it? Deep down, I
knew he was my mate, but I still didn't fully understand
the complexities of that. I was on the verge of giving
into at least some of my instincts where he was
concerned. And I was alarmed to discover the thought
of disappointing him—especially in the physical side of
things where he had so much more experience—*really*
bothered me. And then it made me angry, thinking
about all the other girls who had had what should have
only been mine.

I was a hot mess of writhing thoughts and verging
on a headache by the time Bowen smiled, touched my
arm, and went to his locker and left me to go to mine,
only to discover Skylar's new nickname for me had

been written on the door of my locker with permanent marker. Rage burned through my veins, tinging my vision with red.

"Rave! You made it!" Cade rasped teasingly as he sidled up to me in the hall. His voice still wasn't quite back to normal, even though his werewolf genes had kicked in and healed the infection. "Woah. *What is that?*" He stared at my locker, his nostrils flaring as his jaw set in the way that said heads were going to roll.

"It's a long story," I said as the anger faded and sadness crept in. After the emotional roller coaster of last night and then this morning, tears were close to the surface. I wanted to go home and curl up in a ball with my computer and design something and let the rest of the world fade away for a while.

The bell rang, and we had to get to class.

"I'll take care of this," Cade said. I nodded numbly and stumbled down the hall to first hour.

I made it until lunchtime. The constant snickers, the ripples of rumors about Aria and my supposed involvement, made my heart sick.

At the lunch bell, I dragged my feet back to my locker where a fresh coat of paint dried. Gingerly, I opened the door and put in my books. My back heated, and I could feel him there behind me.

"Why didn't you tell me about your locker?" Bowen asked softly as I turned around. His eyes were dark and stormy, but I realized the emotion wasn't directed at me.

"I honestly didn't think to," I replied. Cade had been there, and he offered to deal with it. He was my protective older brother, and I was too tired to fight that battle this morning. My emotions were in tatters, and I just didn't have the emotional energy to deal with it.

"Next time something like this happens—and I will do my best to make sure there isn't a next time—I want you to tell me. Immediately." He trailed a finger down my cheek, and I caught my breath at such a blatant show of what I considered to be PDA at school. I gulped, thinking it probably was a fairly meaningless gesture to him.

I nodded mutely.

He looked at me hard. "Raven, are you okay?"

I closed my eyes and felt my chin quiver, hating the weak, overwhelming feelings swirling through me. Wolf nudged me, urging me to be real—be honest— with Bowen, instead of shrugging it off and stuffing it down.

"No," I choked out.

"Why don't you call your mom and have her sign you out. Go home for the afternoon. Rest."

I peeked up at him. His face was drawn in concern, and it sent a curl of heat unfurling in my stomach. A pounding headache climbed up my scalp and pulsed behind my eyes. A nap might be the best thing for my battered emotions.

Just then, my fine-tuned hearing picked up Skylar's voice down the hallway. The anger of the injustice done to me and what Aria was suffering sent white-hot flames licking down my spine. Bowen stiffened beside me, and I knew he heard it, too.

I blew out a hot breath. "Because if I go home, then I can't go to tonight's game, and it will feel like I've let *her* win." I gritted my teeth. I wanted to go home and let my body collapse. But I wanted Skylar to know she couldn't beat me. I may not have felt it necessary to verbally defend myself against her, but I wasn't about to run away with my tail between my legs.

Bowen nodded, and I appreciated that he didn't try to talk me out of it. His face turned thoughtful, and he nodded his head down the hallway as we started walking.

"I have an idea then," he said. I lifted an eyebrow at him and tried not to wince as a dull throbbing started at the base of my skull. "Why don't you let me talk to Ms. Librey and see if you can work in the library for the rest of the day. It's quiet, and you won't have to put up with Skylar's crap."

"Actually, I think I'll stop by the nurse's office first. I'm working on a raging headache, and that might be excuse enough."

"I'll walk you there and then bring lunch. I'll text you when I'm through the line, and you can tell me where you are," he said, firmly inserting himself into my world and staking his claim.

I glanced up at him, warmed again at his kindness, but still looking for his hidden motive.

"You know hanging out together is only going to fuel Skylar's interest in you," I mentioned, trying to hide my discomfort by pointing the conversation back to him.

Bowen grimaced. "That is an unfortunate side effect." He looked at me, a mischievous grin hiding in the corner of his mouth while his eyes smoldered, broadcasting his interest. My mouth went dry as Wolf sighed in contentment and urged me to move closer to him. I wrapped my arms around my middle instead. Wolf snorted.

"See you in a few." He tapped my arm again before

he left me at the nurse's office. Something had shifted in our relationship—whatever it was—over the course of last night, and I felt the changes deep in my bones. I was softening. Or I was becoming desensitized to him, I snorted to myself.

"What can I do for you, dearie?" the nurse asked as I mentally shook my head and walked in.

"Um, stampede through my brain." I explained my pounding head and my aching body with enough detail for her to look concerned. Maybe I shared too much?

"I would support you going home for the rest of the day if you want. You actually look quite pale. No fever, but you sound wrung out." She offered with a motherly pat.

"I think I'm okay to stay, but do you think it would be possible to just work the rest of the day in the library? I think the quiet would really be helpful."

She narrowed her eyes at me, assessing my request for hidden intent. Apparently finding none in the black shadows cupping my drooping eyes and pale cheeks, she nodded.

"I'll give Ms. Librey a call and have notes sent to your teachers to have them send your work to the library."

Relief flooded me, pushing back some of the throbbing in my head.

"Thank you," I said with as much sincerity as I could.

I trudged out of her office and shot off a text to Bowen, marveling at myself for seeking out his company. I shook my head and realized maybe part of what was changing between us was my attitude. My cheeks heated as I remembered Bowen's defense of me against Skylar's onslaught yesterday, even after I'd given him next to no reason to defend me. Wolf nudged me and whined as I called up the memory of Cade lying on the ground, blood matting his fur, and Bowen's teeth inches from my brother's throat.

My stomach lurched, but this time, instead of focusing on Cade's exposed neck, I saw Bowen's eyes the second they saw me. There was a visible reaction in the way his eyes cleared and connected to mine. I sighed and pushed it to the back of my overtired brain.

****

My bed was covered in outfits I'd tried on and rejected. Mom had offered several opinions, thrilled to death I had agreed to go on a date with Bowen. I understood Mom's exuberance that I had a true mate—but I didn't understand the complexities of the emotions I felt surrounding Bowen. Wolf was utterly convinced we were meant for each other. I understood her and knew that as mates, Bowen and I *would* be together. But I still felt so nervous around him, unsure of his expectations—or my own, for that matter—and the one thing Wolf and I did agree on was the anger that boiled up every time we thought about the other girls who had come before me.

I sighed and looked again at the multitude of clothes covering my bed. I rejected a skirt. We'd be outside. It would be cold. So jeans then. What clothes broadcasted casual first date? Groaning softly, I scrubbed my hands down my face.

Breathe. I just needed to breathe.

Comfortable. I needed to be comfortable at least in my clothes choice for my first date, because I sure wasn't feeling comfortable in my own skin.

124

Wolf nudged me supportively.

"Why is this so complicated?" I whispered to my empty bedroom.

Chapter 22
Bowen

I knocked on the door, uncharacteristic nerves marching in my gut. Amalie opened it with a wide smile.

"Bowen! Come on in. Raven is just getting her shoes, I think."

"Thanks," I said as I closed the door against the cold behind me.

"Can I get you anything to drink?"

"I'm fine, but thanks."

"Bowen! Great game yesterday," Steve commented as he came into the room.

"Cade had a few pretty great shots." I smiled back. Steve's smile stretched farther across his face at the mention of Cade's two three-pointers in the last minutes of the game.

"Well, that last one wouldn't have been possible without a quick rebound and pass from under the net," Steve said with a wink. I ducked my head, still unsure how to accept praise from this man who was now technically my father-in-law. I was spared from more conversation as the top step creaked, and Raven came down. The breath seized in my throat.

She'd left her long black hair down in a thick cloud that swished to her low back. She had on a blue plaid flannel shirt buttoned up almost to the top, and the lighter blues in the shirt made her eyes look electric. Her long legs were in dark jeans, and she had on sensible casual tennis shoes. She was exquisite. Realizing I was grinning like an idiot, I cleared my throat and walked over to the stairs.

"Hey," I said tentatively. Her eyes were shifting nervously.

"Hi," she said back, her bottom lip tucking between her teeth and making me want to kiss her.

"You look great. You ready to go?" I resisted the urge to give her another once-over with my eyes since her parents were still in the room. I wasn't sure if she'd take my hand if I offered and didn't want to start out on the wrong foot, so I kept them clenched at my sides.

"Raven said you're going over to the carnival at Centerville?" Amalie asked as Raven brushed by me, leaving her scent of cinnamon and plums trailing behind, to retrieve a jacket from the coat closet. I turned to Amalie.

"Yeah, I've heard it's got some pretty unique attractions and food vendors from all over the state."

"Steve, that sounds fun!" Amalie said to her husband. Steve chuckled.

"Well, you two can tell us how it is, and if it's that good, we'll go ourselves." He turned back to his wife and wrapped her in a side hug. I smiled at their easy display of affection and hoped someday things would be so easy between Raven and me.

"Um, not sure what time we'll be back?" Raven said. She finished zipping herself into a dark blue jacket that unfortunately hid some of her curves but did look warm.

"I didn't have a particular time in mind," I

countered, unsure if I needed one. Did she have a curfew? Even though she was technically under my protection now, not her parents'?

"That's fine! No rush at all. Just text us when you head back." Amalie paused. "Or if you decide to stay over."

"*Mom*." Raven's cheeks flamed. I tried to mask the grin tugging at my mouth, realizing Amalie was trying to offer her support.

"Have a great time," Steve called as I opened the door for Raven and gently touched the small of her back to usher her through. Raven waved.

"We'll try," I quipped, and Steve chuckled. Amalie waved beside him as I opened Raven's door for her.

The car was still warm from my trip over, but Raven still sat huddled in her seat like she was freezing.

"You cold?" I aimed a vent toward her. She clenched her teeth and screwed her eyes shut.

"Sorry. No. I'm fine. I," she stopped.

"Raven?"

"I'm actually a little bit nervous," she admitted grudgingly.

"No reason to be nervous." I tried to sound reassuring, unsure why she was so worked up about our date but recognizing that she was. "It's just a date."

I saw Raven roll her eyes and realized I said something wrong.

"What did I say?"

Raven glanced at me, the uncertainty back in her face.

"Um," she faltered.

"Come on. This is all about getting to know each other, right?" I wanted to grab her hand but wasn't sure she wouldn't snap in half if I tried.

Chapter 23
Raven

I twisted my hands together in my lap, unwilling to admit I'd never actually been on a real date, but saw no other alternative to answering Bowen's question without lying or evading it altogether.

Bowen had probably been on hundreds of dates, many of which probably ended in bed. Wolf growled at the thought, and I clenched my teeth and forced the anger back down. I cleared my throat, determined again to try to get to know Bowen better and attempt to enjoy the date—my very first date. At least Mom hadn't mentioned that when she'd casually thrown out her thinly veiled opinion it was fine to sleep over—with—Bowen.

"Raven?" Bowen prompted again as he slowed for a curve in the road.

"I, this is still really new for me," I offered.

Bowen nodded, but a shadow covered his face. "Raven, are…are you afraid of *me*?" he asked, his eyes darting to mine, then back to the road. Some of my nerves eased at the look of vulnerability on his face.

"No, Bowen. I'm not afraid of *you* anymore," I told him, realizing it was completely true. I didn't fear *him*. But feared the unknowns and feared the differences his experiences and mine left between the two of us.

He let out a breath. "Good. Because I've sworn

myself to you. You're my mate. There will never be a reason for you to fear me," he finished quietly. He glanced at me again as my heart beat quicker. Before I could formulate a response, he continued, lightening things as quickly as they'd become serious. "So what do you want to do after high school?" The man was a brilliant conversation starter. My brain was too numb to come up with my own questions. I cleared my throat, trying to center my careening thoughts.

"Well, I guess a lot will depend on whether or not I get this internship this summer. If I get it, then that will be half a graphic arts degree once the internship is finished. And if, it's still a big if, I get in and they like my work, they could offer me a position through next school year, possibly even turning into something more permanent while I finish the degree. But since Meg and Rachel have decided to go ahead and open an online bakery for special events and stuff, they've already told me they'll hire me part time to do some of their icing. As popular as their stuff has become, I'm guessing it will become a full-fledged operation within a year or so. That's also a short-term option," I finished, realizing my future plans didn't currently include Bowen...and they should, since he was my mate, and the two of us were fated to be together now. I felt cold fingers twist my gut. "Um, what about you? What do you want to do?"

"First of all, I think you're totally going to nail the internship. Cade told me some about it the other day. I think it's pretty cool most of the internship is online, but you still get to go into the office and see things from that perspective."

I warmed at his praise, and the icy fingers receded.

"As for what I want to do?" He blew out another breath as his eyebrows rose. "Honestly, I have no idea. Until a few weeks ago, I had no future. Victor controlled everything about my life."

My heart ached at the underlying pain in his words. I knew so little about what life with Victor had been like. I'd heard some of the things Kyp had said, and it didn't sound pretty. And Bowen had been under Victor's control for several years.

"But largely thanks to Kyp and the Wolfe pack, I *do* have a future now." He looked at me again, and I got the distinct impression he was really talking about me, more than any occupation he might hold. "I don't know what sort of career I want. It will probably take some juggling to figure out things with the pack and a job that will offer some flexibility around it. My thoughts right now are to take a gap year and sort things out, really look at options, talk to Dominic, talk to Kyp…talk to you."

Guilt crept in as I realized he was light-years ahead of me in thinking about including me in his future. A flush stole over my cheeks.

"If you could do anything in the world, what would it be?" I blurted to cover my guilty feelings.

"Play pro basketball," he said with a wink.

"Cade has already had scouts looking at him. You're every bit as good as he is. What if someone offers you a scholarship, and that leads somewhere else?" I asked, feeling like I needed to validate him somehow.

He smiled easily. "I would love to play college ball. If the opportunity presented itself, I would be very tempted to take it." He was quiet a minute, and I wasn't sure how to fill the silence. "Basketball was my one out. It was the one thing I had that Victor didn't taint. My status as a basketball player bled into his master plan, so he didn't dictate that. That was the one thing I got to do that I could do by myself. A channel for some of the frustration."

I was shocked at this intimate detail of his life and was unprepared to respond.

"I'm sorry your life was so hard with him," I whispered.

His jaw clenched. "Me, too." I knew he was reliving things and working through frustrations. Tentatively, I put my hand on the console between us. He glanced at it, then at my face, and carefully put his hand over mine, squeezing lightly. It sent a rush of butterflies through my middle.

"Do you like carnival rides?" I offered to lighten the mood.

"I do," he said with a devilish grin. "You?"

"Cade calls me the fearless one of the family when it comes to rides." Bowen chuckled.

The rest of the ride to Centerville was filled with light conversation, leaving the heavier topics alone.

"And here we are," Bowen commented as he parked his car near the back of a crowded lot. We were in a mall parking lot, and ahead of us, I could see towering rides and hear the shrieks of fellow thrill-seekers. Smells that had my mouth watering filled the car, even before we opened the doors. Bowen grabbed his wallet out of the console, stuffed it in his back pocket, and took the keys out of the ignition. The nerves that faded during our conversation on the way over came back now with gusto. Wolf nudged me, excited and energized both by the noises outside and Bowen's attention. I wasn't sure why I felt anxious again, but I did.

Bowen opened his door and climbed out. I started to open my door to follow suit.

"Hang on, I'll get it." Bowen smiled. A quick breath, and then Bowen opened my door. The crisp afternoon air hit me, and Wolf took a good inhale.

"Wow, that sun is bright." I squinted, not realizing how brilliant the late afternoon was compared to the tinted light inside the car.

"You want to borrow my sunglasses?"

"Thanks, but I'm okay. I'll just have to take them off when we go on the rides."

Bowen locked the doors, and without giving me a chance to respond otherwise, he grabbed my hand, confident in his movements, and we walked to the ticket booth. Bowen didn't miss a beat and paid both our admissions—they weren't cheap—and led me into the coolest carnival I'd ever seen.

Everything was themed. We were standing in the middle of a movie paradise. Everywhere I looked, I saw iconic films through the rides, the signs, the booths.

"This is awesome," Bowen said. He pointed to a booth done up in superheroes. The top of the booth was made up yellow with the famous bat-shaped buckle, and the sides of the booth were draped in long black gauzy fabric. "Let's put our wristbands on and then go get in line for something. What do you want to ride first, Miss Fearless One?" He grinned at me as his fingers brushed the inside of my wrist to fasten the sticky part of the band.

My pulse quickened under his touch, and I hoped

he didn't notice. I glanced around and couldn't help the smile that broke out on my face.

"That one." I pointed. It was a giant circle just starting to swing up into the air. The little carriages started out parallel on the ground, attached on spokes to a middle pillar, and spun in a circle. Once the carriages were flinging around at a crazy speed, the carriages were lifted as the pillar moved upward. At the height of the ride, all the carriages were swinging in the circle, but perpendicular to the ground, pitching the riders in a huge loop, upside down and right side up. I'd ridden something similar at another theme park and loved it. This one looked even bigger.

"You weren't kidding." Bowen laughed. He held his wrist out to me with his wristband. My fingers fumbled as I tried to ignore how close he was. Wolf sighed, scenting his dark woodsy smell, and as I felt his muscles tighten, I knew he'd noticed. I slapped the sticky side of the band down, harder than I needed to in my flustered state, and took off in the direction of the *Spider*; I read its name on a sign.

Bowen chuckled behind me as we came to a standstill in the line. The ride was winding down, and there weren't many people in front of us.

"Does she like my scent?" he whispered in my ear and sent chills racing down my spine. I couldn't suppress the shudder wiggling down my back and sensed Bowen reaching out to touch me, but just then, the gates opened, and I scampered down the aisle and found an open car. I managed to get the lid of the carriage open and got ready to climb in, when Bowen's hand came to rest alongside of mine, holding the top of the carriage open. He glanced in the little compartment and raised an eyebrow.

I felt another niggle in my stomach as Wolf chuffed an amused breath. I'd forgotten how tiny those little cars were. We'd be in extremely close proximity.

"I don't think my legs are going to fit in there unless I'm in the back," Bowen commented. I nodded, now self-conscious of my decision to ride the *Spider*. He crawled in, and I refused to check out his perfectly rounded backside. He patted the seat in front of him, and my cheeks reddened further. I chanced a glance at his face, and his eyes were dancing with merriment. I rolled mine and crawled in.

We were closer than close. Bowen's large frame filled the tiny carriage. There was nowhere I could go without touching some part of him. Wolf was thrilled at the contact and tried to push me back against his solid chest. I wriggled uncomfortably, unsure where to put my hands or how far to lean back.

The attendant came by and whisked the lid of the car shut, checking to make sure all was secure. I was sandwiched between Bowen's thighs, my legs smushed up against his. I tried to move my foot slightly to the side and realized the leg of my pants was stuck on something. I leaned over precariously in the tiny space to free my jeans, and the back of my jacket came up.

Suddenly Bowen's warm hands circle my waist over my flannel shirt, but under where my coat had been. I sat straight up, surprised, aware, uncomfortable, and *liking* his hands there. My heart pounded. Wolf rubbed her head against me, telling me this was a good thing.

"Is this okay?" Bowen's words were soft, and the sound of them wrapped around me the way his hands were wrapped around my waist, resting on the top of my hips.

Was this okay? Was I okay? Did I want his hands there? Was I supposed to want his hands there?

A myriad of thoughts thundered across my brain; my mouth opened, but nothing came out. Before I could form a coherent sentence, the machinery creaked to life, and the force of the motion jerked me back against his chest. His hands squeezed my sides lightly. The ride picked up speed, and I was flung tightly against Bowen. His hands inched further around my middle, holding me as the car picked up speed.

I closed my eyes as the wind lashed through the window slits in the car and let myself lean back. There was no place else to go. I felt the steady, albeit accelerated, beat of his heart against my back. His hands were warm and solid. I was cradled against him, his arms around me, his legs on either side of me. As the wind whistled by my ears and stung my cheeks with its chill, I realized in this moment, Bowen made me feel *special*. I wondered at it as we started rising farther off the ground. The machine lurched, jerking us to the side, and I gripped the legs of Bowen's jeans. His hands were hot and pulled me even tighter, telling me he had me, even though he was silent. His chin and cheek pressed against the top of my head. His nose dipped closer to my hair as he scented me. My toes tingled, and Wolf urged me to tip my head back and lean it on his shoulder, exposing the whole length of my neck to him.

I wasn't sure I was ready for that kind of surrender, but my body relaxed into his, and his hands moved so his fingers met and rested over my belly button, only my flannel shirt between us.

We stayed that way the whole ride. My eyes stayed shut, his hands stayed planted on my belly. Wolf simpered. When the ride finally cranked to a stop, I realized my hands were still gripping folds of Bowen's jeans, and I forced them to unlock their hold. Bowen's thumbs smoothed over my shirt, but the intimacy of the gesture sent my heart galloping in my chest. It was innocent enough, but no one had ever touched me like that. No boy had really ever touched me at all. Everything with Bowen was new. It was frightening…and it was exciting.

The attendant clicked our car open, and we walked out, silent. When we had exited the ride, Bowen cleared his throat, and I realized he'd been as affected by the ride as I had. The thought sent a curl of heat through my middle.

"So what next?" Bowen asked, his voice slightly husky. I felt my cheeks heat for no reason.

"Um, you pick. I picked this one."

He nodded, a faraway look in his eye I wasn't quite brave enough to ask about.

"Let's do a good old-fashioned Ferris wheel."

I smiled. It was tame in comparison to what we'd just ridden, and I felt an unusual urge to tease him. "Need something a bit calmer after the aerodynamics of the *Spider*?"

He chuckled and then looked me right in the eye. "Less aerodynamics, possibly. Calmer?" He leaned down, invading my space again. "I'm good flirting with the wilds."

Gooseflesh pimpled my arms. The arrogant, teasing smirk was back on his face. I rolled my eyes at him for good measure but felt a grin tugging one side of my mouth. He grabbed my hand again, his confidence back in place, and started leading us through the crowd toward the giant wheel in the distance.

****

The Ferris wheel line was short, so we got on quickly. We had the cage to ourselves. Bowen patted the seat next to him, and I perched lightly on the bench. After the *Spider*, I was even more unsure what to expect and how to act. Part of me had relished the contact with him, the intimacy I'd never experienced before. But I was still just as unsure how to behave.

"Relax." Bowen smiled and put his arm along the back of the seat. His hand nudged my shoulder, urging me to relax into him.

Pulse thundering, which he could probably hear, I let myself ease into the seat, my shoulders against his arm. He nudged me again, pulling me gently into him. My shoulder met the side of his chest, and heat sizzled through me. Maybe this wasn't so bad.

We were quiet the whole ride. At some point, I relaxed fully, and his hand cradled my shoulder.

I was almost sorry when the ride was over. Bowen squeezed me once and climbed out of the carriage, taking my hand to help me down. He entwined our fingers and tugged me toward a row of food trucks near the entrance of the mall.

"I'm hungry. You want to browse and get a snack before dinner?"

"Sure. What sounds good?"

"Mmmm. Funnel cake."

I laughed. "I smell that greasy goodness already."

"Have you ever had an apple fritter funnel cake?"

"No, but it sounds good."

139

"They are. Let's see if they have them."
****

We found the apple fritter funnel cakes. We shared one. It was amazing.

"How have I never had these before?" I asked as I wiped powdered sugar from my lip.

Bowen grinned. "You missed some." Before I could respond, he ran his thumb over my bottom lip and set loose a fury of fizz inside my belly. Wolf leaned in, and I felt my eyes go wide.

Bowen's fingers feathered along my jaw. "I'm glad you agreed to come today," he whispered.

I was no idiot. This was a perfect moment for him to lean in and kiss me. Anxiety churned as panic jolted through me, so I said the first thing that popped into my head. "Do you suppose they have turkey legs?"

Bowen laughed and dropped his hand. He grabbed mine again, and I exhaled as the intimate bubble burst.

"I'm sure they do. They have a killer taco truck here, too. I know you said you like Mexican."

"Tacos are good." My voice sounded breathless to my own ears.

Chapter 24
Bowen

All considered, I thought our date went about as well as it could have. Raven never quite lost her jitters, but for most of the afternoon and evening, she relaxed. We even flirted a little. And she let me touch her. I hadn't realized how much I'd needed that. Wolf shook his shaggy head out inside me. I needed to go for a run tonight. All that contact with Raven had made Wolf angsty, too.

"Did you have a good time today?" I asked, glancing at her. Her hand was still in mine, but her face started getting that drawn look again.

Her eyes softened. "I really did." She smiled shyly at me, and it was like a vent of hot steam went off inside me.

"You know you're really beautiful when you smile like that." I watched in satisfaction as her cheeks pinked. It was kind of a rush that saying that to her was enough to make her blush. Most of the girls I had experience with would have just turned and kissed me at that point. If I'd even needed to comment on their looks before going straight to the kissing. Lines were lines. But I meant every word I said to Raven. I didn't want anything with her to be a line. Disgust at my past churned in my gut, and I shoved the ugly thoughts away. I didn't want them to taint my first date with

Raven.

Too soon, we pulled into the driveway of Raven's house. I'd hoped she'd come back with me to my house. Baby steps.

Raven's anxiety skyrocketed as I put the car in park and shut off the ignition. I could smell it on her. I scratched the back of my neck as I got out to open her door. I had no idea why she was still so nervous. I thought things had gone well. Did I still make her that skittish, or was it something else?

She all but bolted out her side when I opened the door for her. She went so fast she nearly tripped going up the porch stairs.

"Hey, hang on." I chuckled and jogged up to her. "Thanks for coming today. I think this was good. I had a great time. Maybe we could try another date sometime?"

"I did have fun." A tiny smile hid in the corner of her mouth. Her hands twisted in front of her. I grabbed them, stilling their motion.

"Maybe we could do something again next weekend?"

She blew out a quick breath. "Okay."

I nodded, pleased, and glanced at her lips. She froze. Her body went rigid, and the next thing I knew, she'd ripped her hands from mine and whirled for the door.

"Night, Bowen," rushed from her lips as her front door shut in my face. I stared stupidly at their green door for a few seconds before a laugh worked its way into my chest.

"Night, Raven." I knew she could still hear me on the other side of the door. Chuckling, I went back to my car.

Kissing me. That's what all her nerves had been about. Well, I could wait. Although I wasn't sure why it would be cause for such concern on her part. She was gorgeous. Surely, she'd gone on dates and kissed a few guys at the end of their time together. Wolf snarled at the thought. I shushed him, painfully aware of my less than pristine past.

My shoulders shrugged as I crawled back in my car. I couldn't help myself and sent her a quick smiley face text.

****

Thursday night, we had a home game. Part of me was a little sad I wouldn't have the travel time next to Raven. I'd love to convince her to make my hot tub an after-game ritual. At the very least, we planned to go out for pizza together. That thought alone made me hyped. I was ready to conquer the opposing team and then go celebrate with my mate.

Coach consulted his clipboard, pen tucked behind his ear.

"You ready?" Cade asked me in the locker room as he finished tying his shoes.

I absently traced the thirteen on the front of my jersey as I bounced on the balls of my feet. "Ready to crush them."

Cade snorted, his lips twisting into the mocking half smile he wore often. "Let's do it." He punched me in the shoulder before turning to the rest of the room. "Huddle up!"

We crowded around into a circle in the middle of the room, piling our hands into a giant hand sandwich. Coach Watson put his hand on the very top.

"I'm proud of you all this year. You've worked hard. We're going to up the defense tonight. Bowen, Jamie, you all are starting post tonight. You're tall and strong. Don't let anything inside the paint. Let's show them what we can do." I could smell Jamie's excitement to be starting again. Coach nodded to Cade.

"Boys, we play as a team, just like always. Lester has a new player this year. He's a freshman playing varsity, so we can assume he's good. That's okay. Because when we play together, we're stronger. Remember, any given team can beat any given team on any given day. It's all about how we play. We play together. We carry each other." Pride stirred in my chest at Cade's words. This basketball team had become a second pack with its own acceptance and hierarchy.

"On three!"

"*Wolves!*" And then howls broke out as the group of us pointed our noses to the ceiling and gave it all we had. Wolf rose within me, wanting to literally howl, but I tamped him back down. We'd do that later tonight. Maybe with Raven.

We ran out of the locker room and into a haze of pom-poms, noise, and flaring lights.

"Yeah, Cade! Yeah, Bowen!" Picking out Raven's voice easily from the fray, I zeroed in on her, giving her a flirty grin before running a warmup lap following Cade.

We were just rounding to the half-court line as the opposing team, the Lester Eagles, came charging out of their locker room.

Cade grunted in front of me, and I nearly missed a step. Somebody on the other team *reeked* of body

144

spray. As in, must have marinated in it. It burned my sensitive nostrils and sent Wolf recoiling at the stench.

"Man. That's worse than skunk," Cade muttered. Wolf snorted inside me. I resolved to try to breathe through my mouth if I could. It was awful.

I tried to shove the obnoxious stench to the back of my mind and concentrate on my shots. By tip-off, I was fairly desensitized. As in, my nose was numb. I couldn't smell anything.

That was good, because when I stood on the circle at half-court and my opponent came forward, I realized it was the varsity-playing freshman. And he was the one stinking up the gym.

We were nearly alike in height, but I was bulkier. He had the inches, but I had the muscle. Not that he was a twig. He was built. But I was built bigger.

Brown eyes narrowed at me under a fringe of dark hair. His lip started to curl back in a snarl, and I realized he was trying to look predatory.

Little turd. I'd eat him for breakfast on toast.

A low noise erupted in his throat as we crouched, ready for the referee to toss the ball.

The ball left the ref's hand, and Wolf lunged, muscles bunched, coiled tight in anticipation. The tips of my fingers touched the bumpy leather, and my wrist flicked toward Cade. The ball started moving right as the turd's knee connected to my chest midair and knocked the rest of my hand's momentum off course. The ball wavered as his knee jammed harder into me, shoving me to the ground and crushing the air from me as we landed in a heap; his knee pressed into my solar plexus.

I saw red. Gasping, I shoved him off me, Wolf

growling and ready to launch a full-scale assault. Little sack of crap. That was it. He was going down.

The ball had gone to Cade, but it wasn't clean. He was halfway down the court, both teams trailing after him.

"Bowen, get up!" Zack, a wing, bent and jerked my arm. I was on my feet before he finished, ready to play, using my anger to fuel my focus.

It was a battle. The Eagles played rough. And no one was worse than the freshman bathed in body spray. The referees were not overly indulgent in calling fouls either.

By halftime, we were neck and neck, and all of us were bruised and feeling the heat.

Chapter 25
Raven

It had been a long time since I'd seen a game this intense. I bit my nails in between cheers, and Wolf pawed inside me. I was sure half our team would be black and blue tomorrow.

The halftime buzzer went off, and I moved to the side as the dance squad took the floor. I cracked the lid on my water and took a long pull before capping it and putting it back on the floor. I started to move closer to the other girls, but Skylar broke in.

"Mm-mm." She shook her head. "Don't think you're welcome here just because you've got the same uniform on as the rest of us. You don't bleed the same color. We don't rat out our friends."

Something snapped, sending the docile girl I typically was deep into hiding. Wolf stood to her full height inside me. I'd had enough. I was tired of being accused of something I didn't do. "Skylar. You are full of crap. I didn't say anything to anyone. And I'd bet everything in my bank account you were the one who started the rumor that I did. That makes you a liar and the one who ratted out a team member. You can shove it."

No one moved for a full minute as the dancers continued in the background. Mouths gaped while Skylar's teeth gleamed as her lips pulled back into something ugly.

"You are a pathetic tagalong who got her best friend kicked off the team. You think you're something. *I* am the cheer captain. You will never be better than me."

I snorted. "I don't care if you're the cheer captain. It doesn't give you an excuse to treat people like dirt. I don't know what I did to make you dislike me, but either tell me or get over it. Because I'm done with this." My hands were on my hips, my chest heaving with pent-up anger. It was possible steam blasted out my ears. Wolf puffed her chest, proud of the stand I'd made.

You okay? Bowen's voice echoed in my head, startling me enough that I found his eyes across the gym from where he stood on the sidelines. I nodded as heat curled inside me. His eyes roamed over me in a way that sent Wolf skittering happily.

Skylar didn't miss the way his eyes trailed me either. A very unladylike word dropped out of her mouth but was covered by applause as the dance squad scurried off the floor.

"I'll show you." Skylar snarled the words. She took a few jogging steps onto the gymnasium floor, stared daggers at me, then looked to be sure Bowen could see her. He raised an eyebrow and glanced from her to me. I shrugged a shoulder.

Without waiting for more specific attention, Skylar did back handsprings from one end of the gym to the other. The spectators clapped as she did sparkle fingers and ran back to our side.

"You can't beat me, snitchy."

"Did you forget I did tumbling and gymnastics

most of my childhood?"

Her face paled slightly as her eyes narrowed. And because I wanted to stick it to her, I screwed up my courage and took a running start.

I did my favorite series. I flipped from a roundoff into three back handsprings, from which I launched into a double twist. From that landing, I immediately went into another roundoff and launched myself into the air to finish with a front flip. I stuck the landing so hard my feet could have put down roots.

"Wooo! Yeah, Raven!" Cade hollered from the sidelines. The rest of the team followed his lead, and the gym was filled with noise.

That's my girl, echoed in my head and drowned everything else out. Bowen looked proudly at me, arms crossed, feet planted. I smiled and ran back to the rest of the squad.

"Um, wow. That was pretty amazing," Miranda commented.

"Miranda!" Skylar hissed through her clenched teeth.

"What? It was, and you know it. Get over yourself." I could have hugged Miranda, but it was time for us to move back to our places for the next half.

"This isn't over," Skylar shot at me.

"It can be over whenever you want it to be," I countered.

****

The second half of the game was even worse than the first. There were elbows, deliberate shoves, and my sensitive ears picked up several curses from both teams.

At four minutes to go, Bowen had the ball and drove it hard toward the paint for a layup. Number twenty-three, the one who had tipped off against him, rushed at him. My breath caught. For a second, there was a tumble of arms and a scramble for the ball. Time seemed to slow as I watched twenty-three purposefully reach back with his elbow as Bowen bent to keep possession of the ball. The dark-haired boy's elbow came smashing into Bowen just as he raised his face, catching him full in the nose.

There was a sickening crunch, and Wolf howled inside. My eyes widened as Bowen jerked up, his eyes dilated enough I could see them from where I was on the sidelines. A tremor rocked down his arms as blood trickled from his nose.

"No, no, no," I whispered. *Bowen!* I used our link for the second time since our Claiming ceremony. His eyes snapped to mine, holding my gaze. I didn't dare look away, some baser level understanding I was the only thing grounding him to his skin in that second.

Twenty-three made a move to lunge at Bowen, but Cade stepped in between them, shouting something as both referees threw themselves into the fray about to happen. Both teams swarmed into a standoff with the referees in between, but Bowen just stood looking at me until Cade touched his arm.

Bowen blinked. Cade said something and pointed to the bench. Bowen's eyes focused, no longer dilated, and he tipped his head back and went to the bench where Coach Watson yelled at the refs while Assistant Coach Young had a towel and an ice pack for Bowen's bloody nose.

A few minutes later, when most of the tempers had cooled down, Bowen took his foul shots and sank them both. As it turned out, it was those foul shots that won us the game.

****

The stands were emptying, and people were talking in groups as I waited for the guys. Sarah Thornehill came up and leaned against the wall next to me.

"Hey. Some game tonight."

"It definitely was. I didn't realize you were coming tonight," I told her, trying to keep the curiosity out of my tone.

"Yeah. Cade invited me." She looked me in the eye and gave me a smile that told she knew what was going on in my head, and that I surmised correctly.

"So. You and Cade?" I ventured.

"Maybe." Her pale green eyes glittered as her mouth curved upward just at the corners. "It's complicated."

I was spared answering as Cade and Bowen came tumbling out of the locker room.

"Hey!" Cade wasted no time in greeting us. "Sarah, glad you came. Raven, awesome flips." He winked at me.

Bowen was quiet but looked content enough. His nose was slightly swollen still, but it would probably fade back to normal within the next few hours. He laced his fingers with mine, and my face flushed. He'd showered and had on jeans and a sweater. He looked ready for an alpine modeling gig.

"We'll catch you guys later." Cade waved to us both, and he and Sarah took off to the side door, a careful distance between them.

"Ready for pizza?" Bowen broke into my thoughts.

"Yes. I'm starving. Great job tonight."

"Thanks. I was impressed with your flips. I knew

you did gymnastics, but that was pretty hot."

His praise sent little tingles shooting through me. Maybe I was ready to really try to give this mate thing a chance.

****

I was about midway through my first slice of pepperoni pizza when the chime above the door clanged, and a group of girls flounced in. Bowen glanced at the door, then his head whipped back around. His face shuttered. Feeling my stomach clench, I looked back up and saw one of the girls—a chesty blonde—zero in on our table and flutter toward us, an animated expression on her face.

Wolf bared her teeth as she saw the curvy girl approaching. Wolf outright snarled as the girl waltzed to our table and put a hand on Bowen's arm.

"Bowen Oakes!" she squealed. "I can't believe it's you! We've all missed you so much over at Woodard!"

"Hey, Riley," he offered noncommittally.

"We're out for after-game pizza. Did you guys win tonight? Of course you did. You have that after-game glow. Need any company for *after* after-game pizza? She waggled her eyebrows, and her hand, still on Bowen's bicep, squeezed playfully.

I felt my eyes widen, and my nostrils flared. I clenched the napkin on my lap hard enough my knuckles cracked. Wolf paced within me, ready to leap at this girl staking a claim on Bowen. *My* mate. My earlier resolve to give *us* a chance was quickly disintegrating.

Bowen's cheeks flushed, and he cleared his throat uncomfortably as his eyes flicked to mine. "Riley, this is Raven. My *girlfriend*." He said the words with finality, and while it should have eased some of my tension, it didn't.

Riley's eyebrows shot up her forehead. She turned to me with a fake smile plastered on her face. "You're a lucky girl. No one could keep Bowen off the market back home." Her eyes did a quick once-over, checking out my assets, measuring me up. She straightened up just enough for her generous chest to wobble within Bowen's line of sight. He kept his eyes riveted on my face. She leaned down toward me. "Seriously. He's the best I've ever had. Enjoy him while he lasts!" she whispered to me before giving Bowen another little flirty wave and sashaying back to her group, now seated in a booth on the far side of the restaurant.

My pizza turned to ash in my mouth. I tore my napkin in half before throwing it on top of my half-eaten pizza.

"I'm done." I bit out. My heart squeezed painfully in my chest as waves of anger, embarrassment, and betrayal sliced through me.

"Yeah," Bowen said dejectedly. He threw some bills on the table and slid out of the booth. I didn't wait for him but marched through the restaurant and burst through the door, not waiting for Bowen to open it, and took a lung full of cold air. Once I was at Bowen's car, I screwed my eyes shut, willing the tears of frustration to stay put. I didn't want to cry right then. I was too angry and too hurt.

I heard the doors unlock and again, didn't wait for Bowen, but jerked my door open and slammed it shut behind me.

Bowen crawled in his side slowly. He turned the key and then turned off the radio.

"Raven," he started.

"Take me home," I demanded. Wolf struggled within, wanting to make up with Bowen, but just as hurt and betrayed by Riley's admissions as the human part of me.

Long minutes stretched out in the silence. I stewed in my anger, unhappy, and stuck wanting things to be different. It wasn't like I didn't know Bowen had been with other girls. But it didn't stop me from hating it. With every single fiber of girl and wolf.

Still a few miles from the turn to my house, Bowen pulled the car off onto a little side path I only barely remembered was there. It led to a little alcove and a wooden bench near the river.

With the river in sight and the little wooden bench I remembered directly to the left and the trees soaring around us, Bowen parked. The stars and moon hung bright in the clear cold night, and the river made soft shushing noises as it tripped over the rocks on its bed.

Bowen killed the engine and turned to face me fully.

"Spit it out, Raven."

I looked at him, unsure if pain or fury radiated more from my eyes. Angry heat burbled up from the pit of my stomach and erupted out of my mouth.

"How many more times am I going to be completely humiliated like this?"

He said nothing, but his face was sorrowful. He said nothing, and the blistering words just kept pouring out of me.

"How many more girls are there? I know things were different for you in Victor's pack, and I know you've been with other girls, but it's utterly humiliating and painful to be confronted again and again by your past and your reputation. I'm trying to move past all this—trying to figure out how this mate business is going to work. But every time I'm reminded of the...*others,* it makes me furious!" I scrubbed my hands down my face, realizing tears were seeping out without my permission.

"I feel so completely inadequate compared to all these girls you've been with. Wolves are supposed to mate for life—with *only* their partner. I feel like I've been robbed—like this one thing that was supposed to be mine has been ripped away, and I'll never have it." I sobbed in earnest and couldn't hold it back anymore. Wolf nudged me, and my deepest fears were out in the open before I could draw them back in. "Maybe if I had more experience with guys, I'd feel differently. But you were my first date. I've never even been kissed before—and it makes me feel vulnerable in a way that I hate. And I don't know how to stop being so angry with you and feeling so awful about myself." The words ran dry, and I felt wrung out but somehow lighter for having said all the things that had been churning mercilessly inside me for weeks.

Chapter 26
Bowen

I was the worst kind of dog. Raven was more upset than I'd ever seen her—this was a different kind of anger than she'd shown me before. This was a fury inside herself, and it was tied to her own insecurities. And *she'd never been kissed*? The thought brought heat surging up through my middle and no small degree of terror. It was true—I had miles more experience with girls than Raven had with guys. But things weren't quite as she thought they were.

Dread gripped me and squeezed, making it hard to breathe. There was silence in the car. Raven's words hung like shrapnel in the air. She sniffed. Her eyes were swollen, and I knew I had to share that secret part of me with her now, or I'd lose her forever.

I gulped. I had wanted her to never know this side of me. Wolf pawed at me, restless and antsy.

"Raven." My voice came out in a hoarse whisper. "I've never been past second base." The air in the car evaporated, and I had to get out. I jerked the door of the car open, not even bothering to shut it, and staggered to a tall pine tree. The rough bark became an anchor as I leaned my head against it and shut my eyes.

I heard Raven get out of the car but kept my face pressed against the coarse tree.

"What do you mean?" she asked quietly. Her storm

had passed, but I knew my next words would bring another.

"I never slept with Riley. I never slept with any of them. I've never had sex."

I could practically hear her mouth drop open in shock, but my eyes stayed closed.

"Then how...?"

My heart ached with the weight of the words I knew I had to speak.

"I made them believe we had sex. All of them." I squeezed my eyes tight, opened them, then shoved away from the tree, only to find myself tugging on my hair. I couldn't bear to watch her face as I gave my final confession, so I stared out at the serene water, moving quietly on its way.

"I am my father's son," I said bitterly, the words acid on my tongue. "Just like Victor could, I can control people."

I heard her gasp, and my eyes closed in shame as my head drooped.

"I can't control people quite the same way and not as many at a time. Wolves are harder to control than humans. But it's disturbingly easy to make humans—especially drunk girls who already want to get laid—think something happened that did not. I can insert my thoughts, what I want them to think, right into their brains, and they're never the wiser." I heard my voice, flat and emotionless, as if from outside my own body.

The silence stretched out interminably. My gaze stayed fixed on the water, my guts writhing, waiting for her condemnation. Long minutes passed. I had nothing else to say, but Raven's silence was slowly chipping away at what was left of my soul. Wolf howled. I wanted to shift, to run, to forget this horrible, painful moment.

"Oh, Bowen," she finally said softly into the darkness.

Her words washed over me, and my head came up, looking at her for the first time since I'd left the car.

Her eyes were large dark orbs in her face, the moonlight giving her pale skin an ethereal shine as it shadowed her eyes. Raven's shoulders rose and fell with a heavy sigh.

"Come," she said, her voice soft. "Come sit and tell me everything." She turned and went to the wooden bench. I followed numbly, unsure of her reaction. I had expected her outright rejection—anger, denial, panic— but it wasn't forthcoming. Hope lit inside me, daring me to leave myself totally open.

I cautiously perched next to Raven on the bench, taking in her tear-stained face, her eyes still puffy, dark smudges of makeup left behind that hadn't come away. Her face was pensive as she stared at the rippling water.

She turned and met my eyes. "Have you ever controlled me?"

"No!" I shouted vehemently. She twitched at the abrasiveness of my voice. "Sorry. No," I repeated at a normal level. "I've not controlled anyone since the night Victor died. I know what it's like to have your will taken away." My hand absently tracked to my tattoo. "I never want to do it ever again. Even as Beta to Kyp, I have yet to use Command. It's just too close to what Victor did." I shivered, then braced my elbows on my knees, leaning forward. A torrent of unpleasant memories of Victor and his iron grip on my will flooded through me. I shook my head, forcing them away.

"So why did you convince all those girls—I assume there are several of them—that you slept with them?"

I gave a mirthless laugh. "Did you know that the more a wolf sleeps around, the less he's able to form a cohesive bond with his chosen mate? And the more tenuous his ties to his mate, the stronger his ties are to his Alpha?"

Raven's eyebrows rose. "No, I didn't know that. I mean, I know my own pack puts a high premium on only…doing certain things with your mate, but I've never heard that sleeping around makes your Alpha ties stronger."

"It does. It's a little-known fact, especially since nearly all wolves are instinctually driven to their chosen—or, like us, true—mates. Victor knew this, and that's why he encouraged all his pack to be as promiscuous as he was."

"And that only made the pack's ties to him stronger."

I nodded. "It destroyed the pack's ability to form proper mate bonds with their wives or husbands. And those bonds are meant to be a sort of tether. Without that tether, the only thing keeping them tied to the pack is the bond with the pack Alpha. And in turn, it only increased Victor's ability to exercise his mind control.

"I lived with Victor for two weeks before I knew I was in deep trouble. He'd already forced me to do something against my will, and that was terrifying. So when he instructed me to—" I cleared my throat again and shuddered at the memory of Victor's face as he'd told me to go screw a couple of cheerleaders. "—

to…have a lot of sex," I summarized, "I knew there had to be a reason for it, and that it couldn't be good, coming from Victor. I went to the party like I was supposed to, but I didn't do anything else Victor wanted. When he found out I hadn't banged every cheerleader in attendance, he beat me black and blue. I was fourteen. I matured early, but I wasn't big enough then to take on Victor. I took a good long look at my life while I healed. I already knew I could force people to do little things for me. I was a jerk and a bully the two years before Victor found me. I'd figured out I could make people do things—but I had never done anything on the scale I needed to in order to make girls think we slept together."

I scrubbed a hand over my face and glanced at Raven. Her eyebrows were drawn together, but her face was otherwise unreadable. Laying my soul bare, I continued.

"I started experimenting. I found out I have next to no tolerance for alcohol, so I became a first-rate actor. I can act the part of a drunk like no other. Sometimes I'd pretend to get so drunk that I'd pass out, so I didn't have to mess with some helpless drunk girl's brain. But in order to keep Victor satisfied, I knew I either had to legitimately go all the way or make everyone think I had. It wasn't so much that I didn't want to. I was a fourteen-year-old guy," I admitted ruefully, "But Victor's treatment of my mom didn't win the casual approach any points, and I was still concerned because Victor *wanted* me to go out and sleep around. It took a little trial and error, but I figured out, and then perfected, how to make a girl think exactly what I wanted her to think." The fist squeezing my soul relaxed its grip. It was all out in the open now. It was done. "Say something, Raven," I rasped when I couldn't handle her silence any longer.

"I'm sorry you've had to carry all this. I had no idea," she whispered.

My head whipped up, straining to see every emotion in her eyes as the moon shone down. She turned her face back to the river.

"All this time I've been so focused on myself—on how angry it made me to think of you with other girls, how my own lack of experience would make you feel about me," her voice wobbled, "and I never realized how it tied back to Victor, and how that must be such a heavy burden."

My chest constricted as a wedge of relief and sorrow met in the back of my throat, forcing tears into my eyes. She drew in a shaky breath and turned back to me. Shocking me more than if she'd zapped me with electricity, she leaned forward and wrapped her arms around my shoulders. Stunned, it took me a few seconds before my arms shot out and nearly crushed her against my chest. I held onto her, afraid if I let go, she'd run screaming and never look back. I buried my face in her hair, the shiny black absorbing the few tears that escaped. The relief pouring into me nearly made me lightheaded.

"I'm sorry I didn't see your scars," Raven whispered. She started to pull back. I wanted to pull her back against my chest, sear her lips with a kiss to let her know just what her words meant to me. A quick glimpse of her face set in determined lines, and I released her.

"The mind control doesn't freak you out?" I

hedged.

"Oh, no. It completely terrifies me," she responded and sent my heart to my toes. "But Wolf believes you when you say you haven't used it on me, and I believe you, too. I would like to know a little more about it, though?"

"My secrets are now completely exposed. Ask me whatever you want."

"How exactly does it work? I mean, would I know if you inserted some thought or whatever into my head?"

"It's a little iffier with wolves. Wolves are not as easily mastered. I would have no trouble making you do something, but you'd be aware. If I was being more discreet about it, you may have a little confusion over the thoughts or false memory I gave you, but you probably wouldn't question it."

"Have you ever met any other wolves who can do it?"

I shook my head, relieved no one else I'd met could twist someone's will as horribly as Victor could—or even as much as I could.

She was quiet for a long minute, watching my face. "I want you to tell me to do something. I want to know what it feels like."

My eyes widened in horror. "No. Absolutely not."

"Why not?"

"Have you not heard anything I've just told you? The thought of having to Command someone as Beta practically makes me throw up. I'm not letting this sick, twisted part of me touch you."

She put her hand on top of mine on the wooden bench.

"I want to understand what it's like. I need to understand to feel like I understand you. And I can say that this is the first time I've really *wanted* to understand you. I have railed against being your mate from the very beginning, but I think I'm ready to give this a genuine shot. I want to know *you*, Bowen. And your past, painful though it is, is still you."

I drew in a shaky breath. "No."

"Please?"

It took some more persuading, but I finally allowed her to convince me to do it once.

Touch your toes. You need to stretch, I silently directed her. Wolf watched carefully, his eyes slits. The gift truly belonged to my wolf half, though my wolf was as leery of using it as I was.

"Oh, hang on, Bowen. My back is all tight. I need to stretch it out." My stomach flipped unpleasantly as Raven bent down and quickly touched her toes. Her face screwed up in concentration.

"I have this taste like burned grain in the back of my mouth." She looked up at me, and understanding dawned. "You told me to touch my toes."

I nodded, feeling sick. She gripped my hand again and stared back out to the water.

"Where are we, Raven?" I asked her after another silence.

"We're here on a bench by the river." She looked over and smiled softly. She bit her lip. The way her eyes grew round and the way she worried her lip as she roved her gaze over my face made my blood heat. It was ridiculous that I could still feel so attracted to her in the middle of such a quagmire of emotions.

"Bowen," her voice almost so low I didn't hear it.

"I…I think I want my first kiss," she whispered.

I blinked twice, disbelieving what I'd just heard. Blood rushed through my veins, followed quickly by panic. I'd never been anyone's first kiss. I'd never loved any of the girls I'd kissed. And I knew I was falling in love with the pieces of Raven as she let me see them. I'd never felt so much pressure put on one kiss. I wanted everything about it to be perfect. A light tremor shook my hands as I memorized her face. The way the moonlight fell across her skin and made her hair shine with a blueish tint. The way her lips parted so innocently, waiting, inviting me to taste them.

"Raven?" I asked, even as one trembling hand reached up to cup her jaw.

"Yes." Her voice was breathless with anticipation—and probably nerves. I slowly ran my thumb over the curve of her bottom lip. A little puff of air frosted from her lips. Her heartbeat accelerated, and so did mine.

Wolf danced around, urging me to stake my claim, to kiss this woman who was mine. Never breaking eye contact with her, I let my other hand slip around her waist to her back, drawing her closer. Her eyes widened, and her hands fisted into the sweater covering my forearms.

Before I could overthink it anymore, I slowly dipped my head and let my lips touch Raven's ever so lightly.

Her lips were salty from her tears but sweet with promise. She didn't move, and I held my lips against hers for another moment before pulling back.

Chapter 27
Raven

Electricity charged through my veins as his lips touched mine. Wolf lay down, contented at last. His lips lingered for just a minute before he pulled back. My eyes fluttered open to find him searching my face. His eyes held a mix of awe and concern. I smiled, and his concern melted away.

"Want to go for a run?" I whispered.

"With you? Always." His lips quirked up on one side.

I made myself get up from the bench, part of me wanting to kiss again, but the other part thinking pacing might be a good way to start this.

"Meet you back here in a minute." I walked a few steps away into the cover of the trees, glancing back only to find him sitting on the bench still, looking at the water, a silly grin on his face. His finger traced over his mouth, and heat surged all the way to my toes. Wolf rubbed her head against me. Bowen's expression said our first kiss had been special to him, too.

I hung onto that as I stepped out of my clothes and reached my arms above my head as a frigid wind chilled over my naked body. Flicking my hair out of the way, I let my silky fur shoot through my skin, covering me in a layer of black and melting me into the shadows. Ears pushed through my head, and my canines shoved through my gums. Bending over, my claws buried themselves into the top layer of frozen ground. My tail disconnected from my backbone, sliding out with an audible snap. Senses heightened, breeze floating over my ruff and flickering my whiskers, I caught Bowen's cedar and brown sugar scent. I shivered in anticipation, wanting to be with him in a way I never had before.

Leaving my clothes on the forest floor, I padded back to the bench. The white patch on Bowen's chest caught the moonlight where he waited for me. I stopped just in front of him, gazing up at his shaggy head. He dipped, his nose running up the length of my neck to my jaw and raising the wolf equivalent of goosebumps all over me. My tail wagged, and I scented him back. The freedom I felt as he nuzzled my neck again both amazed and excited me. I'd never wanted him to touch me like this before tonight. But his confession had torn something loose that I'd kept locked close to my heart. Bowen was my endgame. I'd known it before, but now I began to feel it. Exhilaration shivered over my skin, and my fur stood up.

He pulled back. *Ready?* Echoed in my head. I yipped, and his tongue lolled out in a wolfish grin.

****

We ran. The ground disappeared beneath our feet, only for our paws to pound down onto the earth and spring away again. There was solidarity in running just the two of us. At one point, we stopped near a short series of falls in the river. Sides heaving, panting for breath, flanks touching, we sat together, letting our lungs catch up.

It was getting late. School would come early tomorrow. Tingles started in my chest and worked down to my claws.

Ready to head home? Bowen sent to me.

Yes. Let's go home.

Let's...as in us? Together? His wolf chuffed and nudged me with his cold nose.

I pawed his shoulder playfully. *Yes. Let's go home to your place.*

He stood and nudged me harder, mischief lurking in his wolf's irises.

I'm still sleeping in the guest room, I warned him.

He chuffed again, this time in amusement.

****

We made it back to the bench, shifted, changed, and then tried to thaw our frozen fingers as the car zipped down the road.

"I'm going to text Mom and let her know I'm staying with you." My cheeks flushed just thinking about it. It wasn't like I planned on doing anything other than sleeping—alone—at Bowen's house, but it felt right that I should be there.

Mom sent me back three smiley faces.

"So," Bowen started, and a shiver of excitement laced with nerves wiggled down my back. "Can we officially be a couple now?"

"Yes. But define couple?" I scratched my head, still unsure what that looked like.

Bowen's smile came easily. "Let me be your boyfriend. We don't need to be anything more than that right now if you don't want to be."

"Okay...but I'm still not sure what that looks like either. I've never had a boyfriend."

Bowen's face turned serious again. "I love being your first everything." He glanced at me. "I wish I hadn't made so many mistakes." He blew out a breath.

"It's done. There's nothing we can do to change it." My thumb traced over his hand where our fingers twined on the console. "But knowing you've kissed a bunch of girls is a much easier pill to swallow than thinking about you sleeping with a bunch of girls." My face heated as I realized someday, I *would* be his first. Butterflies and lava simultaneously erupted in my belly.

He squeezed my hand. Probably thinking the same thing.

****

The house was dark save the iron lamppost in the driveway. Bowen killed the engine and squeezed my hand.

"You ready to go in? Your shoulders just got all tense again."

I smiled ruefully. "Yes. I'm ready. Just uncharted territory. If you hadn't noticed, that tends to make me anxious."

"You don't need to be nervous with me, Raven." His voice was all low and husky. It woke something inside me. I met his gaze, all warm and chocolatey. It made me all gooey inside. He glanced quickly at my lips.

"We should go in," he whispered as his knuckle brushed against my chin. My breath was coming shorter, and when I didn't move, Bowen found my eyes again. His hand skimmed my jaw and found the back of my head.

With a hint of pressure, he nudged me forward. I didn't need much encouragement and moved of my own volition. He met me halfway, his lips catching mine carefully, reverently. It only lasted a second or two before he pulled back and rested his forehead against mine.

"I'm glad you came home with me."

"Wolf was ready to move in the night of our Claiming."

"She's smart, your wolf." He smirked as his lips stretched wide. "Come on. It's getting cold out here.

Chapter 28
Bowen

Friday night was another win for Rock Falls High, and between the adrenaline from the game and the exhilaration of finally kissing Raven, I was on top of the world.

"Cade, you want to come celebrate over at my place?" I asked him quietly as the team was filtering out of the locker room. "Just some of *us*?"

"Yeah. That sounds good. Raven was talking to Mom about your jacuzzi the other day. I wouldn't mind trying it out. Can I—" he cleared his throat, "—bring Sarah?"

"Thornehill? Sure." I snorted as Cade studiously avoided my gaze. "I'll give Kyp and Sam a call, too."

"It would be good to be just the group of us," he said low enough the other guys wouldn't overhear. There would be no wild partying tonight, as per Cade's orders to the team, as we had a Saturday morning tournament tomorrow. "We haven't really had time to just hang out. I think that's important."

I nodded, a sudden lump of emotion rising. I kicked my shoes off. "Should I order some pizzas or something?" I was starving after playing.

"All the meat." Cade mock punched my arm. "See you soon." He tipped his head at me and clapped a few other players on the back and said a few other words of encouragement before he exited.

I wasn't far behind and shoved my gym shoes in my bag, hitching my warmups over my shorts and sliding into an old pair of athletic sandals. I shot off texts to Kyp and Sam.

Raven met me by the bleachers. Her whole face lit up when she saw me, and my gut flipped. I wanted her. I shoved those thoughts to the back of my brain and smiled as I slung my arm around her shoulders.

"Ready?" I asked.

"Skylar is glaring daggers at the back of my head," Raven whispered, an unmistakable twinkle in her eyes.

"We're happy about this? Want me to kiss you, really lay one on you, and leave no room for doubt?" I kept my voice low and mischievous though I would have happily kissed her for eternity. I leaned my head close to hers, giving the impression of shared intimacy.

Raven giggled. "Maybe not quite yet." But she did snuggle up close to me, and my heart squeezed in a few extra beats.

"Great game tonight, Bowen." Skylar sidelined us anyway.

"Thanks, Skylar." I purposefully let my hand drift to the curve of Raven's waist. Skylar's eyes narrowed, not missing the possessive placement of my fingers.

But not to be deterred, she persisted. "Do you want to go out to eat? Several of us are going out for wings." Her icy glare speared Raven. "You can bring her, too, if you want."

Raven remained completely relaxed at my side, and I couldn't resist giving her a little *atta girl* squeeze.

"Sorry, but we've got plans."

We left her fuming as the chill night air whipped

around the door and brought the scents of motor oil and pavement.

"We have plans?" Raven asked quietly as I let my hand fall from her waist and grabbed her fingers.

"I probably should have asked you first, but I invited Cade and a few others over to the house. That okay?" I asked retrospectively.

"No, it's totally fine. Who else is coming?"

My phone dinged. I fished it out as we crunched over some frozen sludge and reached my car. "Looks like the whole crew. Kyp and Rachel, Sam and Megan, and I think Cade said he's bringing Sarah."

Raven's eyebrows rose. I grinned and opened her door.

****

By nine-thirty, the whole group of us were munching pizza and catching up.

"I feel like it's been so long since we were all together like this," Rachel said as she snagged another slice of chicken and bacon pizza.

Kyp glanced at me, then at everyone else. "You know, this might be the first time we *have* actually all been together like this."

"All friends, you mean," I said quietly. The room sobered, and guilt made a sudden appearance in my middle. This was my house. My kitchen filled with my guests—people I considered friends—and I realized with alarming clarity that a few weeks ago, I was the outsider. The would-be murderer. The air suddenly fled the room, and I felt like all the poison Victor had poured into me was leaking out and tainting everyone in the room. Spots danced at the edges of my vision.

"To friends," Cade said, looking each of us in the

eye as he raised his bottle of root beer.

"To friends," echoed around the kitchen.

A whisper of touch ghosted over my elbow from behind. The black dots receded, and Wolf grasped the emotion behind her careful touch. I took a deep inhale, and cinnamon and plum raced to my brain.

"Anyone else want to try the hot tub?" Cade said with a cheeky wink in my direction.

****

Raven must have had someone bring her over a swimsuit, or Shelby had one shoved in a drawer. Whatever the reason, my eyes about popped out of my skull when Raven came out to the back patio. I was already in the hot tub with the guys, jets frothing bubbles around us. Raven laughed at something Rachel or Megan had said as Sarah slid the door shut behind them.

Raven had a towel wrapped around her but wasn't paying attention to me as she took it off, still talking to the girls. My eyes were riveted. The towel came off, and she stood there in a modest one-piece. Dark red and hugging the most delicious curves I'd ever laid eyes on. I swallowed, trying to bring moisture back into my mouth. I'd seen her in my wet shirt, and that was more of a turn-on than I'd expected. But I'd never seen this much of her perfect skin. And I was actively ogling it now.

"Dude. My *sister*." Cade hissed between his teeth.

It jolted me enough to make sure I wasn't actually drooling, but then I looked slyly at Cade. "Dude. My *wife*," I whispered back just as quietly.

Cade made a small gagging noise and turned a slight shade of green. I resisted the urge to chuckle, and he quickly turned his attention to Sarah, who was decidedly more aware of the effect she had on Cade than Raven was of the effect she had on me.

Sweetly oblivious, she stepped into the hot tub and finally met my eyes. I hoped my pupils weren't dilated.

They must not have been since she crossed, the water bubbling up and making a wet line just underneath the swell of her chest. She sat on the ledge next to me, her bare thigh brushing against my knee as she situated. I was going to combust.

"Hey," I squeaked out.

"Hey." She smiled back. I wasn't sure if I should comment on her looks in the swimsuit or not. She was still getting used to the boyfriend idea, but as I'd just reminded Cade, Raven was mine, and I was hers. I opted for boldness.

Carefully leaning over, so my nose brushed her ear, I whispered, "You look *hot*."

An embarrassed but pleased smile hovered in the corner of her mouth.

"Kyp, does your house have a hot tub?" Sarah asked before Raven could respond.

"No. There's a pond on the property, though. I haven't tried swimming in it. Been a little too cold for that," he said good-naturedly.

"Do you have any pack members living with you yet, Kyp?" Sam asked. I knew Kyp and Rachel had picked that monstrosity with the intention of helping needy pack members. It was a decision that had earned them both my respect.

"Two right now. It's been good for everyone, I think," Kyp said.

"I'm glad it's worked out well. Something positive

that came out of Victor's mess." Though I didn't think Sam's words had been meant in anything but kindness, a hush fell over us, each of us thinking the ways Victor had somehow touched our lives.

"How is Shelby?" Megan asked after a moment of silence.

"She's still in the coma, but her body is starting to deteriorate," I found myself answering. "I talked to her nurse earlier in the week. No change."

"I still haven't forgiven her for trying to kill Meg, but part of me feels so sad for her," Rachel said.

"Me, too," Megan agreed.

"She got wrapped up in something bigger than she realized," Sarah said. Cade bumped Sarah's shoulder with his.

Of the group of us, I had probably known Shelby the best. She was not a nice person.

"I feel guilty thinking about her sometimes," Megan confessed to the group.

"Why?" Sam asked, his blond eyebrows pulled together. He put his arm protectively around Megan, water streaming down her shoulders.

"Part of me wonders if I'd been a better friend, or I don't know, I guess I just feel like there's something I could or should have done differently. And if I had, maybe she wouldn't be in a coma now." She shrugged.

Heaviness settled in my middle as Wolf gnashed, thinking about Shelby. "You shouldn't feel guilty." Heads turned at my words. Raven's hand found mine under the water, and Wolf settled inside. "She did get in over her head. But killing you was her idea. Victor just helped her work out some kinks in her plan because it fell in line with what he wanted. She was cruel and manipulative." It didn't please me to say the words, but it was no good feeling guilty for what you couldn't change. And I knew Megan didn't have anything to feel guilty about.

"She grew up with Victor. She learned from the master manipulator," Kyp said softly. We'd talked about our half sister. She'd been with Victor since she was a little girl.

"Why didn't all of you grow up with Victor?" Sarah asked.

Kyp shrugged. "He didn't even know I existed until I showed up at his doorstep."

"Right. I guess I knew that. Bowen?" She turned to me. My stomach dropped like lead. I didn't like talking about my past with Victor. It was painful and dredged up things I'd rather leave forgotten.

"He got my mom pregnant right around the same time as Kyp's. He knew she was pregnant but didn't care. Left her and then showed up fourteen years later. He had decided to decimate the Wolfe pack and was amassing his own pack. He already had a pack, but he was adding to it. Blood ties make the strongest leaders. I'm older than Shelby, so he hunted me down. Threatened my mom. She had no choice but to let me go with him. I became his Beta. Drew had been the functioning Beta, and I don't think he ever forgave me for usurping his place." I shuddered. Raven squeezed my hand.

"It's over," Raven said quietly.

"It's over," Rachel echoed.

Chapter 29
Raven

It was later than it should have been for having a tournament the next day when we all climbed out of the hot tub, fingers and toes all pruney. I walked Cade out to the front door.

"So you're staying here?" There was an odd tone in his voice.

"Yeah. I think so." He looked like he'd sucked on a lemon. "Cade, what's wrong?" I asked with a chuckle.

His lips widened in a grimace. "It's weird, you know. You're all...deflowered and stuff now." He scratched the back of his neck, and his cheeks flushed.

I nearly choked on the groan somersaulting up my throat. "Are you kidding me? I am not...*deflowered*," I said between my clenched teeth.

An imperceptible look flashed over his face. "Okay. I'm not sure which of those scenarios is weirder, to tell you the truth."

"Why don't we just stop discussing my nonexistent sex life, yeah?"

"Brilliant idea. Night, Rave." He slung his arm around my shoulders and gave me a quick hug. I squeezed him back, so glad he was my brother, weirdness and all.

"Thanks for having us over," Sarah said with a quick smile as she came up to us from the other room.

"Anytime," I said, meaning it. She flashed me another grin and grabbed Cade's hand, tugging him out the door.

I didn't miss the excitement that lifted my brother's features and hoped he wasn't going to do anything that would get them in trouble.

****

It wasn't long before it was just me and Bowen left in the house. I turned back from waving to Megan and shut the door behind me. Bowen leaned casually against the wall near the stairs. A lazy grin stretched across his face, and my heart kicked up.

We were very much alone.

"Early morning tomorrow. I'm ready for bed. You?"

There was no teasing in his words, and my heart slowed down.

"Yeah," I whispered. Haltingly, I walked to the stairs. He met me there and motioned for me to go up first.

Halfway up the stairs, a thought popped into my brain. I stopped and whirled around to face him, only slightly taller than him one stair up. "Are you checking me out?"

"Oh, I definitely am."

The bluntness of his words startled a giggle from my throat. "And here I thought you were being polite. Ladies first and all."

"I can be polite and check you out at the same time." He winked. "It's a good view. I really liked the swimsuit."

I felt my cheeks heating and resisted the urge to dash up the rest of the stairs, forcing myself to take them at a normal pace.

"Raven."

I stopped and turned again, just outside the guest room door. Bowen came up slowly, carefully coming into my space. His wide hands slid lightly around my waist, and my breathing hitched.

"You're beautiful." The sincerity in his words kindled something inside me. His eyes tracked to my lips and back up. "Can I kiss you goodnight?"

I tilted my face and let my eyes fall closed as his lips captured mine. They moved against mine, and I wasn't quite sure how to reciprocate.

"Don't overthink it." There was a smile in his words as he pulled back. Insecurity still fluttered in my middle.

I bit my lip. "I feel like I should apologize for not knowing how to kiss."

His eyebrows shot up his forehead. "You should never apologize for that. Do you have any idea how much it turns me on that you've never kissed another guy?"

I gulped as that kindled sensation in my middle flared to life. "I guess you just told me?" The words were breathy, and I knew he heard the trepidation in my tone when he stepped back.

"Good night, Raven." His eyes twinkled as he ran a finger over my cheek and headed into his room.

****

I woke up sometime way early, convinced I was dying of thirst. Probably all the salty pizza before the hot tub. I snuck to the bathroom and drank straight from the faucet. I padded silently down the hall, planning to sneak back to my room now that I'd had a drink. I paused as I tiptoed past the master suite and saw Bowen sitting on the window seat, staring out the window. His knees were bent, his arms draped loosely around them. Though his face was to the window, I could still see his profile. My heart picked up as I let my eyes have their fill of his squared jaw, his strong nose. His dark hair was messy and fell across his forehead. Never taking his eyes from the window, he leaned his head back against the bookshelf bracketing the window seat. He closed his eyes and swallowed. He was sad. I'd never seen him look so sad and lost. It broke my heart. Bowen was always so confident, so poised—even when he was angry. Bowen was a mountain of immoveable stone, but right then, he looked like he was about to crumble.

Without meaning to invade his privacy, my feet took me into his room. His eyes opened, and his eyebrows rose slightly as he saw me walking toward him. I had never come into his domain.

The cushion was soft as I sank down into it opposite him. He said nothing, but his eyes held a deep sadness I wanted to erase.

Wolf nudged me, and I felt my cheeks flush even as I agreed with her. Hesitating only a moment, I leaned forward slowly into his space and placed a soft kiss on his lips.

His breath stuttered in surprise as my lips met his—firm and inviting. I pulled back, still unwilling to go further than that, but wanting to comfort him.

"What was that for?" he asked quietly into the stillness of the room.

I gave a one-shouldered shrug. "You looked like you needed it."

A half smile tipped one side of his mouth. "I did.

Come here." He dropped one leg off the edge of the seat and opened his arms. Biting the edge of my lip, I moved toward him and sat with my back to his chest. He wrapped his arms around me and leaned the side of his face against my head. I could feel the strong muscles of his forearms beneath the thin cotton of his long-sleeved shirt as I rested my hands against his arms.

We sat in silence for several long minutes, the sound of our breathing and the light patter of snowfall as it hit the roof and trees outside the window the only noises. I wanted to know his thoughts but feared breaking the calm between us.

"I love to watch it snow," he finally whispered.

"It's peaceful."

He nodded against my hair. "It's more than that for me." I held my breath, wondering if he'd continue. "I've made a lot of mistakes in my eighteen years. Some worse than others, some I was compelled to make, most I've done all on my own. Talking about Victor last night broke open some old wounds." His chest rose and fell with a deep sigh. "In winter, everything is bare and ugly—like my mistakes. But when the snow comes down, it covers it all, making it white and clean. I want to leave the winter of my life behind me. I want the snow to come down and cover me, so I can be rid of the darkness my father left. I know some of it I'll struggle with all my life, and I'm okay with that. I just want to be done with *him*. With the mistakes I made because of him." His voice cracked.

I didn't have words. His confession tore something loose inside my chest, and I felt a tendril of heat curl its way around my heart. My arm tracked up his bicep and rested over his tattoo.

"You are not him, Bowen."

His chest rose and fell again. "Sometimes I feel rage building in me that terrifies me. It reminds me of him, and I just want to claw it out of me, but I don't know how."

"What calms the rage?" I asked as my thumb absently stroked over the material of his shirt covering his tattoo.

"You do," he whispered so soft I almost missed it.

I turned my head so I could see his brown eyes. They were swimming in emotion.

"Then I'll make sure the rage doesn't take you," I whispered back, conviction in my voice. I felt it down to my toes as Wolf puffed her chest in agreement. I might not be ready to feel for Bowen everything mates felt for each other, but I cared. He was slowly working his way into my heart. I would not lose him to his dead father.

"Always?" His voice was hoarse.

I nodded. "Always." He swallowed and blinked hard several times before his gaze raked over my face as if memorizing every inch. His eyes lingered on my lips, and my heart sped up in response. He glanced back up to my eyes, searching carefully, then slowly—so I had time to back away if I wanted to—he lowered his lips to my mouth.

His confession had opened something between us. I could feel it in his kiss. I didn't know if it was him or if I was more receptive, but this kiss was different. His lips teased me, closing over mine lightly, coming up only to touch down again with more pressure in a dizzying dance that left me wanting more. His hands slid so one braced against my back, and the other found my hip, holding me to him like I was made of glass.

We kissed slowly for several minutes, each kiss feeling more intimate than the last. Just as I started to become more confident in returning his kisses, Bowen pulled back, his eyes warm, cheeks slightly flushed. I was embarrassed to hear my own breathing coming harder than it had a few minutes earlier. My cheeks heated, and Bowen smiled as he noticed, which only made me blush harder.

"I've got to get ready. Tournament today."

"Two more minutes?" The words slipped out before I could rein them in.

Bowen groaned, his hand pulling me closer. "I'd sit here and kiss you all day if I could."

Well, I wasn't sure I was ready for that yet, but I couldn't say it didn't have serious appeal.

****

It was one of those rare times I wasn't going to Cade's—and Bowen's—game. Since it was a Saturday tournament, cheerleaders weren't required. And while I normally might have gone anyway, Megan and Rachel had had a giant custom cookie order come in on short notice, and I'd promised to help them.

"Kiss for luck?" Bowen asked as he pulled into the school parking lot. I smiled and met him over the console.

"I like kissing you." The words exited my mouth without my permission. Wolf snorted inside.

Bowen chuckled. "Glad to hear it. I vote we practice more later." He winked as I blushed again.

"I'll catch a ride back with Cade, and we can get your car and drive back to the house at the same time."

He paused. "If you're coming back?" The sudden vulnerability in his voice melted my insides.

"Yeah. I need to take things slow, but Wolf is most content with you. And…well, mates." I floundered for a better explanation.

"We'll take things as slow as you want." With another quick peck on my forehead, he was out the door and headed toward the school with his duffle thrown over his shoulder. He waved at the door before going in.

I switched seats and let myself inhale Bowen's lingering scent before pulling out and heading to Megan and Sam's cabin.

****

It was about ten-thirty, and Rachel's car was already there. I smiled to myself. Rachel and Megan had been friends since the dawn of time, but I never felt like an outsider with them. I really appreciated that. I knocked briskly on the door.

Rachel threw it open, seized me by the wrist, and hauled me bodily into the cabin.

"Look!" She shrieked as happy sparks danced in her eyes and lit up her whole face. She thrust her hand three inches from my eyes, and when I could focus, I realized she had a ring on her finger.

"Rachel!" I squealed with her.

"Yes! He asked! Officially!" She threw her arms around me and did a happy little jig with me right there in the entryway while Megan laughed, spatula in hand.

When we calmed down, I took her hand and got a good look at her ring. It was huge. I was no diamond expert, but it had to be in the two-carat range. It was a round diamond but arranged in a hexagonal setting of white gold. It was simple, stunning, quietly dramatic, and so Rachel.

"He picked out the ring, but we're going to go together to look at sets for the wedding band." Bliss radiated off of her, and Wolf nudged me, so happy for Rachel and Kyp.

"Based off your expression, I'd say you think he did a good job," I said.

"She may have mentioned it a time or twelve this morning." Megan laughed. My finger absently traced over my own ring. Still on my right hand.

"Well, tell me everything—how did he propose?" I asked and stilled my finger.

"It was *so* romantic." Rachel fanned herself dramatically before taking up a stainless steel bowl and giving the contents a vigorous stirring. "I didn't know he did this, but apparently, he talked to Mom and Daddy days ago and asked their blessing. Which they obviously gave. I mean, Kyp is amazing. Anyway, he let them in on the plans. Then, this morning, he texted really early. I'm usually a morning person anyway, so I was awake, but not up yet. He asked me to come out to the front yard.

"I did, and right there on the porch, he had electric heaters plugged in and running with a gorgeous breakfast spread out on a little table with two chairs. We had breakfast together, and then he got down on one knee and asked me." Her smile nearly stretched off her face. "I mean, we're already Claimed and married as werewolves, but Kyp wants a human wedding to make things as official as they can be. I think being only half wolf has a lot to do with it. And honestly, the desire to have a regular wedding has crossed my mind.

My mother can't wait to go dress shopping."

"I think that's wonderful." Thoughts of my own Claiming and Ancient Rites of Marriage ceremony— different from Rachel's Claiming because Bowen and I were true mates—floated through my brain.

Megan winked and handed me a sheet of paper with the cookie designs to pipe, and I sat at the table facing them.

"It is," Rachel sang. "I did have one other thing I wanted to ask you." Her green eyes flashed up at me cheerfully. "Will you be a bridesmaid?"

Excitement bubbled up. "Are you serious? Yes! Of course, I will!" I got up and gave her a quick hug. She squeezed me back tight.

"We don't have the date set yet, but it will be June. Anyway, enough about me. How are you and Bowen doing?"

"I am all ears for this. Are things going better than they were?" Megan asked.

I swallowed as heat trembled up my spine.

"They're definitely better." Wolf preened.

"Have you guys, you know, done stuff?" Rachel asked, never one to mince words. My belly squirmed.

"Rachel," Megan said with a roll of her eyes and a smile. I didn't miss the way she waited for an answer, too.

"No. I mean, we've kissed, but nothing else."

"Don't look at me. That's all Kyp and I have done, too." Rachel winked at me. "Megan, on the other hand..." She trailed off and wagged her eyebrows suggestively at her best friend.

Megan blushed and giggled. "If I didn't need this ball of dough in my hand, I'd throw it at you."

We shared a laugh, and conversation and wedding plans continued as we worked on our various tasks.

I was concentrating on the last of the purple squiggles on a complicated design when my ears picked up the crunch of gravel as a car rolled into the driveway. Shifting in my seat and working out a kink in my back, I glanced out the window. Wolf jumped up, and my insides went all tingly when Bowen's dark head emerged from Cade's car. Sam's car pulled in, and he and Kyp got out, too.

I stood and went to get the door. Rachel beat me to it and flung it open. Kyp's face broke into the most adorably goofy grin I'd ever seen. The second he stepped foot inside the cabin, Rachel leaned up on her tiptoes and planted a big kiss right on his mouth.

Kyp let out a little surprised groan, and his ears went red.

"I'm glad you're back," Rachel said sweetly when she surfaced for air.

Kyp cleared his throat and took her hand. "Me, too."

"Can we come in now?" Sam laughed from the porch step.

"Oh. Sorry. Impulse control issues, you know." Rachel shrugged, and she and Kyp moved over by the couch.

Sam nodded to me, and Cade squeezed my shoulder.

"Hey, Raven," Sarah said as she followed Cade in.

"Hi." I was surprised to see her but not disappointed.

My heart thumped hard in my chest, waiting for Bowen to come through the door. When he did, my eyes widened, and my mouth dropped open.

"Bowen?"

"Hey, Raven." He smiled ruefully, his eye squinting around a purple bruise cupping his whole eye socket.

"What happened?"

"That little punk—Kyle Mason is his name—from the game the other night. We played the Eagles again today. I think he's decided he has a major rivalry or something to prove, being the only freshman on his varsity team." He snagged my fingers and brought me with him to a chair where he plopped. He raised his good eyebrow at me, and I knew he was offering his lap as a second seat.

Wolf's tongue lolled, and her tail beat the air furiously. Biting the inside of my cheek, I perched on his knee. His hand, warm and solid, slid around my waist, and my nerve endings caught fire.

"Major inferiority complex," Cade offered as he eyed the cookies.

"Only the broken ones." Megan handed him a plate of cookies that were rejected for the order.

"Why do you say he's got an inferiority complex?" I asked.

"I mean, he's the only freshman playing varsity for his team. And there aren't many this year in our whole conference, I think. He's good enough skill-wise to play varsity, but he's got a temper that gets in his way." Cade nodded at Bowen's eye before continuing. "He reeked of body spray so bad I still can't smell properly. The only upside was that we couldn't smell all the sweat. He's not ready to play with upperclassmen, and he knows it. I think that's why he tries so hard. Plays so rough."

"We've got to play the Eagles at least twice more this season, don't we?" Bowen asked. His thumb moved slowly back and forth against my side. Wolf reacted strongly. So did the human part of me. Heat sizzled up my spine.

"More if we both continue winning more than we lose." Cade took a bite of cookie. "Man, these are good. What kind is this?"

"We experimented for this order. It's for a lady's luncheon. You're eating an Earl Grey tea biscuit," Rachel told him.

"I have no idea what half those words mean, but this is delicious."

Sarah snorted. Cade looked at her and shrugged. "Here. You try it." Sarah rolled her eyes and took the last bite of Cade's cookie.

"I'm not a big bergamot fan, but these *are* pretty good," she confessed.

We munched on leftover cookies and chatted a while longer.

"Anybody want to go for an early afternoon run?" Sam asked once the cookies were gone. The suggestion was well received, and we spent a good hour or so running wild in the forest behind the cabin.

Wolf relished the bite of the wind, the companionship of my friends, my brother, and my mate. Wolf shook her head and yipped as the tang of January ran over our nose and brought Bowen's distinctive cedar and brown sugar scent.

My feelings toward Bowen were warming dramatically. I didn't see a hidden agenda behind every action now. I wasn't afraid of him anymore. I could relax, knowing his reputation wasn't exactly what the rumors said. He nudged me gently from where he ran beside me. For the first time, I let myself acknowledge the attraction that had been building and growing from the second I saw him, bloodied and battered on the battlefield.

Heat slithered down my limbs, and a flash of desire, hot and potent, nearly knocked me off my feet. A wave of pheromones crashed over me, and Bowen growled appreciatively beside me, nudging me off the path and slowing us down. We paused and took a few minutes to ourselves. Bowen rubbed his head against my neck and behind my ears and licked my cheek.

It was easier to surrender to the wild rush of emotion as my wolf. I tipped my head back and howled. Bowen joined me. I scooted closer, my shoulders touching his, and leaned my head against him, his ruff tickling my whiskers. He leaned down, putting his head against mine. We sat like that for a long time.

****

Sometime later, we made it back to the cabin, changed, and went over to my house.

"Raven!" Mom gave me a big hug when she answered the door. "Hi, Bowen! Come in, come in." She ushered us into the heat of the family room, the familiar crackle of the fireplace welcome.

"Hey, Mom. We dropped by to grab a few things. Can you come upstairs and help me?"

"Of course." Mom smiled, knowing I wanted to talk. "Bowen, help yourself to anything in the kitchen. Steve is back there marinating something for dinner. Do you all want to stay?" She turned her last question to me.

I glanced at Bowen. He smiled and shrugged, leaving the decision to me. "Dinner would be great."

Mom followed me up the stairs to my room while Bowen went to chat with my dad.

"So how are things? I know we talk on the phone every day, but it just hasn't been the same." Mom's eyes were full of excitement as she sat down on my bed and patted the spot next to her.

"Things are going well. I had my first kiss." I smiled shyly.

Mom clasped her hands under her chin. "I'm so pleased, Raven. Really. You look happy. Is your wolf happy, too?"

"This is the happiest and most in sync we've been in a while."

Mom nodded knowingly.

I found the end of my ponytail, twisting the strands around my finger. "I think I'm ready to move into Bowen's house. I'm still staying in the guest room, but Wolf is more content there, and I mean, I guess I'm kind of supposed to be there since we are married." I bit the inside of my lip. "And I wanted to ask you about joining Kyp's pack. I don't really want to leave ours— I'm kind of scared to leave you guys and the only pack I've ever known. But eventually, I'll have to since Bowen is Beta. He won't be coming to the Wolfe pack." The thought of leaving the safe haven of the pack I'd been born into sent little shards of ice through my heart, but at the same time, there was a sense of peace, too.

"You don't need to be scared, Raven. I left my pack when I wasn't much older than you after I met your dad. We knew instantly that we were true mates, and after we talked it over—with our parents, too—we decided I'd join his pack. I was excited. Nervous, sure. It's a big step to leave your own pack behind to join another. But it's not unheard of. And it's not like we're going anywhere. You'll always belong here. You'll always be our daughter." She cupped my chin, her eyes filling with tears. "I'm so proud of you, Rave."

"I'm not sure why. I've fought this almost every step of the way," I confessed.

"What changed?"

I sighed. I wouldn't betray Bowen's trust by telling my mom everything he'd told me. "I guess I just got to know him. The real Bowen. Not the Bowen everyone thinks he is."

"And you like what you've found?"

"I really, really do." I smiled, and Mom hugged me.

"You'll know when it's time to join Kyp's pack. I think you're getting close to that point. You'll want to be with Bowen and won't want the separation of packs. It's not as hard as some of the stories make out. You'll talk to Kyp and surrender your allegiance to him—and to Bowen."

Surrender.

I grappled with the implications of that word.

Chapter 30
Bowen

Monday afternoon in science, Mr. Shaver had us split into pairs.

"All right, now I'm letting you choose your own groups, but choose wisely because a big ol' fat chunk of your grade is going to ride on this project. In just a minute, I'll turn you loose, and you can get to work. But let me first draw your attention to this list up here on the digital board." He tapped a few keys on his laptop, and a list with pictures appeared on the board behind his desk.

"Now," he continued, "this is the list you can choose from for your topics. There is an Internet video that goes with each one. You'll watch it on your own time. Together or separately, it doesn't matter, so long as you watch so you can contribute to the group. Let me know if you have no way to access it on your own time, and I'll set up computer lab time on a one-on-one basis. After you watch the movie, you'll find several questions for further research. In your groups, you'll discuss these questions and follow up on the topic. You'll put a presentation together and submit it for your grade. All of this and additional details are in your packets. Any questions right now?"

"Mr. Shaver, do we have to present this to the class?" someone asked from across the room.

"You knew it was coming. You will be presenting these to the class as part of your final grade. You can be creative in your method of delivery. Videos, reports, oral presentations, check with me if you're wanting to do something unorthodox. Anyone else? No? Okay. As soon as you find your groups—no more than three in a group, I prefer pairs—pick a topic from the list. Once that topic is picked, you're out of luck. Only one group can cover each topic."

I scanned the list. There weren't a lot of particularly interesting ones. I stopped looking at the list and stared at the back of Raven's head. She had her hair up today, and I could see the curve of her neck right where it joined her shoulder. I wanted to kiss that spot.

"And go!" Mr. Shaver said. Noise and a flurry of activity flew around the room.

"Raven," I said quietly, knowing she could hear me. She turned in her seat to face me, her blue eyes wide and innocent, a teasing light filling them.

"Oh, did you want to be partners?"

I smirked. "I thought it might be convenient." I lifted an eyebrow as she grinned.

"I suppose I could be talked into it."

I scooted out of my chair and came to the one left open beside her. Her regular tablemate had gone elsewhere in search of a group.

"Oh, wow, these people are serious about their topic choices." Already several were knocked off the list.

"Okay. Any preferences?" Raven squinted at the list. "I'm not seeing anything that really strikes a fancy."

"Cells wouldn't be all bad. Oh, never mind. Looks like that one's gone, too."

"Amoebas? How bad can amoebas be?" she asked, not looking convinced.

"Works for me. I don't have to like something to research it. Besides, I figure my partner will provide a distraction should the material become too boring." I winked at her, and she rolled her eyes, her lips turning up.

"If we're good with amoebas, I'll go tell Mr. Shaver."

I nodded and then watched her walk to the front of the room to talk to Mr. Shaver. She had on jeans today and another button-up flannel shirt. Those were good jeans. They hugged her butt in all the right ways.

She turned and caught me staring. Her cheeks heated as she slid back into her seat. She lifted an eyebrow at me in challenge.

"You object?" I asked her, teasing.

Her mouth opened, but she didn't answer for a second. "I guess not," she finished shyly.

I put my hand on the back of her chair, letting my thumb graze her back. Her eyelids fluttered briefly, and Wolf lunged to the fore, realizing that just maybe, I affected her as much as she affected me.

Chapter 31
Raven

Tuesday night, after practice and a quick bite to eat, Bowen and I curled up on the couch to watch our required science video. It was atrociously dull. Finally, the amoeba movie came to an end.

"That was one of the worst things I've ever had to watch." Bowen turned mournful eyes to me. "I think I need that partner distraction. Please tell me we can make out now or something?"

I giggled, his mock-seriousness wearing off as he grinned suggestively at me and tugged the bottom of my ponytail. I smiled back and lifted my face as he impishly put a quick kiss on my lips.

He pulled back, still grinning, his eyes like melted chocolate, the curve of his mouth teasing and sexy all at once. My knees felt weak, and my stomach did a few somersaults as I looked at his lips. Wolf wiggled inside me, and heat flared in my belly. Desire swept over me in a rush of tingles and a pull so intense it physically gnawed at me. I glanced back up to his eyes, wondering if he felt the same wrenching *want* I did. My answer came as his lips came back to mine, capturing me in a sweet, still playful kiss. I didn't want playful. Wolf thrashed. I didn't want sweet either.

It took about two seconds before the kiss stopped being playful. My hand snaked up behind his head, pulling him closer to me. With a sharp intake of air, his lips moved over mine, his arm across the back of my shoulders sliding down and turning me to face him. My lips were moving with his, dancing together. His tongue deliberately swept over my bottom lip, asking for permission, and a breathy little noise escaped. I wanted *this*. I wanted *him*. Wolf urged me, and for the first time in a long time, I felt the two halves of me fuse together, desires righted. Bowen. He was mine. I *needed* him to be mine. I hadn't believed Mom when she'd said the mate pull could be immediate and crazy intense—not until now. His tongue followed the curve of my mouth. Bowen's phone vibrated on the end table. We ignored it.

Inhaling, his scent shot straight to my head and sent my belly quivering. I opened my mouth fully as my fingers twisted into his hair. His hand slid down my side and gripped my hip as his tongue stroked against mine, creating sparks where they met. Bowen's hands were like firebrands, holding me tight against his chest as his tongue did magic things in my mouth, inviting, encouraging me to respond, drawing noises from me that danced between our lips.

Closer. I needed to be closer. He loosened my hair tie, and my black mane cascaded down around us. His mouth worked over mine, his hand tangling into my hair, holding my face to his. Fire raged through my veins. I could feel his wanting through his lips. His thumb by my hip swept across the skin just above the waist of my jeans.

As desire consumed me, all rational sense fled. Without another thought, I broke my lips away from his, kissing behind his ear and down his neck. His hand left my hair, and suddenly he gripped both my hips.

A noise somewhere between a growl and a groan that was both terrifying and thrilling ripped from his throat as he tipped his head back, giving me full access. It was a sign of surrender but also of trust. He sucked in a breath as my lips grazed his skin.

"Raven," he murmured, his voice thick and gravelly. His fingers pressed deliciously into my flesh, and he pulled me harder against him, moving his head so our lips pressed together.

The phone vibrated again as Bowen kissed me more insistently, his tongue probing into my mouth, his lips demanding the response I readily gave. The fire in my blood turned to lava as his lips pulled away only to kiss the underside of my jaw and down my neck.

Gasping for air, I let my hands slide down his biceps, coiled and bunched as he held me against him. My hands trailed down his sides until I found the hem of his T-shirt.

Faster than I thought possible, Bowen leaned us forward and yanked his shirt off, flinging it back behind the couch as his lips crashed against mine again. Somewhere in the back of my brain, I registered noises—little grunts and gasps for air that made the lava bubble inside me. The phone vibrated again, and without stopping, Bowen grabbed it and threw it down the hallway as my fingers found the solid planes of his chest. Passion flooded me. I was completely lost in primal sensations, desperate for more of what we were doing, but I was sidetracked as Bowen took one of my hands in his, placing it on his bare chest over his thundering heart. His lips moved with intensity against mine and my palm pressed against his skin.

"Raven." He gasped, voice deep and heavy. "I... Ah!" His head jerked back forcefully against the back of the couch, and I pulled up, confused.

Bowen's eyes screwed shut as his hands clenched my sides.

"I am going to kill Kyp."

Kyp?

"What?" I tried to slow the painful pounding of my heart and rested my hands on his bare shoulders. His hands gripped me harder again before releasing me to run through his hair. With satisfaction, I noted his chest heaving like he'd just played an intense game of basketball.

"Kyp. He just did everything but command me to get over to his place. Right now." He searched my face hungrily. "And believe me, I can't tell you how bad I want to do more of this." He leaned in for one more kiss but pulled back before things could get heated again. "But I can't do this properly with him in my head." He grimaced.

I scowled. I was still turned on like I'd never been before but starting to come to my senses. *Wow.* Wow, as I looked at Bowen's bare chest. Wow, as I thought about where we were headed. Wow, something must be really wrong for Kyp to use the link. My whole body flushed as I looked at my hands still on Bowen's shoulders, then realized I was sitting on his lap. My eyes darted everywhere but his face.

"Don't," he whispered, catching my jaw in his hand and turning me to look him in the eye. "Don't be embarrassed." He shook his head. "Not with me. Not about this." I swallowed as I watched him sigh and bank the fires raging in his eyes. "We are definitely not finished here," he said with a wink. "But in order to get to Kyp's, you are going to have to get off my lap." His hands squeezed my knees as I blushed even redder.

Chapter 32
Bowen

It took *all* my willpower to get up off the couch and not pull Raven back down and continue where we left off. The memory of her fingers on my skin, the way her lips moved, the way I felt her wanting, the way I wanted her, about brought me to my knees. Wolf whined. Kyp's insistent message over the link was the only thing—*the only thing*—that could possibly drag me away from what we'd been doing.

As it was, I leaned down and grabbed my shirt off the floor, my gaze skimming her legs and hips, over the rest of her curves as I stood back up. Heat poured over me, and I seriously wondered if we had time for me to back her up against the wall of the hallway where she stood and sneak in one more minute of kissing. I blew out a hot breath. I couldn't do just one more minute. It would be a lot longer than that if we started again.

"I think I need a drink before we go," she rasped and walked around me to the kitchen.

"Grab two glasses down, will you?" I needed more than a cold drink to cool me off.

****

I called Kyp once we were in the car.

"Kyp, what's wrong?"

"I'd rather not say over the phone. Just get here." He bit the words out, terser than I'd ever heard him. Ice lodged in my chest.

"We'll be there in ten."

"Raven's with you?"

"Yes." I was hesitant about bringing her with me for the first time. I hadn't even thought about it. I just assumed we'd both go. Now I wasn't sure. What could have possibly gone so wrong that Raven's coming was circumspect?

"Okay. It might be best if she stayed at the house. Mom is here. Jonathan Stone is here, too." Jonathan, a member of the Wolfe pack, hung around Kyp's mom a lot. It was pretty obvious they were interested in each other even though Jennifer was human. Regardless, I liked him. He was a welcome voice of rationality and experience. But tonight, I got the distinct impression Stone was there as protection. From what, I didn't know.

"All right." My voice came out hoarse, and Raven's eyebrows drew together as she looked over at me. "Be there soon."

"Bowen, what happened?"

"I don't know, but nothing good." I put my phone down and grabbed her hand, needing her anchoring influence.

****

The porch lights were on at Kyp's house. He was out the door before I'd even pulled the keys from the ignition.

"Raven, you need to go wait inside with Mom and Jonathan. Rich and Lucy from our pack are here, too. Bowen, come with me. In fur."

Kyp had never taken charge so ferociously since the night he assumed Alphaship of the pack. I didn't question him.

"Raven, I'll be back as soon as I can. You okay?"

"I'll be fine. Be careful."

Two minutes later, we were in fur, and I followed Kyp through the woods on his back property.

Bowen, there's a body. The face has been ripped off just like Victor's victims, Kyp sent to me as we went silently deeper into the forest. Panic he hadn't shown earlier now laced his words.

What? I nearly tripped on a root as shock raked over my back like claws.

It's right on the edge of our land. Just like when Victor dropped his murder victims at the edge of Wolfe territory. I need you to confirm something for me when we get there before I call Dominic Wolfe and Austin Thornehill.

The unmistakable tang of blood woke deep places in Wolf, a primal, base response that propelled me closer.

It's in the clearing. Kyp nodded with his nose. I knew to keep to the edges of things so I wouldn't mess up any possible trace evidence. Skirting around the clearing, the scent of blood was strong. And under the blood, another scent snagged my attention and made the hair along my back stand up. A growl ripped low in my throat.

It's Drew. Two others with it. Both from Victor's time.

Are you certain? Kyp asked, his voice echoing tiredly in my brain.

I'm certain.

Kyp's wolf let out a heavy breath. *I thought so, too.*

****

We got back to the house, and Kyp immediately called Dominic and Austin. Within the half hour, they were pulling up in the driveway, Sam and Sarah with them, too.

"You found another body?" Dominic's face showed his dismay. Austin ran a hand through his blond hair, cursing under his breath.

"Victor is dead. Who is behind this?" Austin asked.

"It's Drew. Victor's right-hand wolf, aside from his Beta. I took Drew's place as Beta. Drew never forgave me either. His scent was there. Beneath the blood," I said.

"And I forced him out of the pack, too," Kyp added. "That can't have been an easy thing to take. Getting thrown out of what you consider to be *your* pack by some half-breed whelp?"

"Is he making a power play?" Sam asked as we moved into the living room. The information would be all over the human news tomorrow. Best our packs were informed first. Jennifer, Jonathan, Rich, Lucy, and Raven all joined us in the sitting area. Raven sat close to me, our legs touching. Nervous energy seemed to thrum through her.

"Either a power play, or he's just trying to make trouble," Austin offered.

"Can he frame any of us for it?" Jonathan asked. Dominic raised his eyebrows, considering the thought.

"Not that I know of," Kyp answered. "I found the body this evening, but I was Wolf. I had Bowen come and take a look, too, to confirm it was Drew I smelled." Kyp nodded solemnly at me. Being only half werewolf, Kyp's nose wasn't quite as good as mine.

"I'll call Gordon Rockwell. He'll know how to

handle it and keep us in the loop." Dominic got his phone out with a resigned sigh. Gordon Rockwell was on the police force and a member of the Wolfe pack. He'd been a tremendous help when they were trying to solve Victor's murders.

"We should start patrols again," Sarah said. There were grunts and nods around the room.

"We need to find Drew. Find out what he's after—power or trouble," Kyp said.

And when we did find him, I would make sure he paid.

****

It was after midnight when we got home. Raven was dragging, tired, but jumpy.

"I really thought this was all behind us," she said, running a hand over her face.

"So did I." I double-checked the door was locked tight behind us. I checked the back door and garage doors, too.

"You're worried." Raven's eyes were big in her pale face.

"I've learned not to underestimate a wolf with a grudge. Drew is vindictive and mean-spirited. And he blames me for losing his place in the pack hierarchy and probably blames Kyp for kicking his sorry tail out of the pack. I don't know if he's doing this out of spite to hurt us or if it's something else entirely, but I do know he's involved. And that's enough reason for me to be concerned."

We were at the bottom of the stairs. I cupped her face, my palms large and rough against her smooth skin.

"I'm glad we're on the same side this time." Her

hands came up and covered mine.

"I'm always on your side."

****

Miraculously, things were kept quiet about the body. The cops were involved, but everything had been done so discreetly that as far as we knew, word hadn't broken to the public yet. Wednesday night, Kyp called again as we were leaving practice. "Bowen, can you come back over here? No more bodies, but something else new for us."

"Sure. I'm bringing Raven. We're just getting ready to leave school. Practice just got done." I glanced at her as I opened the car door for her and let my fingers graze her elbow before I shut the door.

"That's fine. I agree you shouldn't leave her alone at your house or anywhere else. I think we should put an all call out for all pack members to go in pairs."

"Agreed. So what are we facing tonight?" I resisted the urge to shudder. Raven arched an eyebrow, watching me as I turned the engine over and an icy blast from the heating vents raised the sweat-dampened hair on my forehead.

"Well, Jonathan would like to formally join our pack."

"Seriously?" I knew he was interested in Jennifer Kypson, but he must be intensely serious—like planning to marry her and change her into a werewolf serious—to leave his pack of origin and join ours. "How do you feel about this?"

"I think he'd be a great addition to our pack," Kyp skirted.

"And your mom?"

"I'm still processing."

"We'll be there soon."

I clicked the phone off and pulled out of the parking lot. "Jonathan Stone wants to join our pack," I told her before she could ask. I didn't want her to feel like there were secrets between us. There weren't. Not anymore.

"Wow. I wonder what Dominic will have to say about that?"

"I'm guessing he's already discussed it with him." Wolf lurched inside me, but I shoved him back down. I wanted to bring up a timeline for when Raven might join my pack, too. Shushing Wolf, I let it alone.

She was quiet, staring out at the frozen landscape as it blurred beside the car as we left town and headed for the surrounding meadows near Kyp's house.

"Raven?" I finally broke the silence. We'd been easy with each other since the other night. We hadn't picked back up where we'd left off with the kissing—which was disappointing—but we hadn't taken any steps backward either.

"I will, Bowen."

"Will what?" I glanced at her, confused.

"I will join your pack. Soon. Wolf wants to. I want to. I'm just working through the anxiety that's following the decision."

Warmth seeped into me, knowing the desire was there. I squeezed her hand.

"You're so much farther ahead than I am...with everything." She swallowed and fiddled with the ends of her ponytail.

I could feel the underlying questions, but I wasn't sure which one she was stuck on. "Like?"

"Like including me in your future plans, ready for

me to join your pack…ready to…do all the physical things. I mean, don't get me wrong, I really enjoyed the other night. You're like, an amazing kisser, and I kind of lost my head to the wolf for a while," she tripped over her words, her cheeks flaming even in the dim moonlight filtering in through the windows. "I, I want to be ready to do all of those things with you, but it scares me when I think about them. I kind of freeze and just…I can't move forward." She let loose a frustrated sigh.

"Raven, do you feel like I'm pressuring you to do more than you're ready for?" The thought left me feeling hollow. I didn't want to make her uncomfortable. I didn't want her to do anything she didn't want to do. I was trying to take things slow, let her tell me when she was ready. I was absolutely ready. For anything and everything. But I knew she wasn't.

"No. You've been really great about not asking me to do things I'm not ready for. But I *want* to be ready. I guess a part of me feels like I'm still in competition for your attention. I see the way Skylar looks at you, and it makes my blood boil. I hear all these rumors still about you—guys like you—who don't, you know, go without, and that insecure part of me kind of drives me nuts thinking about it. Even though I know the truth, that little part of me feels like I need to do more to keep you interested or something. I don't know." She swiped a quick hand under her eye. This must have been bothering her more than she let on.

"I won't lie to you, Raven. I'm *very* interested in losing my virginity." I paused and met her gaze for a second before turning back to the road. "But I'm *only* interested in losing it with you. We'll wait as long as you want. We've got the rest of our lives to figure this out, and there's nothing that says it needs to be now."

"You really mean that?"

"Every word." I pulled into the drive of Kyp's house. "But I need you to do something for me, too."

She looked at me, her blue eyes shining in the porch light, her face vulnerable.

"What?"

"I need you to tell me if you want me to slow down or if you don't like something I'm doing. Okay?" I reached out and let my fingers graze her jaw, my thumb stroking once over her lips. "It's easy for me to lose track of the line when you're involved."

"Okay."

My lips curved into a devilish smile. "You can tell me what you like me to do, too," I whispered, my voice deep and throaty. As I'd hoped, a smile flitted over her face.

"I'll keep that in mind." Her eyes twinkled. "I really like it when you put your hand on my waist to show everyone I'm yours."

"My hand will be sure to find that spot."

Chapter 33
Raven

Dominic and Sam showed up a few minutes after we made it into the house. I was already feeling a little emotionally worn with not a lot of sleep and then the unplanned bearing of my soul to Bowen on the way over. Wolf felt lighter and more in tune after I'd tried to explain what I was feeling to Bowen, but little seeds of dread cramped in my belly as we all gathered in Kyp's living room for Jonathan's change of pack alliance.

There were several of us there to witness. Dominic, Sam, and Megan from the Wolfe pack, Kyp, Rachel, and Bowen, Jennifer and Jonathan…and me. Technically I still belonged to the Wolfe pack, but I felt like I was in no-man's-land. An old proverb about how fresh and salt water couldn't come from the same spring flitted through my brain. The Wolfe and Kypson packs were the salt and fresh water. And I was some muddy mix in between with a foot in each world, my heart torn between the two.

But as I watched Jonathan kneel in front of Dominic and Kyp, Wolf backed off, watching, waiting in the shadows. Legend said leaving a pack was a painful experience.

"Jonathan, it's been an honor and a privilege," Dominic said and put his hand on Jonathan's bowed head.

"It has been *my* honor and privilege," Jonathan said back. Not by rote, the meaning was clear in the words of both men.

"Go in peace," Dominic said. He took his hand back. Jonathan's shoulders straightened, and his eyes shut though no pain flashed over his face.

Kyp jolted, and Bowen's hand twitched, but otherwise, everyone was still.

"Welcome to the pack, Jonathan," Kyp said.

Jonathan's shoulders relaxed, and his face broke into a wide smile. He glanced at Jennifer, her hands clasped tightly under her chin, her eyes luminous with a sheen of tears. Jonathan stood and immediately tipped his head back in front of Kyp, exposing his throat. Kyp leaned forward and scented him, Jonathan returning the gesture. Bowen was next.

We went around the room, refamiliarizing ourselves with this new adjustment. When it was my turn, I was surprised to find Jonathan smelled the same as he always had, but with an added tag that was unmistakably Kypson. It was like a different surname had been put on his smell.

Jonathan smiled at me, knowing someday I'd be a part of his pack again. Wolf nudged me. There hadn't been anything particularly frightening about Jonathan's transition. Wolf whined. She wanted to be with Bowen. Wanted to be a part of his pack. With an internal sigh, I realized I wanted that, too.

Wolf nudged me harder. My Alpha was here. Kyp was here. What was stopping this from happening right now?

I wanted my parents and Cade, too. This was a massive decision, and one I wouldn't make without them present.

"Bowen," I tugged gently on his sleeve as people stood around talking, preparing to leave. Bowen turned the full force of his chocolate gaze on me, and my knees weakened. "I think I want to stay at my parents' house tonight."

His eyebrows drew together, and hurt flashed across his eyes.

"No, no, nothing like that," I said quickly. Wolf gave me a reproachful stare. His hurt turned to confusion. "I'd like a night to process. To talk to my parents and Cade." I looked back to his eyes. "I want to join your pack. But I don't want to do it without them."

"Want me to take you over there now?"

"Let's just go back to your place. I'll drive my car over and then follow you home from practice tomorrow."

"I'm not sure I like you driving all the way to your parents' house by yourself. Not with Drew and the others loose."

"How about if Dominic follows me?"

"That's acceptable."

****

I popped into Bowen's house after him while the Wolfes waited in the driveway. I wanted to grab my brush and straightener for tomorrow.

"You sure you don't want me to take you over and bring you back tonight?" he asked as he leaned against the doorjamb of the bathroom. It was a spacious room, big enough I didn't feel crowded with Bowen's large frame filling the doorway. I zipped my things into my backpack.

"It's already late. We both need to sleep." I glanced

at him, and the look he leveled at me made my toes curl. "I'll be back tomorrow." My voice came out as a whisper.

"Good," he said back, voice equally low. He stepped closer and electricity charged up my body. "Because I like you here with me." He was in my space now. His hands slid around my waist. My backpack dropped to the floor with a thud as my breath came shorter. He nudged me back half a step, and I bumped against the sink.

Flashes of the other night on the couch crowded into my brain. Wolf wasn't helping. She fidgeted longingly inside me. My fingers trailed up to his biceps. His head dipped, and he caught my mouth, his tongue gently sliding along my lower lip. With a little shiver, my mouth opened. His hands slid up under my shirt, resting on the skin just above my jeans as his tongue flicked into my mouth.

"Are you sure you need to go tonight?" His lips punctuated his question. His thumbs rubbed over my skin, drawing breathy noises from my throat. He trailed light kisses down my neck, and I nearly forgot why I was going back to my parents' house. He moved a few inches closer, his body whispering against mine.

I groaned. "I should go. They're waiting." My hands fisted into his shirt.

"Tell them to go. I'll take you over. Or we can stay here." There was a teasing lilt in his voice, but then his lips found their way behind my ear, and my belly quivered.

"I really have to go. I'll see you in the morning."

Something between a growl and a groan rumbled under my fingers. I reached up and jerked his head back to my lips, kissing him hard. He froze beneath me, and I pulled away before we completely lost our heads.

Snatching my bag, I dashed down the stairs. "I'll see you tomorrow."

"Let me know when you get there." He followed me to the door, kissing me once more on the forehead before I shivered into the chilly night air.

****

Morning was cold, crisp, and full of promise. After talking with Mom, Dad, and Cade the night before, I finally felt ready to move forward and join Kyp's pack. Join Bowen's pack. I texted him a smiley face.

—*On the way out the door. See you soon.*—

He sent me a thumbs up, and a sudden wave of longing washed over me through our link. I smiled, my fingers absently touching my lips.

He met me in the parking lot, waiting for me in his spot.

"Hey," he said, coming around and getting my door.

"Hey," I answered, suddenly feeling shy.

"So was your conversation worth missing some good make-out time?"

An absurd bubble of laughter leaped out of my mouth. "Yeah." I shifted my backpack over my shoulder. "I think I'm ready to—" I glanced around, "—join your pack."

Heat lit his eyes and sent a warm rush over me.

"Name the time and place." He laced our fingers together, and we went into the building. "Ugh. Go that way. Skylar is over there." He nudged me the opposite direction.

Wolf snarled in Skylar's direction, and I shushed

the insecure part of me that flared to life anytime another girl gave Bowen attention. I shook my head. Was I really that jealous? Bowen had told me he didn't want anyone besides me. I believed him. Didn't I?

****

School breezed by, and so did practice. Tomorrow was an in-service day for teachers, so we had an extra-long weekend. Cheerleading practice let out a few minutes before basketball. I had agreed to wait for Bowen, but then, remembering I had my own car, I felt the urge to just go ahead and leave.

I hit the parking lot and had to take a minute to find my keys. They'd slipped into the bottom of my purse, and I had to fish them out.

My hands closed around them, but as I looked up, my blood froze.

There across the parking lot by the doors of the gym, I saw Bowen's back. Skylar was turned toward me. Though I was far enough away, I doubted she realized I was there. In horror, I watched as her hand cupped the back of his neck. She kissed him. She kissed him, and he did nothing.

Wolf gnashed and snarled inside me. I was immobile. Rooted to the pavement. Bowen didn't lurch away. Didn't move. Until his fingers reached out and slid over her hip.

I was going to be sick.

Before I could heave the contents of my stomach up, boiling fury took over, and red tinged my vision. I got in my car and slammed the door shut. Peeling tires screeched against the blacktop as I sped far faster than was legal out onto the highway toward Bowen's house. I'd wait for him there. And when he got home, Wolf and I would let him know exactly what we thought about his actions. I might rip his face off. Maybe a different body part he'd miss more.

I stewed in angry desperation for several miles when I felt the flavor of burnt grain mixed with something acrid in the back of my mouth.

My fury iced to a sudden stop as my foot faltered on the gas pedal.

What had I done?

What had Bowen done?

What had he made me do?

Frantically, I searched my memories. I could recount nothing other than what I'd seen after practice—Bowen and Skylar. I swallowed hard to keep the nausea at bay. Had Bowen made me leave so he could go with Skylar for some quick action before returning to me, ever the picture of the devoted mate?

My mind had been tampered with.

The ice boiled, and steam probably came out my ears. Rage, hot, potent, and near eruption, coiled in my veins.

All his pretty words. All his passionate promises. All his special looks.

Lies.

The bitter taste of burnt grain hung heavy in my mouth and intensified the closer I got to Bowen's house. I pulled in, slammed my car into park, and stormed inside, flipping the lock behind me.

I paced. Wolf snarled and growled inside me.

Betrayed.

We were betrayed.

Chapter 34
Bowen

"She was really okay with it?" I asked Cade as I shrugged into a hoodie in the boys' locker room.

"Yeah. She's serious. I think she's ready to move forward." Cade made a face like he'd swallowed sour milk. "It's weird to think about you and my sister." He shook his head. "Anyway, I mean, you guys will still be close. You're...you're not leaving the area anytime soon?" A fine edge of panic bled into his voice. A smile tipped the corner of my mouth.

"No, Cade. We're here for the long haul unless Dominic wants us to move on."

Cade's shoulders visibly relaxed. "That's cool then. All right. Catch you this weekend, probably." Our eyes met, grim at the thought of running patrols and making sure everyone was accounted for.

Speaking of, Raven should be waiting for me outside the locker room in the gym. I planned to follow her home. I didn't want her out of my sight for long, but I wanted to double-check with Cade that she had seemed totally on board with joining my pack.

The first tendrils of dread snaked down my back when Raven wasn't in the gym. My heart started galloping when her car wasn't in the parking lot. Skylar was, though, and I rolled my eyes as she waved a few fingers at me. Her expression was hard and cold, but less predatory than usual. I ignored her.

The barest hint of scent caught my nose, but I was too distracted to focus on it.

I tried Raven's cell. Straight to voicemail.

Raven? I tried our link.

I could feel her presence at the other end and realized she was deliberately ignoring me. Wolf snorted. Not cool. My heart slowed a fraction, but irritation wormed its way under my skin as I slammed the gas down and made better time than I should have back to my house.

The main floor lights were all on, and Raven's car was in the driveway when I pulled in. Still aggravated she was ignoring me on purpose, I stalked to the front door, jammed my key in, and entered.

The arctic held more warmth than Raven's eyes as she cut to my face.

"Bowen, what did you make me do?" Her words ground out like shattering glass. She stood in the archway separating the kitchen and den from the main part of the house. Light from the kitchen flooded behind her, giving her an angry glow.

Wolf pricked his ears forward. "I didn't make you do anything. What are you talking about? Why didn't you wait for me?"

She snorted, fists clenched, nostrils flaring.

"I know you made me do something. What was it?" Each word was like the scrape of nails on a chalkboard.

Wolf simmered under my skin as anger roiled through me. "Raven, I have no idea what you're talking about."

"Are you seriously going to look me straight in the

eye and lie to my face? I saw you with Skylar. In the parking lot. I know you made me leave or do something so you could go do who knows what with her." Furious tears wet her cheeks. She wasn't finished. I opened my mouth to say something, but she cut me off with a shuddering breath and words like a death shroud. "You stay out of my mind. You are just as sick and twisted as Victor. *You are his son.*"

I stopped in my tracks, robbed of breath.

An ache so deep I thought my chest might literally open and spill my heart out onto the floor cracked down my middle. Wolf whined. My limbs shook with pent-up fury, despair, and shock.

Without another word, I stormed past her, flung the back doors open, and stormed into the murky night.

Stripping so fast I wasn't even sure I had everything off, I shifted and bounded out of the yard. Sobs and snarls alternated deep in my chest as Wolf and I tried to figure out what had just happened—why Raven would intentionally hurt us so deeply.

And it did hurt deeply. Her words had flayed me open and left me raw and bleeding. I stumbled to a stop at the edge of my property. Anguished and confused as I was, I still didn't want to get too far away. The shred of rational brain left in me knew Drew could be lurking.

Black as the shadows around me, I paced. I walked the perimeter of my substantial yard. I don't know how long I stumbled, too grief-stricken to pay attention to where my feet fell. Hours passed. The midnight chill descended, wind whipped through my ruff, and dulled some of the pain inside.

Sometime in the wee hours of the morning, the wind blew toward me, and I jerked to a halt.

Instantly alert, my senses heightened, my eyes focused like laser beams.

Shad.

One of the wolves Kyp exiled from the pack. One of Victor's. And he was here. On my land.

A growl ripped from my throat as two red eyes materialized out of the brush several yards in front of me. We were at the very back of my property. Wild forest butted up against the invisible barrier I'd made around my house and my landlines.

White teeth gleamed in the moonlight as Shad snarled, baring his sharp canines. My muscles bunched as I crouched, my ears flat against my skull, the ridge of hair along my back standing on end. A twisted part of me was glad for the coming confrontation.

A warning rumbled menacingly in my chest as Shad stared at me from the bushes. Shad growled, and with two running steps, he leaped.

I didn't wait and thundered toward him, catching him midair. Of the two of us, I was bigger and more powerfully built, but Shad was older and more experienced. And I was no longer his Beta. He was no longer subordinate to me.

With a crash of bodies and mash of fur, we hit and landed hard on the ground. He barked, snapping his teeth, trying to catch me. I danced out of the way, his teeth catching air where my flank had been.

I snapped, catching a mouthful of fur, but nothing more. He was at me again, thrusting his bulk into my shoulder to knock me off balance. My teeth met him instead, and blood seeped into my mouth, rousing the primal instincts of the wolf.

Shad yelped and backed away, staring after me like

he couldn't believe I'd actually bitten him or that he'd gotten close enough to let me. Regrouping, he hunkered down, muscles coiling.

I was incensed. He came onto my land, challenged me, and I was done being tested for one night. Channeling all my fury, my rage, my sorrow, I lowered my head, and my paws left the ground, barreling into Shad's side in one gigantic leap.

He flew tail over ears and shook his head hard to clear it once he landed.

Wheezing and whining, he scurried away, limping back into the underbrush. I wanted to run after him, to pursue, but Wolf acknowledged Raven was still at the house. She'd be utterly unprotected if I left the grounds.

I rubbed my neck against several trees on the way back, my scent permeating the air and marking my land even more specifically. Doing a perimeter run, I found nothing else out of the ordinary. No more scents, no more wolves. Just the ones from my pack that should be present.

Mentally and emotionally exhausted, I made it back to the porch, padding softly between the pool and the hot tub.

Letting myself have one final shake in my fur, I shifted and put my clothes back on, freezing from being out on the cold ground all night.

Hesitating again before the sliding doors, Wolf cringed inside me. My hand shook. Pain lanced my heart all over again as Raven's words replayed with crystal clarity in my head.

You are his son.

I swallowed as tears pricked the back of my eyes. Grinding the heels of my hands against them, I exhaled and slid the door open, wondering if Raven was asleep.

She'd turned most of the lights off, but the lamp by the couch in the den was on. She sat, huddled, clutching a pillow to her chest. Her eyes were red and swollen, her face mottled like it was splattered with strawberry jelly.

Raven's eyes snapped up the second the door clicked shut. She jumped from her seat on the couch, the pillow still clasped to her chest. "Bowen." Her voice was breathless. "I'm *so* sorry." Fresh tears tracked down her cheeks. "I'm so sorry," she whispered again. "Can you forgive me?"

I was too shocked to answer. My brain was still trying to catch up to the events of the night. The giant hole punched in my chest still ached, the adrenaline from the fight with Shad faded, and I was drained. I blinked.

She continued, her sobs interrupting the words that ran together in her effort to get them all out. "I didn't mean what I said. I was angry, and confused, and scared. I'm still scared. But I don't think *you* controlled me. I keep going over and over everything that happened, and I know what you told me that night about your abilities. What I know of you, you wouldn't control me. I don't know what you were doing with Skylar. I don't care. Just, please, don't do it anymore. I'll sleep with you. Right now, if that's what it is. Just, please, not her. Don't leave me—we're *mates*." She cried so hard I could hardly understand her, but the words I did hear cracked my heart open again.

In three steps, I crossed the room and crushed her against my chest. Her arms came around my waist and held me like a lifeline. She sobbed into my chest, and more than one tear fell onto her hair, even though I screwed my eyelids tight shut.

We were a mess.

Relief, sadness, and confusion mixed inside me. We held each other for long minutes.

"Bowen, I'm sorry," Raven whispered into my rumpled shirt once her tears stopped enough for her to speak.

I sighed, her head moving with the motion.

"What happened?" I didn't know what else to say. I was still smarting from her callous words. I was afraid they were true. That despite my efforts, too much of Victor had been left behind, and I would never be free of his influence. That she didn't want me because of it. Wolf howled inside.

She backed up a few inches, wiping at her eyes. Glancing up at me, her chin quivered again. "I'm so sorry. I never should have said those hateful words. I didn't mean them. You are *not* like Victor."

Some of the tension in my back started to ebb, but my muscles were still rigid with apprehension.

She took a deep breath and tentatively grasped my fingers. With a tug and an imploring look, she brought us to the couch. We sank down onto the brown leather, not touching except for my fingers she still held.

"Today after practice, I waited for you but decided to go ahead and come here since I had my car. When I got to the parking lot, I saw you and Skylar together. She...you let her put her hands on you and *kiss* you. Then you ran your hand all the way down her hip." She gulped.

Confusion knit my brow. I hadn't seen Skylar but for the three seconds she waved at me. But that was after Raven had already left. And I certainly wouldn't touch her like that. I hadn't even been that forward yet with Raven's hips.

She continued, "I saw red, got in the car, and came here. But before I got all the way here, I tasted that burnt grain flavor in the back of my mouth just like when you told me to touch my toes. But as I've been sitting here, obsessing over my colossal mistakes, I realized it tasted different. It was still the charred wheat taste, but it was bitter. When you did it, it tasted smokey sweet. This was harsher, more...dirty." She glanced at my face. "I don't think it was you who controlled me."

"No. I didn't, and I wouldn't."

I watched helplessly as her eyes filled with tears again. "Why Skylar? I...I can be ready."

My shoulders slumped. "Raven, I didn't do anything with Skylar. I only saw her a few seconds in the parking lot as I looked for you. I don't like her. I don't want her. I've never lied to you. Especially about that." Emotion seized my chest. Anger and betrayal tinged with love. Different emotions directed at different people.

Raven's eyebrows drew together. "Then how..."

"It has to be a false memory. Or a suggestion. You never actually saw my face, did you?"

"No. I didn't. But it looked exactly like you from the back." She looked me over. "Same gray sweatshirt and everything."

"I stayed behind in the locker room a few extra minutes to talk to Cade. I wanted to be sure you were really okay with joining Kyp's pack."

Her eyes slid shut again, and she massaged her

temples. "I have never screwed up this royally before in my life."

A harsh laugh escaped my throat. "I have."

Her hand came down and grabbed mine. "Why would someone do this? *How* could someone do this?"

I gulped. Wolf whined, and I felt like I'd swallowed a lead weight. "There's someone else out there who can control minds. Like me. Like Victor did."

We stared at each other for a full minute.

"What if Victor had another kid?" Her whispered words sent a shiver of dread skittering over my skin. My father hadn't been known for his celibacy. Victor hadn't known about Kyp, and Kyp hadn't known Victor was his father until Kyp had recognized him from the one picture Jennifer had of his father. It was possible— plausible even—that Victor had other children. A weird sensation tingled in my gut. Another phantom sibling could materialize at any time. "It's definitely possible," I said after a long pause.

I scraped a hand through my hair, bringing a few errant twigs with it. "One of Victor's wolves was here tonight. On the property. We fought."

She gasped beside me. "Are you all right?"

"I'm fine. But I'm frustrated. And if I'm totally honest, I'm hurt and angry." My chest loosened at the admission. My emotions were in a knot I didn't know how to untangle.

"It's my fault."

I looked at her, and Wolf tapped against me. "Not all of it."

"Tell me. Tell me how to fix what I've broken."

I looked over and met her gaze. Her face was

wrinkled in sadness and puffy with sorrow. More of the tightness left. Her eyes were sincere. I swallowed. "I'm frustrated that you won't believe me when I tell you I don't want anyone else. I don't want to be with anyone else. I'm not interested in anyone else. I want you to trust me the way mates are supposed to. I've never lied to you, never shown an ounce of interest in anyone literally since the first time I laid eyes on you. I'm trying so hard to be what you need. To be who I want to be and not who I was forced to be the past four years. I thought we were making progress, but then..." I drifted off, floundering for the right words.

"Then I said things that hurt you worse than anything else could have." Tears gathered in her eyes again. My chest constricted. I couldn't deny it. She swiped at her eyes and took a shuddering breath. "My lashing out has more to do with me and my insecurities than you. I hurt you because I meant to. I was scared. Scared of what I thought you'd done to my mind. Scared of losing you to Skylar or someone else. But it was wrong. *I* was wrong."

She looked up at my face, her eyes roving over me and lighting a little fire in my gut. Despite everything that had just happened and the reeling swirl of emotions tangled inside me, I realized I'd fallen in love with her. And the thought of losing her was like a strike of lightning straight to my heart.

"Forgive me?" she whispered.

"If you'll forgive me, too."

She gave me a weak smile. "I don't think there's anything for me to forgive."

"I'm sure there will be at some point."

Her weak smile stretched and grew. She leaned

forward and kissed me softly. I ran my hand through her tousled hair, sliding my hand along her jaw.

"I like it when your hands go down my back."

"Yeah?" A grin tugged at my lips. My hand slid down her back while the other one rested at the top of her jeans.

She kissed me again, harder, waking my insides and fanning the flames she'd kindled. Her arms twined around my neck, and she pressed herself against me.

Resisting the urge to groan and feel her skin under my fingers, I pulled back slightly.

"It's almost seven o'clock in the morning. I need a shower. I need a nap. We've got to call Kyp."

"I suppose." She sighed and backed up.

"Raven, you're drooping. Your eyes are hardly staying open." I let my finger trail over her cheek.

"I could use a nap, too."

"Okay. I'll call Kyp and see if he can come over later."

"Go ahead and get in the shower. I'll call Kyp. I won't tell him about your mind control, though."

I nodded. "Raven," I started, wanting to say the words that floated on the tip of my tongue.

Bracing one hand on my chest, she leaned over and hugged me one more time.

****

I ran the water as hot as it would go, washing away the dirt, sweat, and lingering bitterness toward my father down the drain. Wiping my face with a towel, I put on a pair of pajama bottoms, not bothering with a shirt.

My chest seized, and I stopped in my tracks as I walked back into the bedroom. Raven lay curled up on

227

one side of the bed, her dark hair spread out across the pillow. She'd changed clothes, and her tank top gave me a clear picture of her neck, collarbones, and shoulder where one arm fell across the top of the comforter. My heart constricted. She was soundly asleep, but she was asleep in *my* bed. Any remaining hurt melted away. At this juncture, there wasn't any bigger way she could show me her trust.

Flinging the towel back into the bathroom, I crawled carefully into bed. Letting my arm go around her middle, I snuggled myself next to her. She sighed in her sleep, not waking, and my pulse spiked. If I weren't so tired and emotionally drained, this would be an entirely different experience.

As it was, I sent a quick message over the link to Kyp, to use the link when he was about twenty minutes away, put a soft kiss on Raven's shoulder, and was asleep within seconds.

Chapter 35
Raven

Bowen groaned next to my ear. "Kyp is going to be here soon," he mumbled, sleep heavy in his voice. My blood raced, and adrenaline rushed away any lingering slumber. My back was firmly planted against Bowen's chest, our legs tangled up together under the blankets. The events of the past twelve hours crashed in on my awareness, and I took a staggering breath.

Leaving the heat of Bowen's chest, I twisted onto my back, so I could look at him. He propped himself on one elbow and looked down at me. His expression was open, which was probably more than I deserved, given my behavior last night.

Reaching out, I let my fingers trail over the dark stubble on his jaw. His eyes widened, but he didn't pull away.

"Are we okay?" I whispered.

"We're okay," he whispered back. His hand found my side and slid down over my ribs to the hem of my shirt. It didn't quite meet my pajama shorts, and his fingers ran over the strip of skin between the two. My hand trailed from his jaw, over his neck, down his bare chest, his muscles tightening under my touch and filling me with a heady sensation. My fingers drifted over his abs, hesitating as they encountered the line of hair above his pajama bottoms.

He made a rumbling noise in the back of his throat.

"This is not a good time to start something," he rasped as his hand slid under the bottom of my tank, his palm flat against my stomach.

"Probably not," I agreed breathlessly. Wolf whined, wanting to continue, even though I knew we only had minutes before we'd have company, and then we'd have to relive yesterday's terrifying ordeal. My fingers didn't move, poised under his belly button. His heart audibly picked up, and his Adam's apple bobbed as he swallowed. His eyes sizzled with…anticipation?

For a long minute, neither of us moved, trapped in a state of arrested suspense.

A knock at the door downstairs shattered the moment. Wolf startled. Bowen shut his eyes, growling quietly.

Instead of getting out his side of the bed, Bowen rolled over on top of me, his body pressing mine back deliciously into the bed.

I gasped, every nerve ending on fire. My hands reflexively gripped his sides.

"I'm going to go get the door." He said it like he was convincing himself of the words. For another second, neither of us moved. Then Bowen got up and grabbed a shirt from the top of his dresser. With one more lingering look at me, he disappeared into the hallway.

I sat up slowly, relishing the euphoric, foreign sensation tripping through my jagged pulse. I blew a hard breath out my mouth.

Kyp's voice trickled up from downstairs, and I knew I needed to get up and get dressed so I could explain what happened to me yesterday. But I wanted to linger just a minute, letting myself feel and process the way Bowen made me react. The way I responded to his touch. The way the human part of me wanted him.

****

Kyp was just as shocked as we were. His head dropped to his hands, elbows braced on his knees. He scrubbed his face like he could take away the information we just gave him.

"So you were controlled? Completely? Like Victor could?"

I nodded, my lip tucked between my teeth. Wolf paced within me, disconcerted thinking about yesterday.

"Did you ever meet or hear about any other wolves with mind control when you were in Kentucky?" Bowen asked.

Kyp frowned. "No. I heard and saw plenty of questionable stuff, but never anyone with mind control. Until I moved here, I'd never heard of any wolves who had any extra abilities at all. Just the ability to take the wolf form and the enhanced senses while in skin."

Trepidation washed over Bowen's face. He glanced at me. Wolf was restless.

"Kyp, I should tell you something else." Bowen swallowed hard. "Something about me."

Nerves swarmed my belly, and I sat up straighter. He was going to spill his secrets to Kyp.

"What's wrong, Bowen?" Kyp's frown turned to concern.

Bowen took a big breath and leaned back in his seat, hands on his knees, bracing himself. "I can control people. Like Victor did."

Kyp said nothing for long minutes. He just sat

there staring at his brother, blinking a few times. His gaze swung to me, his eyebrows hiking up as he realized I wasn't surprised by this news. "Okay. That wasn't what I was expecting." Kyp ran his hand over his face again. "Who else knows?"

"You and Raven are the only ones. Victor never knew. My mom never knew. I never told anyone."

Kyp studied his brother, his eyes slitting. "How powerful are you?"

"I don't really know. I can't do as many, as much as Victor could. I don't think I could control the whole pack at once like he could. But—" He swallowed hard again. "—I can give people false memories. Make them do things I want them to."

Kyp was quiet a minute. "Do you think you could teach someone how to do your mind control?"

Wolf perked her ears forward. Teach someone to do it?

"What are you thinking?" Bowen's voice was wary.

"What if Victor had started teaching Drew how to do it before you became the Beta? What if he's had all this time to perfect what Victor might have taught him?"

A gasp escaped my throat.

Bowen's eyes grew huge in his face. "I…I have no idea. But if he could have, Drew would have been the obvious choice to teach. He never broached the subject with me, though."

"Yeah, well, Daddy dearest wasn't exactly big on including others in his plans for world domination," Kyp said dryly.

We were all quiet a minute, processing.

"We know Drew was behind the murder a few days ago. And that he may be able to control people." Kyp's finger rubbed over his thumb.

"And last night Shad attacked me. Here on my land," Bowen interjected. Kyp's head snapped up.

"Shad?" Kyp groaned. "Who else that was kicked out of the pack has Drew recruited? Any possibilities from anyone else that may generate mind control capabilities?"

"None I know of," Bowen said on a sigh.

"It sounds like Drew is forming his own pack. But why commit another murder mimicking Victor's? Why come onto pack land? Why not move on?" I asked.

"Revenge," Bowen said simply. "Drew wants what he thinks is his. He's always been vindictive and sneaky. Drew always resented me. He thinks the pack should belong to him, not Kyp or me. If neither of us had come on the scene, Drew would have maintained his position as Beta, unless Victor let Shelby take the Beta spot. But she's a female, and half off her rocker, so he wasn't obligated to have her as Beta." Pack law stated Alphaship and Betaship passed to the eldest male offspring of an Alpha, but if a girl was born first, if instated by her Alpha father, she could take Betaship. It was some ancient-held tradition that most packs, the Wolfe pack included, had done away with. But some packs still held tightly to the patriarchal codes. Victor's must have been one of them. My nose wrinkled in disgust.

"At least we have more of an idea what he might be after if he's rounding up the leftovers." Kyp stood and popped his back. "I'm going to call Dominic and Austin. We can't, and we shouldn't keep this information to ourselves."

Bowen stiffened beside me as Wolf perked her head up.

"We won't let your mind control out of this room, though," Kyp said, looking his brother in the eye. His gaze swung to me, and I nodded at my soon-to-be Alpha.

Chapter 36
Bowen

The rest of the day passed in a blur of pack meetings and planning, brainstorming, and making new patrol routes. Drew's threat—of what exactly we didn't know—hung over us like a storm cloud, heavy with impending rainfall.

My house became the headquarters of the three packs as we laid out a map of Rock Falls and the surrounding areas on the table.

"Put an X on all Victor's murders." Dominic nodded his head to Gordon Rockwell. With the police force, Rockwell had been involved in Victor's murder cases, both from the werewolf and human sides.

"Better mark where we found Shelby, too," Sam commented. Gordon nodded and drew another red X after consulting his notes.

"And then here is where Drew's murder victim was left." Kyp pointed.

"I don't see any correlation at first glance. Anybody else?" Austin said.

Sarah's eyebrows drew together, and her eyes squinted up. "Drew's murder is closer to the river. Look." She pointed. "Victor's victims were left just outside Wolfe territory lines. Drew left his here. Isn't this almost directly halfway between Kypson land and Wolfe land?"

My blood iced. Drew was vindictive. And he liked thinking he was smarter than everyone else. "Someone grab a ruler?" I knew the way he thought. His pattern wouldn't be so obvious.

"I'm not sure we have enough data just from this to make any sort of calculated guesses," Gordon said as he ran a thumb along his chin.

"Here." Raven handed me a ruler. Megan stepped closer as Rachel bit her fingernail.

I put the ruler on the map and stilled the tremor threatening my fingers. I drew a line.

"Is there any chance that's coincidence? There could be any number of points that match within that radius," Sarah whispered.

Kyp met my gaze across the table.

I'd drawn a line straight from my house to Raven's, with Drew's murder scene smack in the middle between the two.

****

The sun sank below the horizon and left the backyard wreathed in shadows and darkness. I watched the shadows gather as I sipped a root beer and braced my arm against the doorjamb as I contemplated.

"What are you thinking?" Raven whispered as she stepped up beside me. Several of the wolves had gone home, and only a handful remained, still discussing and talking. Raven stepped closer, her shoulder grazing my chest.

"I'm wondering if it would be safer for us to be closer to the pack. If you'd be safer with your parents." The words left a bitter taste in my mouth.

"You want me to go?" Her voice was tiny, and my eyes immediately swung to her face.

"No. I want you with me. But I also want you to be safe." I glanced out the glass doors into the yard again and took another sip. "I didn't know if you'd feel safer with them." It cost my pride to force the words out. No one would try to protect her the way I would. I was her mate. But there were two of her parents and Cade. And all three of them would die to protect her. There was also the lingering question of her pack allegiances. She still belonged to Dominic's pack.

Raven leaned her head against my shoulder, and my arm came down to wrap around her waist.

"My place is with you." Tension bled from my shoulders. "Dominic's still here. So is Kyp." She looked up at me. "I want to join your pack. Tonight."

Wolf lurched, filling me with a primal sort of desire to have her joined to me that way. "Yeah?" I whispered, my voice hoarse.

"Yeah. It's time."

I squeezed her waist and turned us back toward the living room. She didn't waste time and immediately went to speak quietly to Dominic. His head bobbed, and he glanced at Kyp. A few more steps into the room, and I snagged Kyp's shirt, dragging him with me over to Dominic and Raven. I had a one-track purpose.

"Little rough with the brother there?" Kyp laughed as he disengaged his sleeve. He smiled at me, the corners of his eyes crinkling. I grinned, shrugging my shoulders unrepentantly.

"I'm going to call my parents and let them know." Raven squeezed my arm as she passed to make her call in the kitchen.

Twenty minutes later, full dark had fallen when there was a knock at my front door. Steve, Amalie, and

Cade waited on my stoop.

"You take good care of her," Cade whispered as his parents went on into the house. We stared at each other.

"I will. With my life."

Cade nodded solemnly. He clapped me on the shoulder, and I shut the door behind us.

Soon after, the remaining wolves were gathered in a semicircle. My heart thundered as Raven hugged her parents and then Cade. She glanced shyly at me, then knelt in front of Dominic like Jonathan had done.

Dominic's smile transformed his craggy features. "Raven, you've been like a daughter in a lot of ways. Go in peace." He put his hand gently on the top of her head.

The room seemed to hold its breath.

A searing awareness ripped through my chest. Wolf tipped his head back as Raven's presence in the pack filtered in and filled a hole I hadn't realized was there. My eyes slid shut as the gaping hole sealed itself as her presence settled. She was in my pack. She was my mate, my pack.

Tears suddenly pricked the back of my eyes, and I kept my lids shut for a second longer to keep them at bay.

"Welcome home, Raven." Kyp's words were soft.

Raven rose from her knees and immediately came to me. We wrapped our arms around each other. It was more gratifying than I could express that she came to me first, not her parents, not Cade, not Megan or Rachel, who were smiling at us on the other side of the room.

"It's done," Raven whispered.

"You're home," I whispered back.

****

We decided it would be safer for us to stay a few nights elsewhere.

"You know I was just getting used to being here," Raven said as she zipped her backpack full of stuff for the second time this week. "Have you seen the light blue top I had on yesterday? I was going to put it in the wash over at Kyp's, but I couldn't find it in my cheer bag."

"Sorry, I haven't seen it. But better safe than sorry. I don't like that our house and your parents' house is a straight line through Drew's murder scene. That's two ties too many to you." I handed her the scarf she indicated from the closet.

"No. You're right. And...so long as you're with me, I'll be fine." She glanced up shyly, a light blush staining her cheeks.

Wolf wiggled in pleasure, nearly giddy with everything that had happened this evening.

"You know I'm not going anywhere." I would really miss the privacy of our own house.

"How many of your, *our*, pack are staying with Kyp right now?"

My mouth tipped up as she changed her word choice. "Lucy and Rich were the only ones, but there may be a few more filtering in since it looks like our pack may be more specifically targeted."

"Okay. I like Lucy. Rich...he seems like a wounded animal."

"Rich about had the spirit beat out of him by Victor. He's very much a wounded animal." I frowned, flashes of memory floating through my brain. I shut it off. "Does it make you uncomfortable to be in the house with Rich?"

"No. I want to help him if I can." She bit her lip as we went downstairs. "Will you tell me more about our pack members as we drive over to Kyp's?"

"Sure." I was pleased she'd asked. I locked the door, leaving the porch light on.

"I haven't been very gracious about getting to know a lot of our pack like I should have. I regret it now."

Our fingers tangled together for the short walk to my car.

"It's been a rough road for you the past few months."

"I haven't made it very easy for you either."

"We're still figuring it out. We've got plenty of time."

****

Jennifer met us at the door. "I'm glad you guys are here. I do not like the idea of Drew on the loose!" She ushered us in.

"You okay here? Is Kyp back?" I asked as we shrugged out of our coats.

"No. He took Rachel home. I wish there were a good excuse for her to stay over here on pack land, too. If her parents were in the loop," she drifted off with a shrug. Jennifer took our jackets and put them on a coat tree beside the door.

"This is the first time I've been inside Kyp's place. This is beautiful," Raven commented.

Jennifer smiled. "It's definitely more than we're used to, but he's put it to good use. Lucy and Rich have their rooms on the lower level. Kyp and I have bedrooms on the second floor. Jonathan will be moving into the lower level for additional protection while this mess is going on, too. In fact, he should be here any minute." She glanced at her watch. "I've heard back from five other pack members from the outskirts who are concerned, too. So we may be having more guests." She led us into a kitchen that could have belonged to a five-star restaurant. "Can I get you guys anything? We've got snacks and sandwich stuff. Anyway, help yourself to whatever whenever. Is it okay if you all are on the top floor?"

"Sure. Good view up there." I grinned. I'd been to the top floor of Kyp's house.

Jennifer led us up the stairs. "I mean, if it's not all right, just let me know. We've got room. Even with other people coming in, we'll juggle things around."

Jennifer left us at the door to the in-law suite at the top of the house.

"Oh. I see what she meant. One big bedroom." Raven's eyes were wide.

"And an attached bathroom," I offered sweetly and ushered her fully into the room.

The queen-size bed dominated the room, tastefully done in dark blues and greens. There was a chair and ottoman next to the big window looking out into the snowy hills surrounding the house.

Raven still hadn't moved. She took in the room. My sensitive ears picked up her accelerated heartbeat.

"Relax, Raven."

She glanced over at me, and her uncertainty mixed with desire sent shock waves rippling to my toes and woke a hunger in Wolf I knew we couldn't satiate. Not yet. This morning's events tripped through my brain, and I sighed, shutting them off.

She innocently licked her lips as she stared up at me. My gut constricted. Measuring my actions, I took her hands and brought us to the middle of the room.

"Relax," I said softly again. "Our first time is not going to be in my brother's house with half the pack downstairs." I smiled at her, and her cheeks pinked as her heart stuttered again.

"I...I wasn't sure what you were thinking after the way we left things this morning."

I resisted the urge to groan. There was nothing I wanted more than to revisit the way we'd left things this morning.

I brushed the pad of my thumb over her cheek instead. "I won't do more than kiss you here."

"Just kissing?" Her shoulders lost some of their tension.

"Just kissing," I confirmed.

****

Bowen, wake up.

You are making the worst habit of interrupting very good things, I shot back over the link as I cracked my eyes open, Raven still asleep and pressed against me. The barest hints of dawn streaked through the curtains.

Do you think I'd be interrupting very good things if it weren't important?

I'm coming.

I shut the door quietly behind me so I wouldn't wake Raven. Kyp stood across the hall, arms crossed, leaning against the wall. His forehead was lined with worry, his finger going over this thumb furiously where it stuck out from below his opposite elbow.

Yanking a shirt over my head, I followed him

down the hallway to the opposite side of the house, where a media room had been set up. Several couches framed a giant screen on one wall.

"He killed again," Kyp started without preamble.

"Where?" All vestiges of sleep fled. "Who?"

"Gordon said it was a vagrant from what they can tell. Small, emaciated. No one connected with us that we know of. They were left right off Munzee Creek Road, by the creek bank, not hidden or concealed. Face ripped off and slash marks through the gut."

I scrubbed my hands through my hair, shutting my eyes and pulling up a mental map. Munzee Creek Road and the creek itself wove a direct path between my house and Kyp's if you took the woods. Wolf snarled inside.

"He's targeting us. Toying with us."

"I know. But that's not the worst part."

My heart sank to my toes. "What's the worst part?"

"It's not as bad as it could be."

"Spit it out, Kyp." My heart thundered, waiting for the information as dread formed a boulder in my throat.

"Jake Rockwell—Gordon's son—was on patrol with one of the wolves still here from Austin's pack. They found the body. And one of Raven's shirts covered in the victim's blood."

My head jerked up, nostrils widening, eyes dilating. He was messing with not just my pack, not just me, but with my mate. I would rip his head off with my bare human hands.

Kyp continued. "Jake took it from the scene before it was discovered. He knows her scent, obviously, since they grew up together. Jake pinged Dominic, who called Gordon. Gordon went out to check things over with Dominic in their wolf forms. No other traces of Raven were left. Just the shirt. But if a human had found the body first, and it's pretty clear that was part of the plan since it was left in such an open place, it would have thrown Raven into the middle of the investigation and tied up both packs into more publicity and scrutiny than anyone wants."

I groaned into my hands. "What do we do now?"

"Part of me wants to go hunt Drew down myself, but if he has mind control abilities, then, and I can't believe I'm saying this, it might be better to make him come to us. If we go looking for him, he could pick us off one by one. Assuming I'm still immune to the mind control like I was to Victor's, I may be able to get close enough to him, but unless he's alone or it's just him and a few others, I can't take four or more grown wolves down by myself."

"What if we target Shad? We know he's involved. Drew won't have him with him all the time. He'll have others do his dirty work. If we go after his pack to get to him, maybe we can pick them off one by one—weaken him enough so it's just him we have to take down."

Kyp nodded. "Rachel's parents are not going to be pleased I need to put off wedding shopping again." He smiled ruefully. "I had to make an excuse for Friday. We were supposed to go to the city. I told them Mom was sick. We were going to try to go again today. I don't have the first clue about wedding anything. They said something about needing my input about cake." Kyp shrugged.

"I think I'm glad Raven was good with the Ancient Rites." I gave him a strained grin.

"Well, true mates and all. Things going better? I'm not trying to pry—just checking. As your brother."

I sank back into the couch cushions. "We've certainly had our ups and downs. Several this week. But I think we're moving in the right direction now." Wolf nudged me. She was coming to us. We didn't have to seek her out every time now. Wolf nodded in satisfaction. "She joined the pack." Happiness lit up my chest.

"She did." Kyp smiled. "I'm glad things seem solid."

I nodded. Now I just had to keep her safe from another raving lunatic.

Chapter 37
Raven

Monday morning, school was abuzz with news of the latest murder. Tensions were high, people were on edge. There was talk of canceling the homecoming dance on Friday, which put people in even more of an uproar.

Honestly, I'd kind of forgotten about it with everything else going on. But if it was still a go, all the cheerleaders and basketball teams were required to go as the homecoming king and queen were always chosen from the teams or squad.

I felt the presence of the murderer follow me through the hallways. Sit beside me in class. Trail me to the locker room. It was all in my head, but Wolf and I were on all kinds of high alert after being controlled Thursday and then being targeted. My light blue shirt had to have been taken out of my bag Thursday. Because I'd worn it to school that day.

Bowen had about gone ballistic when I'd told him.

He checked in with me over our link at least once an hour. Kyp checked in frequently, too. Instead of feeling smothering, it was comforting. It made me feel less alone.

"Rave." Cade caught me before practice. "Your day go okay?" His hand wrapped around my lower arm and paused me in the hall. Wolf relaxed with my big brother next to me.

"I'm okay. Just…really on edge."

"Good. You should be. Keep your eyes open. You stick with Bowen. Or me. Or Sam or Kyp. Or Mom or Dad. Or Dominic."

A shimmer of a laugh ghosted past my lips. "I get it."

One side of his mouth tipped up in a grin. "Yeah. Seriously, Rave. Don't go anywhere by yourself if you can help it."

"I won't. You, too."

He nodded. Wolf rolled her shoulders as we felt Bowen's presence at the end of the hall. Cade glanced in that direction. "Come on. I'll walk you down to Bowen, and we can all get to practice before we're late."

Chapter 38
Bowen

Wednesday afternoon brought me another shock. My pocket buzzed as I was headed to meet Raven to go to the cafeteria together. It was unusual for my phone to go off during the day. Fishing it out, I read what Sam had sent.

—*Police caught Shad. Pinning all murders on him*—

I stopped in my tracks, sucked in another breath, and read it again.

Did you see the news? Kyp broke into my jumbled thoughts.

I'm reading Sam's text now. What happened?

I don't have other details yet.

"Bowen? You're all pale. What happened?" Raven found me, and I berated myself for getting distracted enough that I didn't get to her first.

"The police are pinning the murders on Shad. They have him in custody," I whispered.

Her blue eyes got round.

"But—"

"I know."

****

It was all over school by the time practice rolled around. The dance was on, and normal life had resumed for the rest of the world. But for the werewolves, we were still vigilant. I wouldn't rest until Drew was caught and caged.

Cade met my eyes across the locker room. A quick nod, and I knew we were on the same page. We hurried, eager to get back out into the gym where we could keep at least partial tabs on Raven. I didn't like having her out of my sight.

Skylar is excited about not having to cancel her date for homecoming.

I snorted. *Who stooped low enough to bring her?*

I don't know. She won't say, but she's excited about it. Thinks it's one up on you. So at least she's not staring daggers at me anymore.

She'd better not be.

Breathing was easier after my quick check-in with Raven. The ball swung effortlessly through the hoop every time I shot the ball.

****

By Friday, we still hadn't caught Drew, and there had been no other episodes of anyone being controlled. Raven and I were still staying at Kyp's to be on the safe side. Our pack had closed ranks. Several more of them were living in the house, and others who were still in mobile homes from their time with Victor had moved closer, too.

"Okay. So you want to get ready at your house?" I asked, trying to organize myself, as Raven slipped into my car right after school. No practice today since everyone was required to be at the dance that night. Plus, they were getting the gym ready.

"Yes. My dress is there. And I already talked to Megan, Rachel, and Sarah. We're all going to get ready at my house. Rachel is going to leave early so she and

Kyp can go see Joanie at the rehab place while they're all dressed up and then meet us back at school."

"Is she doing better?" I hadn't had an update on Rachel's sister in a while.

"She is." Raven's smile lit her eyes. "So is Aria. She still won't talk to me, but her mom called my mom. Aria is getting help." I pulled out of the parking lot.

"That's great, Raven! But back to tonight, your parents will be there the whole time?"

"Absolutely. And Dominic has extra patrols running, too."

"All right. Sam offered to let me get ready at the cabin. That's not far."

"I think Cade said he's getting ready there, too. Too many females clogging up the bathrooms at Mom and Dad's." She smiled, and I followed suit. It sounded like a cloud of hairspray and a lot of fuss. Part of me was relieved I didn't need to be involved.

"Who do you think will be king and queen tonight?" Raven asked.

"I have no idea. I haven't given it much thought. I'd guess Cade stands a good chance since he's the captain of the team."

"I think he's hoping it's not him. For all his antics, he's not wild about being the center of attention up on stage in front of everyone."

"I can understand that. So tell me about this dress. Will I like it?" I glanced at her and saw her cheeks flush. I grinned and put my hand on her knee.

"Maybe."

"Raven, if you're in it, I'm sure it'll be gorgeous." Or if it was on the floor and she was standing out of it…

"This would be so much more fun if Drew wasn't still out there somewhere."

I squeezed her knee. "At least Drew is old enough he wouldn't blend in easily with the students. He looks too old to be in high school but a little too young to be a teacher."

"You look older than high school, too."

I winced. "Yeah."

"In a good way, though." I glanced over and found her unabashedly checking me out. Wolf preened, and my grin widened.

"Glad you think so."

Chapter 39
Raven

Mom and Dad were glad to have me home, even if it was just for a few hours to get ready for the dance. The other girls hadn't made it over yet, so Mom and I took the opportunity to talk.

"Tell me, Raven, how are things going? Are you okay? You've had so much thrown at you the past few weeks." Mom ran her hand down my hair like she had when I was little. Wolf snuggled up next to her.

"I'm okay. Not great, but okay. Bowen and I," I paused, and Mom raised her eyebrows expectantly, fighting a smile. "We haven't done *that* yet." My face flamed.

"I'm surprised. Mate ties are intense." Concern drew her eyebrows closer. "Is everything…good? There's nothing wrong, is there?"

"Well, what I was going to say, is we had a pretty major fight last week. I said things I shouldn't have, and I hurt him." Wolf growled. "I thought he had done something he hadn't. Anyway, he left to cool down and while he was gone, I realized how much I need him." I paused as Wolf rubbed her head against me. "I think I might be in love with him."

Mom's face beamed. "Have you told him?"

"No. Not yet. I still get really anxious thinking about…going farther. And there hasn't been the right time, you know?"

"You don't need to go any farther than you're comfortable with. He's not pressuring you, is he?" Mom's voice took on a hard edge.

"No. Not at all. When I first realized we were mates, I thought he would, and that scared me."

"Why didn't you tell me, Raven?" Mom patted my hand.

I shrugged. "I don't know. I guess admitting it out loud was like admitting I was scared of Bowen."

"Oh, sweetie."

"I'm not scared anymore." I cleared my throat. "Just unsure what to do."

"Are you asking me to tell you?"

My stomach revolted. "Um, not in any amount of detail." We chuckled.

"Well, it's okay if you want to take the lead. He's probably waiting for your cue."

He was. I knew he was.

The doorbell rang downstairs, and Mom got up off my bed.

"That's probably your friends." She smiled down at me. "Tell him how you feel if you're ready. The rest will come. Or if you really want to frenzy him, show a little skin." She winked and went downstairs.

I sat on my bed, thinking about what Mom said. Wolf brought up flashes of the morning after our fight. The way his muscles had rippled under my fingers. The way his hand had felt on my skin. The way his eyes told me he loved me. The way his body told me he wanted me. The way I had responded. Did I want to frenzy him? Before I could change my mind, I went over to my top dresser drawer and grabbed the one thing I knew I had that would cause a frenzy if I were ever brave enough to put it on. I stuck it in my bag.

Shaking my head, I tried to get a grip.

"Raven! Are you okay?" Megan's head popped through the door. Rachel's wild red curls bobbed behind.

"I'm good. Just thinking."

Megan smiled slyly. "Yeah. I can guess about what, too."

"Only because she knows that look from experience," Rachel retorted with a giggle. Meg wiggled her eyebrows.

"You all starting this party without me?" Sarah said from the hallway as they all spilled into my room.

"Ooh, I want to see everyone's dresses! I've seen Meg's, but only because I was there when she picked it out." Rachel twirled into my room, cradling her dress bag.

****

Two hours later, the four of us had laughed together, done makeup, hair, and zipped each other into our dresses. And truthfully, it had been a blast. For a while, I had been able to shake off the surrounding gloom and just enjoy being with my friends.

Kyp had come and picked up Rachel in her green satin dress that swished when she brushed down the stairs. I hoped Joanie would enjoy seeing them all dressed up.

Sarah was an ice princess, her light blonde hair piled on top of her head with sparkly pins, and her deep blue dress shimmering to her knees. Megan was simple and elegant, as I expected, in a long wine-red dress that dusted the floor. She'd left her hair down and loose in big waves.

I felt beautiful, but also a little risqué. My dress showed more of me than I was used to. In fact, I probably wouldn't have chosen this dress at all, but I loved the rhinestone detailing along the thin straps and the bodice. They sparkled against the red of the dress. It had also been on a great sale, and at the time when I bought it, I wasn't worried about anyone noticing it was mostly backless or that I couldn't wear a bra with it.

With Mom's earlier comment about flashing some skin hanging between my ears, I couldn't not be aware now. Wolf wiggled, excited to show Bowen. And he'd have a clear look, too. Megan and Rachel had styled my dark hair in an elegant bun while Sarah had done my makeup. With my hair up, *all* of my back was there for his perusal.

The doorbell sounded again, and with one final check of ourselves and one more bobby pin for Sarah, we went downstairs.

I hung back just a little, letting the others go down first. Bowen was waiting at the bottom of the stairs. While Meg found Sam and Sarah found Cade and my parents snapped pictures, I was locked in Bowen's gaze as he watched me descend.

His eyes traveled over every inch of me. From my silver strappy heels, the slit that came up the side to just above my knee, the way the red material clung to my hips and dipped in at my waist, over the curve of my chest, to my face. He swallowed hard as I reached the bottom step.

He glanced around. Everyone else was busy. Mom looked over and gave me an encouraging wink and a quick nod toward the dining room. Bowen noticed too, and a boyish grin broke out on his face as he grabbed my fingertips and tugged me into the solitude of the other room.

The breath left him in a rush as he took me all in again. I let myself take a good look at him, too. He had on dark dress pants, a crisply ironed white shirt, and a black tie. Wolf fluttered. He smelled clean and crisp over his scent of cedar and brown sugar. Wolf moved to the surface, and I leaned in and scented him.

"Turn for me." His voice was low and had that sexy edge that curled my toes.

I turned slowly. Heat prickled along my spine as he saw my exposed back, and an appreciative growl sounded in his chest.

"I like the dress," he said, his eyes dilated slightly, his voice rough. "No maybe about it."

I smiled as he took another step into my space. Mere inches separated us in the shadows of the dining room. The rest of the world faded away, and it was just the two of us.

"Can I tell you how bad I want to kiss you right now?" His fingers reached around and ghosted from my neck, over my shoulders, the middle of my back, all the way down to the edge of the dress.

My breaths were coming shorter, and my heart picked up. I had to work to focus with the pads of his lightly calloused fingers running up and down my spine. "Why aren't you kissing me?" It came out like a squeak as I tried to center my thoughts.

"I don't want to mess up your lipstick." He cleared his throat. "But I plan on kissing you a lot later tonight when the lipstick won't matter." His fingers skimmed the bottom dip of the dress again, way low down on the small of my back.

"You guys coming?" Cade hollered.

"In a second," Bowen called back, never taking his eyes from my face. "What is it with brothers interrupting significant moments? Yours is as bad as mine." His lips quirked up at the edges. Hesitating a moment, he cupped my jaw lightly and brushed his lips against the opposite curve where my neck met my shoulder and where my pulse pounded. My eyes slid shut, memorizing the feel of his lips against the sensitive skin. "Consider it a down payment."

I was too flustered to respond.

****

Many pictures later, Bowen and I pulled into the lot at school. Darkness shrouded the landscape, and unease twinged in my middle. Anything could be hiding in the shadows.

Thoughts of dread flew straight out my ears as Bowen's fingers disengaged from mine and landed lightly on the skin above my knee where the slit in my dress stopped. His hand was warm and steady.

"You okay?"

Was I okay? "I think so." The words were all breathy.

"You look and sound all nervous."

A titter escaped. "I am a little nervous about who else might be here tonight. But I probably sound nervous because your fingers are creeping their way up my leg." I swallowed. "And I like it."

Bowen laughed, and the sound thawed me, melting some of my nerves. "Do you still like this?" The teasing lilt was back in his voice as his hand inched up under the slit of my dress.

I did. I really did.

Bowen's phone buzzed, and he rolled his eyes, his hand sliding back to the visible skin of my knee.

"If that's Kyp or Cade, I'm going to—" He didn't finish his threat as he fished out his phone. "Kyp. Of course it is." He answered. It was quiet enough in the car that my wolf ears had no trouble overhearing their conversation.

"Bowen, we're going to be late," Kyp said.

"What happened?"

Kyp sighed on the other end. "We're in between Joanie's rehab center and school in the middle of nowhere, and completely out of gas."

"Are you kidding?" I couldn't tell if Bowen was amused or annoyed.

"No, I am not." Kyp was not amused. "We had a fourth of a tank when we pulled into the rehab. I planned to fill up in town tonight. And we just ran out. I don't know if the gauge is busted or what. Jonathan and Mom are coming out with gas. I just wanted to let you know you've got two fewer pairs of eyes tonight. Be careful. I'll let you know when we get there."

"All right. Watch yourselves. I don't like it."

"Me neither."

Bowen clicked his phone off, his head resting against the back of his seat for a second. I touched his arm.

"I guess you heard everything?" His eyes slid to me.

"Yeah. What are you thinking?"

"That it's very coincidental."

Chapter 40
Bowen

I didn't want to let on how worried Kyp's call made me, so I pasted on a smile and turned back to Raven.

"You wanna go dance?"

"Or at least watch from the sidelines."

My smile grew. "Didn't you tell me you like it when my hands are on your back? I think it would be a shame to waste such a prime opportunity." I let my gaze grow suggestive, which wasn't hard since seeing that much of Raven's skin had about sent Wolf over the edge. No way she could be wearing a bra under that dress. And that about sent the human side of me over the edge.

"Well, if you put it that way."

We made it to the gymnasium. Half my attention was on Raven, while the other half was focused outward, listening, searching, probing for any information that things weren't as they should be.

"Hey!" Sam caught us just inside the doors of the gym. Lights flashed, and music boomed, the bass vibrating under my feet. Wolf disliked the overload. It was harder to pick out anything useful.

"Why don't we step back outside the doors?" Megan suggested. She pointed to where she'd dropped her coat on the bleachers. Raven put hers there, too, and we followed them back out into the hallway, where it was dramatically quieter.

"Did Kyp call you?" I asked Sam.

"Rachel called me," Megan said.

Sam's lips were set in a grim line. "Just keep an extra eye out. It may be nothing."

I nodded in agreement. "Well, I guess we should try to enjoy the dance in the meantime." I shrugged, and Wolf shook out his ruff at the thought of pulling Raven close.

"Might as well," Megan said with a smile as Sam held the door open for all of us.

The heavy beats of a fast song gave way to the slow strains of something quieter, and I was pleased when Raven let me pull her into a corner of the dance floor without resistance.

"Do you like dancing?" I asked next to her ear, realizing I had no idea.

"This kind is nice," she said. My fingers skimmed her skin, and I had to agree. I couldn't decide where to put my hands. I loved the feel of the silky skin of her back but equally loved the curve of her waist.

A ripple of commotion drew our gaze.

"Woah. Skylar is really getting into that kiss," Raven commented dryly.

"Are you serious? She brought Kyle Mason?" The snotty little turd who crushed the air from my solar plexus and singed my nostrils with his nasty body spray was practically sucking the face off Skylar.

"Ew. I do not need to see their tongues." Raven grimaced.

I snorted. "You don't want to see where Kyle's hand just went either." I turned us and edged us farther away from the passionate couple.

We danced and sat on the bleachers, watching everyone else dance. In turn, we talked with Sam and Meg, and Cade and Sarah.

About an hour into things, it was time for the crowning of the homecoming king and queen. We'd lost track of the others, but I wasn't feeling worried. I knew they were all in the gym.

"And it's the time we've all been waiting for! Let's give it up for this year's homecoming queen…" The principal paused and tore open the envelope with the results of the vote, dragging it out for suspense. "Skylar Jones!"

The gym erupted into noise, and Wolf shuddered. My thumb traced over Raven's palm as Skylar sashayed up the steps to the stage and accepted her bouquet of roses. She waved at the crowd, lapping up the attention.

"And now, for our homecoming king—" Principal Angelo's eyebrows drew slightly together before his expression cleared, and he announced, "Bowen Oakes!"

Wolf jolted inside me as Raven squeezed my hand.

"Are you kidding?" I muttered. Raven smiled at my bewildered expression.

"That's you, handsome," she quipped.

"Yeah, I know." I frantically scanned the crowd. Wolf relaxed as I snagged Cade's eye. He and Sarah were opposite the gym from us. We were on the bleachers near the door. I nodded at Cade, and he and Sarah started making their way over to us through the throng of bodies on the dance floor. "Go find Cade. I'll come back to you as soon as I can." I kissed the side of Raven's head and pointed with my chin toward Cade before going down the bleachers and to the stage to be crowned next to the simpering Skylar.

Wolf rumbled with unease.

Chapter 41
Raven

I watched for just a minute as Bowen's wide shoulders went through the path opening for him. Wolf wagged her tail. A smile hid at the corner of my mouth. I wasn't worried anymore about Skylar or anyone else. Bowen belonged to me.

Sighing in contentment, I stood, intending to look for Cade and hang out with him as Bowen had asked me to. Before I could find my brother, my feet propelled me toward the door. My eyes widened, and panic flared in my gut as I watched my arms push the door open, and the flavor of bitter burned grain flooded my mouth.

Wolf whimpered inside me, and I tried to stop. My feet wouldn't obey. This hallway was deserted. Everyone was inside the gym for the crowning.

In horror, completely aware and unable to do anything to stop myself, my arms pushed open the back door of the school that would take me toward the football field. I tried to use my link, but it was like trying to tune into a frequency and getting only static.

My feet hit the edge of the grass, and Wolf thrashed. I'd never been more terrified in all my life. Not even when Bowen had been poised to rip out Cade's throat. I was being controlled, and I was completely aware.

Shaking my head, desperate to clear it, I did the one thing I still could to protect myself. I shifted. Wolf leaped out of my skin, heedless of any who might see us. I couldn't hold my paws back any more than I could my feet. Leaving the tattered remains of my red dress on the curb beside the back parking lot, my footpads fell on cold grass.

Wolf scented, and we recoiled as the tang of blood mixed with the green smell of the football field. Rounding the side of the bleachers, I whimpered.

There in the middle of the field was a body. Ripped in bloody shreds, entrails spilling from its middle. I would have wretched, but fear overtook my gag reflex. Standing beside the body was a man. Too old to be a student, but too young to be a teacher. And he was wolf. I could smell his dark musk beneath the coppery smack of the blood. It had to be Drew.

"Ah. Little she-wolf. You were supposed to come in skin. It would have been much easier to place you at the scene of this murder that way. No matter. We managed at the last, we'll manage this one, too."

I was close enough to see his eyes slit. Fear, cold and constricting, ratcheted through me as my feet remained rooted to the ground. I was still unable to move. I could do nothing but watch in helpless terror as Drew stripped, taking his time, like he knew no one was coming. My heart thundered in my chest as Drew let his shift roll over him, showing me the rippling muscles, the corded sinews, the long dark fur whipping from his skin like tiny snakes.

Bowen! My desperate cry through our link snapped something. Dirty burned grain flavor coated my mouth, but my feet moved. I backed up so hard and so fast I fell flat on my butt.

Drew snarled, realizing his control over me had broken. He bared his teeth. Saliva dripped in strings from his wicked canines. The growl that ripped from his throat sent skitters of adrenaline shooting over me and kicked my fight response into gear.

Coiling my muscles under me as I sat, I crouched. Just as Drew gouged the ground, racing to me, I leaped. Higher and stronger than I ever had before.

I cleared the top of him, my paws brushing his ruff. Snarling, he turned and clipped my tail. Yelping, I whirled around, dancing out of reach of his teeth as I pulled my tail back. He didn't break the skin, but I doubted I'd get another easy pass.

Drew was bigger than me, more heavily muscled. I shook in fear that he'd control me again, but instead, he circled me. His canines glinted in the moonlight, and his eyes glowed unnaturally gold.

Paws pounded the ground at the edge of the field, and Drew's focus was momentarily torn from me as he glanced back toward the field house. I knew who was coming. The scent tickling my nose on the hush of wind was as familiar to me as my own. Buoyed and relieved help was here, I launched myself at Drew and caught him around the underside of his neck.

He howled and thrashed, his paws coming down painfully hard on my chest as I hung on. Drew slung his head and knocked me loose right as Cade slammed into Drew's side. Drew flew back several feet, whimpering and landing hard on his back leg.

Cade didn't wait. With a snarl that raised the hair on my own neck, he pounced on Drew, catching hold of his throat in a vice-like grip that made me wince. Cade menaced a growl and pushed his heavy paw down on Drew. Drew could do nothing under the might of Cade's teeth and claws.

"Here!" Sarah called as she dashed across the field in her bare feet. Pale hair streamed behind her as her blue dress puffed and her knees pumped.

On shaky legs, I stood and went over to Drew and Cade. Drew glared up at Cade, a gurgling growl trying to exit his mouth but getting stuck where Cade had him clamped. I grabbed one of Drew's legs in my mouth, biting down hard enough I felt his muscles tighten. I didn't draw blood. I didn't want it in my mouth.

"Okay. Everyone all right?" Sarah panted as she uncoiled a length of rope. She made quick work of hog-tying Drew. All four legs pinned together. With the extra and the end, she cinched his muzzle shut. Then, with one almighty kick, she brought her bare foot down on the side of Drew's head. He slumped into unconsciousness.

"Well, that ought to hold for at least a little bit. No more mind control for him for a while. Raven, Cade, you both all right?" Sarah glanced over both of us. I whined. I wasn't hurt, just petrified and probably emotionally scarred for life.

Cade finally eased up, and Drew wheezed even in his unconscious state, sucking in as much oxygen as he could through his nostrils. Sarah had tied the rope tight around his snout.

Cade rubbed his head against me and then snorted at Sarah, pushing his nose against her arm.

"I'm fine. I had to break a window to get into the field house and find rope." A little trickle of blood ran down her arm. "Okay. How are we getting our pretty little captive off the football field?

Cade yipped, and I knew to turn around.

"Ah, Cade! A little more warning next time?"

"I barked. Didn't you see Raven turn?" Cade snorted in his human form, and I latched my wolf lips down to keep from exposing all my teeth in a wolfy grin. "Sorry if I've ruined every other male specimen for you," Cade groused. "Look. I can't drag him like this in my wolf form. Go get my pants, and we can all three drag him into the field house and keep him trussed up until Dominic gets here."

"Fine." Sarah started to stalk off toward the concession stand when a snarl ripped from the tree line on the other side of the football field.

"Oh crap." Cade spat.

Apprehension throttled through me. Where was Bowen? Where was Sam? Kyp?

"Raven, go find Bowen, Sam, anyone you can. I don't know why they're not here yet. Sam knows what's going on. I linked him. Use your link to Bowen. We need back up."

I risked a look at my brother's face. He was grim and determined.

An unladylike oath burst from Sarah's mouth. "I knew I wouldn't get to enjoy one night in a fancy dress." She yanked the zipper down and morphed into a huge white wolf the moment it hit the ground.

Two sets of glowing eyes burned from the tree line, and slowly the hulking shape of two grizzled werewolves materialized.

"Go, Rave. Use that speed. We'll hold them off as long as we can." With his last instructions given, Cade was back in his wolf form.

I didn't waste any more time. With a whimper, I sped over the ground, my nose searching for any familiar scents to lead me to help.

Bowen?

No answer. Why wouldn't he answer?

A chill descended deep in my bones and gave unnatural speed to my paws. There was no way he wouldn't answer me unless he *couldn't*. Fear threatened to freeze my paws to the ground. I stumbled but forced myself forward. I found Cade's shirt and pants by the field house. I scooped up his shirt in my mouth when a breeze fluttered in and brought Megan's scent with it.

Where Megan was, Sam would be, too.

Chapter 42
Bowen

I foraged my way through the sea of bodies as the colored lights flickered. Skylar batted her eyes at me from the stage like I was some prize she'd won. Wolf grit his teeth.

Once on the stage, Skylar latched onto my arm with a force that said she meant to keep her hands there as long as possible. What was her game with Kyle Mason? Did she think she could make me jealous? Wolf snorted at the thought. I scanned the crowd for Raven and Cade, but the lights turned onto the stage made it impossible to see a few feet beyond the steps. Everything past that was just a dark blur.

Skylar had a heavy dose of perfume on, and I wanted to sneeze, to clear it from my nostrils, but I held it in, not wanting to be remembered forever as the sneezing king. Thankfully, I didn't have to hold it in long.

We each got crowns, and then we were released back into the wild. Skylar kept her death grip on my bicep as we descended the stairs, and I kept a smile plastered on my face. But once we were down on the main floor and no longer elevated, I forcefully tugged my arm away.

"Congratulations, Skylar," I said as politely as I could, even as I started to back away.

"But aren't you going to dance with me? It's tradition!" Her eyes were round and a little lost looking.

"I came here with Raven. I'm *with* Raven. Why don't you dance with your date? It looked like you guys were really enjoying yourselves earlier."

Her face seemed to crumble slightly, and I almost felt sorry for her. Almost. I shrugged with another polite smile and turned to search for Raven.

After about two minutes, when I didn't see her or Cade, Sarah, Sam, or Megan, Wolf took charge. I let him up to the fore and scented. Which was pointless. There were so many bodies packed into the gymnasium, I had no chance of picking out individual ones. That and Skylar's perfume still lingered in my nose. I did let myself have a tremendous sneeze then. It cleared my sinuses, and sensory information came flooding back in.

Then one scent stood out among the others.

My blood turned to ice, and Wolf recoiled, howling inside. A tremor rocked my arms.

Victor.

A twisted version of his scent filtered into my nostrils.

Kyp, I smell Victor. Here. At the dance. Where are you?

We're on the way. I'm calling Dominic and Austin now.

Fear hammered my heart against my breastbone. I thought I'd never have to encounter my father again. But there was someone here who reeked of him.

Raven?

No response. She was silent. Biting back a whimper, I forced my feet to move. I followed the stench. Out the gymnasium doors. Down the hallway. With a shuddering breath, I pushed the back doors of the school open. The night swallowed me whole, shadows taking me in with grasping fingers that clutched at my flesh and grappled for my soul.

There. Raven's scent was overlaid with the Victor-like one. Terror and horror clashed together in my gut. I immediately shut off the dark thoughts that followed. He'd keep her alive—whoever it was—long enough to toy with me. To dangle her in front of me. He had to. Because I wouldn't consider the alternative that she was—

I ran, following the mixed scent trails. Sarah. Raven. Victor. Cade. They all mixed together and muddled in my brain.

Come into the concession stand. The door is unlocked.

My feet rooted so hard I nearly toppled over.

No. No, no, *no*!

It wasn't Drew. I knew his voice. His thoughts. This was someone else. And they had complete control of me. Just like Victor.

Resisting was futile. I couldn't shake the bonds drawn around my brain. Staggering under the weight of despair and panic, my shaking hands turned the round knob of the shadowy concession stand building and entered. The door clicked shut behind me.

Darkness swarmed my vision, and Wolf immediately compensated. My eyes adjusted to the weak light filtering in from a high window, and my heart plummeted to my feet.

"Hello, brother."

Kyle Mason leaned casually against the far wall.

AJ Skelly

Victor's twisted stench reeked off him. His scent was familial. I could not deny this freak was my half brother.

"What do you want?" I rasped. I tried to use my link to reach Raven, to warn Kyp, but my voice just bounced around inside my own head. I was trapped. Immobile and cut off. But Raven wasn't here. I wasn't sure if I should be relieved or more panicked.

"What do I want?" He pushed off the wall and stalked a few feet so he stood in the middle of the room. He swung his arms wide. "Isn't that obvious? Victor was my father. I deserve a place in his pack. Not only that, I'm his most powerful son. I should *lead* his pack." A maniacal grin slid over his face. "And I will. Just as soon as I take you and your pathetic Alpha down. Then everything that's rightfully mine will actually be mine."

My mind moved at a frighteningly fast clip, trying to figure out how to get out of this. "Drew put you up to this, didn't he?"

An angry snarl clouded his face for an instant. "Drew was the one who told me who I was. Who showed me how to develop my abilities. He told me Dad tried to find me, but *you* kept him from it. You knew I was the powerful one. That I'd take your place. Guess who's going to have the last laugh now?"

He stepped closer, jeering in my face.

"I was with Victor's pack for four years. He never mentioned you. He had no idea you even existed."

"No! He tried to find me. Drew was personally in charge of finding me. Only it was too late when he did. Kypson—filthy mongrel half-breed—*murdered* my father. He should be here soon. I had him followed. It was only too easy to have his gas siphoned out. When he gets here, he's going to pay for killing my father. And you're going to watch. Then when his Alpha power has passed to you, I'm going to slit your belly open and take out your intestines while you watch me. I'm going to pierce you with my claws so you slowly bleed to death and watch your Alpha power leak from your broken body and flow into me. I will be the Alpha. I will take what you have stolen from me."

"Kid, you need to get out more. Get yourself a girl, something. Fantasizing about disemboweling your brother isn't healthy," I goaded him. Seeing where his triggers were. Maybe I could make him overcompensate and break his hold.

"Shut up!" Spittle flew from his lips as he swung his arm back and slammed his fist into the side of my head.

Sparkles tinged the edges of my vision as the back of my head connected to the cinder block wall behind me. Wolf gnashed inside, whimpering. That hurt.

"That all you got? You'll have to do better than that."

"I'm not going to wait for Drew. I'm going to kill you right now."

Fear cramped my belly, but I was powerless to do anything about it.

Before either of us could react further, the door slammed open. Sam charged straight in and tackled Kyle to the dusty floor.

"No! Back off!" Kyle shrieked as Sam's fist crunched against Kyle's nose. Blood streamed down Kyle's upper lip. Sam jerked his arm, trying to bring his fist in for another swipe, but he couldn't. Kyle shoved him hard in the chest, and Sam toppled backward.

"Go stand against that wall," Kyle said, his eyes murderous as he wiped the back of his sleeve against his nose, smearing blood across his cheek.

Sam's eyes were round enough I could see the whites all the way around his blue irises, but his face gave nothing else away.

I tried to move my feet forward, but Kyle still held me firmly in his will. Wolf quaked. It was too much like Victor. Memories of control, humiliation, and horror threatened to overtake me, but I shoved them back. Kyle hammered his fist across Sam's cheek. Wolf shrugged off his trepidation, righteously angry.

"Is that it? You can't fight unless you make them hold perfectly still?" I found my voice. My head throbbed. "You *are* just like Victor. *A coward.* He couldn't fight his own battles unless he cheated, too."

Even in the dim light, Kyle's face mottled with pent-up rage. I braced myself. His retaliation would be painful.

But before he could get across the room to me, the unthinkable happened.

The doorknob turned again, and Raven stood there like a ghost as moonlight washed over the white dress shirt she wore.

"*You.* Is Drew completely incompetent? You are supposed to be out on the football field." Kyle sighed and flipped his fingers toward Raven. Panic choked me. She moved woodenly to the far wall. We each had a wall, Sam, me, and Raven. Tears pricked the back of my eyes.

"You know, I had so much fun impersonating you, Bowen. But I have to hand it to you." He hooked his thumb toward Raven. "She took a lot more convincing than I expected. After what Skylar told me about the two of you, I figured she'd dump you like a bad crap. Do you know it's disgusting the way Skylar wanted you? She didn't once she had me, of course. But she made it easy. She got Raven's shirt—that was my idea—to leave with the first body. We made sure it was a body light enough Raven could have killed it and dragged it herself." Kyle smiled to himself, remembering his gruesome deeds. "It was also my idea to use my…gift…to have you crowned king. It should have actually been Cade. But it was just too perfect a way to get you out of the way and away from her for just long enough for Drew to take care of her. Which he obviously didn't." His eyes slit as he stared at Raven.

Wolf struggled inside. My hands clenched uselessly at my side.

Sam grunted, and Kyle turned on him. "You be still, or I'll go after your little she-wolf, too."

Sam growled threateningly, and Kyle gripped one hand to Sam's hair.

"I said be still!" As he shouted, he punched Sam in the gut. Sam sucked in a hard breath. My muscles twitched. Aching to be free. To pummel Kyle into a pulp.

Kyle looked knowingly at me, a slow, menacing smile lighting his face.

He crossed the room until he stood in front of Raven. "Nice mate, brother. Brothers should share, shouldn't they?" He leaned in and scented her.

Red tinged the edges of my vision as Wolf and I gnashed and snarled together in my human form.

"*Mi voluntatis meae est,*" Raven whispered, her

terrified gaze locking on my face.

"What did you say to me?" Kyle got in her face, eyebrows drawn down.

"*Mi voluntatis meae est*," Raven said, her voice stronger.

Torrents of tainted memories, of control, of abuse, of hate, roiled under my skin. Chains that bound me inside myself, bound me to Kyle's will, bound me to the black traces left by my father, snapped under the fiery determination surging through my blood.

Mi voluntatis meae est. My will is my own. *My will is my own!*

He would not touch her.

With a mighty roar that shook the charged air of the room, I tore my arms free of the invisible shackles and took a giant step into the room.

"Wha—" Kyle didn't get to finish. Fear scrawled across his face.

"Back away." My wolf spoke through my voice, every ounce of power I possessed poured into my words.

Fear morphed to horror as Kyle stood rigid like his backbone had soldered together. He took a halting step away from Raven. Another.

"How?" he squeaked.

My eyebrows drew down, my eyes slits as rage boiled through my veins.

Sam slumped over, clutching his stomach.

"Did you think you were special? That you were the only wolf with powers? I'm Victor's blood, too." The bitterness in my voice startled me.

"Bowen!" Raven's relieved whisper echoed. She ran to me. I crushed her against my side, never taking my eyes from Kyle's shocked face.

"Sam, you okay?" I called.

He groaned. "I'll live. Just had the wind knocked out of me. He's a basketball player, not a boxer. Nice trick, by the way. Came in handy. Would have been nice to know about it beforehand."

Guilt niggled inside while hate flashed across Kyle's face.

"We've got to go. The rest of Kyle—Drew—whoever's pack is on the field with only Cade and Sarah!"

"Sam?" I asked.

"I'm gone. Take care of him." Sam charged out the door. Snarls ripped through the night as the door opened.

"I've got to go help," Raven said. Desperation tinged her voice.

Wolf nudged me inside.

"No. I can end this." I marveled that the thing I loathed most about myself, I could now use to protect my family—those I loved.

"Out to the football field. Now. Sprint," I commanded Kyle.

The three of us set out at a dead run.

As soon as we were out of the building, barking and echoes of growls surrounded us. Once I was close enough to make out three hulking werewolves alternately attacking Sarah and Cade, with Sam latched onto a fourth, I let Wolf have his head.

"Stop now." I didn't have to shout. The words carried my authority.

Instantly the fighting ceased.

Bowlegged, bloodied, and exhausted, Cade and

Sarah leaned against each other. Sam growled and put himself between them and the enemy wolves.

"Sit." The four brutes sat. Drew, fully human and stark naked, whined from his trussed-up spot a few feet away.

Cade and Sarah's wolf eyes burned into me as they realized what was happening.

Rapid footsteps hit the pavement behind us.

"We're here!" Megan called, coming to stand beside Raven.

Dominic, Austin, and several other adults swarmed the field. Behind them came members from my own pack.

"What do you want us to do?" Rich asked me as my pack paused beside us.

Gordon Rockwell took charge. "You all need to get out of here. Right now. Let the adults do this. The police will have enough questions they can't answer without finding all of you here."

Without Kyp here as Alpha, I was in charge of our pack. They'd follow my orders. I glanced around, unsure.

Raven grasped my arm, her touch centering me. I turned back to Rockwell. "Is it safe to let go of their wills?" I didn't know how else to explain it. His eyebrows rose as understanding dawned.

"Probably," Gordon said.

Dominic and Austin had taken charge of the bullies on the field while Resha, a wolf from Austin's pack, took care of Drew, still hog-tied on the ground.

"Sarah, you do that? Those are some tidy knots." I heard Austin ask as he looked at Drew's snarling form.

Sarah's white wolf nodded, her tongue lolling out

at her father's praise.

The man next to Drew cut him loose and kept a tight hold on his arm as he heaved him up.

Slowly, I eased back my control of the werewolves once belonging to my father's pack. Released from my will, they slumped, outnumbered and defeated. I kept a tight hold on Kyle Mason. I wasn't about to let go of him. If I did, he'd just control his way right out of the situation, and we'd be back where we started. Wolf bared his teeth at him.

Rockwell fished cuffs out of his pocket and locked Kyle's hands behind him. Kyle turned pleading eyes to me.

I sadly shook my head. There was nothing I could do for him. Raven's fingers found mine. Still keeping Kyle's will immobile, I turned to my gathered pack members.

"Go on home. Tell Kyp what you know happened. I'll come along as soon as we're done here and fill him in." I met the eyes of my pack. They nodded and melted back into the shadows.

A scream of rage cut through the night and raised every hair on the back of my neck.

Before I could stop it, Drew, dragged nearer to us and the exit, lashed out, catching Resha across the face and opening a wide cut across her eye. She howled, loosening her grip enough that Drew charged.

Morphing in midair, faster than I'd ever seen a shift, Drew latched his wolf's incisors around Kyle's throat. Blood spewed from Kyle's neck, a wet gurgle all that marked his final words.

Growling, Rockwell yanked his giant human hands around Drew's neck, and Wolf recoiled as the cracking snap echoed around the field. Drew's head lolled, Kyle's blood matting the front of his chest.

Stunned, I startled when Raven wretched beside me.

"Get her out of here before she leaves any more DNA. All of you, go. I'll get the tapes from the cameras." Rockwell ordered.

Dominic nodded somberly. "We'll take care of things out here."

It was over.

The madness had ended.

Chapter 43
Raven

"Is it done?" I whispered as I kept my eyes screwed shut and breathed through my mouth. Bowen didn't reply but instead scooped me up into his arms and ran with me into the darkness of the parking lot.

"Okay. You can't smell the blood anymore."

He put me down gently. I shivered, realizing for the first time that it was freezing out and I had no shoes on, and I only wore Cade's dress shirt.

Bowen jingled his pocket. "My keys are still here. Come on." He held his arms out again, and he lifted me into his arms again. "You're frozen." His car wasn't far, and once we were inside, he blasted the heater.

His knuckles turned white on the steering wheel, gripping it, but not driving.

"Bowen, you saved us tonight. All of us." I couldn't imagine how hard it must have been for him to use the genetic abilities he hated more than anything, but he had.

He turned his face to me, chocolate eyes sorrowful. "Raven," he whispered. His arms shook. Wolf longed to comfort him. The human part of me did, too.

Getting on my knees in the seat, trying not to flash anything, I leaned over and wrapped my arms around him. A light tremor rocked through his shoulders, and then his arms came around me, locking me to his chest.

We both took a shuddering breath.

I was surprisingly calm, given what had happened. The relief of knowing Drew and Kyle and their pack were done and over lifted the weight I'd been struggling under.

"Do you want to go back to your parent's house? Where would you feel safest?" He finally asked me as we broke apart.

I buckled my seat belt and pulled the ends of Cade's dirty shirt down as far as they'd go. "No. I want to go back to your house. Our house." I looked up at him. It was time to go home. Wolf nudged me, content.

A grin tipped the corner of his mouth, and his face lost some of its haggardness.

"Yeah?"

"Yeah." I smiled. "I think after tonight, a soak in the hot tub together sounds amazing."

"I can't argue with that."

He pulled out of the lot and zipped to the highway. His hand ghosted onto my bare knee. "This still okay?"

"I like your hand there."

He smiled. "You know, this is really not the appropriate time for this, but you look *hot* in a man's dress shirt."

"I'll make a note. Maybe I'll borrow one of yours sometime." Wolf was pleased. Bowen squeezed my knee lightly.

"You should. I'm going to use the link and fill Kyp in." The rest of the drive was made in comfortable, tired silence as Bowen explained our side of the story. Bowen had just finished giving him the short version when we pulled into the driveway, porch light still gleaming merrily against the night.

My backpack was still in the back seat, my phone tucked safely in the front pocket. My coat had been left at school. And Dominic would dispose of whatever remained of my once beautiful red dress. I sighed. I was glad I'd at least gotten to wear it for Bowen and that he'd enjoyed it. A flush crept up my cheeks, remembering I'd shoved something else in my backpack that Bowen would probably enjoy.

I cracked the back door and reached in for the pack. A breeze shot up the back of Cade's shirt, and coincidentally, up the back of my rear end, and had me moving. The driveway was freezing under my toes as I slung the bag over my shoulder.

"Want me to carry you again?" Bowen met me at the front of the car. He'd hurried and unlocked the front door and flipped the inside light on.

"Almost there." I chattered and skipped inside, where the heat immediately soothed my aching feet.

"Mm. But there's so much of you...uncovered...like this." Bowen grinned lazily at me as he shut the door and locked it behind us. My flush deepened. He stepped closer, in my space. Gently, his thumb traced my jaw to my chin. "I'm glad you're safe."

My heart melted at his tone, and I covered his hand with mine, cupping it to my face. "I'm glad you're safe, too." Wolf nudged me. Was this the right time?

His lips came down and closed softly over mine, stealing any words I might have uttered. A moment later, he pulled back. "I think my trunks are in the laundry room. I'll meet you in the hot tub?"

I smiled as Wolf wiggled. "Sounds good."

Taking my backpack with me, I went into the guest

room where I'd stayed. Glancing around, Wolf lolled her tongue out. I took my bag and hesitated only a moment before entering the master bedroom and going into the en suite.

I'd only purchased the swimsuit to use in my own backyard in the rare event I wanted to lay out. It had been cheap at the end of last year's season. I'd never even worn it. I pulled out the tiny triangles and strings and looked at it. Wolf snorted.

I would never wear this. Not even in my own backyard. But I did love the deep magenta color. And I knew Bowen would love how little it covered.

It took me a minute to get the strings tied—one at the neck, the back, and then two low on my hips—and get the tiny bits of material adjusted. Ooh. It covered even less than I thought it would. I swallowed. Wolf pranced. Glancing in the mirror once more, I quickly put up my long hair in a knot on top of my head. Now all the strings were visible.

"It's time," I said to myself in the mirror. My husband waited. I slipped my ring off my right hand and put it onto my left. The diamond glittered against the metal creases of the oak leaf. A smile touched my lips as I stared at it there on my ring finger.

Giving myself a quick mental shake, I snatched a towel and wrapped it around my chest, covering me, and let myself out the back sliding doors.

Bowen was already in the tub, water burbling, his eyes closed, head resting on the stone ledge around the pool. His chest glistened in the soft yellow lights, muscles firm. I licked my lips.

"I was starting to wonder if you'd changed your mind," Bowen said as he opened his eyes and sat up straighter. His face was relaxed, already leaving this evening's events behind.

My heart kicked up, and my hands clenched the corners of the towel.

"Raven?"

Instead of saying anything, I let the towel drop.

Bowen's eyes got huge, and his lips parted in an audible groan. He watched my every step, devouring me with his gaze.

He did nothing to hide how much he liked what he saw, and it filled me with a sweet heat that burned brightly, filling me with confidence and assurance.

Slowly I stepped into the water opposite him. A deep rumble sounded in his chest as the water hit my thighs, my hips, then over my waist as I touched the bottom. I didn't stay on my side. His nostrils flared as I came to him.

"Rave." His voice was like gravel, his eyes were dilated, his chest moving rapidly. My legs brushed against his, knees pressing against him, my arms twining around his neck as I moved onto his lap.

My heart thundered in my chest as his breathing grew tight. His fingers traced from my knees to my thighs, brushing the ties on my hips, up my sides, his palms resting along my ribs and moving to my back, touching all of my skin.

Ripples of pleasure shivered over me everywhere his hands grazed. He swallowed hard, and I leaned close enough my chest brushed against his.

"This is so much better than your dress," he said hoarsely, his eyes trailing down to the two tiny triangles pressed against him, leaving next to nothing to the imagination. He cleared his throat. "Although there is a very serious issue that's come up that we should probably talk about if you're going to keep wearing this." A tiny noise somewhere between a giggle and a whimper escaped my lips as his hands swept back down, pulling me tighter against him. His lips traced my collarbone up the side of my neck. My head tipped back, eyes shut, hands gripping his biceps. He trailed kisses down my throat, his lips dragging over my skin to my shoulder. He shifted underneath me, groaning against my skin.

I couldn't form the words out loud, so I used a more intimate method.

I love you.

He pulled back, his eyes searching my face. "I've felt it for weeks, but I was afraid you weren't ready."

"I'm ready now," I whispered.

"I love you. I love you, I love you, I love you."

I kissed him hard on the mouth then. Our bodies rubbed together, gasps mingled with the bubbles, hands sliding over wet skin.

Long minutes passed while the heat inside me only grew. His lips teased me, tasted me, brought lava boiling beneath my skin.

I broke away, leaning my head against his. He pulled me against his chest, one hand on the string tied at my back, the other flirting with the top of my swim bottoms.

"I'm ready now," I whispered again.

With a hungry growl, he lifted us both from the water, took us into the house, and straight up the stairs to the master bedroom.

Laying me back on the bed, he hovered over me for a minute.

"I love you," he whispered again.

"I love you, too." I smiled up at him, my arms splayed beside my head. "Untie me?"

A devilish glint rose in his eyes as one side of his mouth tipped up.

****

Surrender had never been so sweet, so strange, or so fulfilling. After months of fear, fighting my attraction to him, weeks of despising who I thought he was, it all culminated in the moment I freely, willingly gave myself to him. He took that sacred trust I put in him, and he treasured it, guarding it with his own heart.

When sunlight streamed in the window and finally woke me, Wolf rubbed her head against me. We were complete in a way we'd never been. We were part of Bowen now, just as he was now a part of us. A lazy smile stretched my lips.

Bowen's phone rang somewhere downstairs. He groaned and let his fingers wander as he kept his eyes shut.

"What do you want to bet that was Kyp or Cade?"

A silvery giggle erupted from my throat. "Who else would call right now since we're just waking up from something significant?"

Chocolate eyes cracked open, staring at me. "I don't know about you, but I was kind of hoping we were in the middle of something significant all over again." He grinned.

****

When we finally did make it downstairs, there was a voicemail from Kyp.

Bowen snorted. "I knew it." He flashed me the phone screen and pressed play.

"Bowen, it's Kyp. I wanted to let you know I got a call from a pack out in Ohio. They've heard about what happened with Victor. I'm not sure how—maybe they had dealings with him in the past. Anyway, they want to consider forming an alliance. I'd like to talk it over with you. Call me later."

"You know, when Kyp gets married, I think we should call them on their wedding night. Repeatedly. What do you think?" Bowen chuckled.

"Maybe we'll be busy doing other things ourselves."

"On second thought, that might be one night we can escape the brotherly interruptions. At least from my side."

My eyes sparkled.

"We should probably practice. Just to be on the safe side." That sexy smile spread across his face as he reached for me.

"Bowen," I warned teasingly.

I laughed as he pounced, scooping me up in his arms and holding me to his chest, eyes twinkling. He kissed me soundly before putting me back on the ground. He kept his hands on my waist, pulling me gently against him and drawing a breathy little squeak from me.

"You know, a year ago, I was hopeless, trapped by Victor. There was no way out. It was an endless cycle of hate, control, and misery. And then I saw you. You broke it."

"No," I said softly, reaching up and brushing some hair from his forehead. "You broke Victor's curse yourself. Our mate bond just gave you the incentive you needed."

"I fought the darkness that tied me to Victor with everything I had—I never thought I could use it for something worthwhile. Using it to protect you and the others last night…I don't even know if I can explain it." His eyes focused inward as he searched for the right words.

I kissed his jaw, and his eyes slid shut. Opening them again, acceptance shone from them.

"I don't hate that part of me anymore. I'm still afraid of it, but I think I've accepted it's a part of who I am, for better or for worse."

"For better," I murmured.

The chains of fear no longer bound either of us, and as our lips met, I knew we were both finally home.

A word about the author…

AJ Skelly is an author, blogger, and lover of all things fantasy, medieval, and fairy-tale-romance. As a former high school English teacher with a master's in Creative Writing, she's always been fascinated with the written word and has spent many years working with teenagers. She lives with her husband, children, and many imaginary friends who often find their way into her stories.

http://www.ajskelly.com

Thank you for purchasing
this publication of The Wild Rose Press, Inc.

For questions or more information
contact us at
info@thewildrosepress.com.

The Wild Rose Press, Inc.
www.thewildrosepress.com